To: Risa,
Happy Reading!
Misty Jae

See You Never

Misty Jae Ogert

Copyright © 2015 Misty Jae Ogert

Moon and Back Books

All rights reserved.

ISBN: 978-0-9963214-5-7

DEDICATION

I would like to dedicate this book to the Love of My Life. My husband, Donny has kept me focused when I wanted to turn my head and say, "Squirrel". Those of you with kids will probably understand the reference. He is responsible for taking my drawings and making digital magic, together spending no less than ten hours in front of the computer we designed my book cover. He has encouraged me throughout the whole process of making my dreams come true. I love you.

CONTENTS

This book is a work of fiction.
Names, characters, places and incidents are products of the of the author's imagination or are used factiously.
Any resemblance to actual events or locales or persons, living or dead is entirely coincidental.

ACKNOWLEDGMENTS

There are several people I would like to thank. First of all my parents for sharing their love of books with me. To my mom who found one of my first books in the typewriter then called a family meeting to read it to everyone. Afterwards she told me what a great job I had done. To my dad who gave me the book The Horse Whisperer by Nicolas Evans and told me it reminded him of my writing. To my friend Courtney who I swear is in Witness Protection. She is the best person to bounce ideas off. I hope it continues with all my books.

To ALL my editors, MB, DM, CC, and AW.

Last but certainly not least, my partner in crime, Ashley. We always find a way to have fun.

Chapter One

Boston International Airport

Harper Quinn was ecstatic to be going away with her husband Brody and their best friends Kara and Bennett. They had been planning this kid free vacation for the past seven months and it was finally here.

Her stepdad, Frank was driving them to the airport in their SUV. She had already said good bye to her mom. They were going to be watching the kids while they were gone. She and Brody had three beautiful kids, two girls and a boy. Chloe was twelve, going on twenty. Colton was ten and their baby Paige was four.

They had all insisted on riding to the airport with Grandpa to say good-bye to their parents. Harper was finally letting it sink in that she was really going to miss them. They pulled up to the curb and Frank put it in park. Brody jumped out of the front seat and walked around back. Frank pressed the button to lift the tail gate and got out.

She opened the door and all the kids all jumped out onto the curb with her. Her friend Kara and her mom, Judy pulled up right behind them. Kara's, parents were going to be watching her boys while they were gone. Kara and Bennett had two boys. The oldest Lucas was fifteen and their youngest Griffin was in the same class as Chloe.

Frank and Brody pulled the luggage out from the back of the SUV and placed it on the curb. "Ok guys," Harper held out her arms and gathered the kids around her, "I want you guys to be good and listen to Grandma and Grandpa."

"Yes, Mom," Chloe said and the other two nodded.

"Good. Alright, I'm going to miss you guys. I love you very much."

"We love you too Mom." They all said almost in unison.

She hugged Chloe who was almost as tall as she was. "Good bye, Sweetie Pie."

"Bye, Mom. Can you bring me back something cool?"

"Sure, honey. You take care of the other two for me ok?"

When her daughter nodded she turned to say good bye to Frank who she considered her Dad. She hugged him tight and gave him a kiss on the cheek.

Harper turned to Colton who was buried in his phone. “Hey bud. Try not to spend too much time on the Xbox while we are gone ok?”

He looked up his eyes were wide like she was asking him not to breathe while they were gone. “Mom,” he whined.

“What? You will be fine. I love you, take care of your sisters for me,” She whispered in his ear as she bent down to give him a big hug.

“I will Mom.” He gave her a big squeeze and went right back to his phone.

Harper turned to Paige. When she picked her up Paige’s legs wrapped around her waist. Out of all her kids she was most worried about her youngest. She squeezed her tight inhaling the scent of her watermelon shampoo in her big red bologna curls. She had no idea where the red hair came from seeing as neither she nor Brody had red hair. She had been told it was a recessive gene from Brody’s great grandmother.

She kissed her on her neck causing her to go into a fit of giggles. “Mommy!” she cried out. “That tickles!”

“What?!” she fringed surprise.

“That tickles, Mommy.” She giggled and tried tickling her back with her chubby little fingers in her neck.

She gave her a huge kiss, squeezed her tight then put her down. Frank came over and took Paige's hand. She gave him one last hug and while she was hugging him, Paige gripped the lower half of her leg.

"Thank you so much, Dad."

"Anytime, my girl, you go have fun. I'll see you when you get back." He gently peeled Paige off her leg and held her hand.

They checked in their bags curb side and took their carry-ons with them. They waved good-bye as their parents pulled away with their kids.

"I miss them already." Harper turned towards Brody.

He kissed her. "They will be fine."

"I know but will I?"

He kissed her again, "Yes."

She smiled at him; his eyes were alight with mischief. "Let's get this party started."

"Let's do it." Bennett chimed in enthusiastically. Kara and Bennett were holding hands waiting for them to go inside.

Brody slipped his hand in hers and they took the lead into the airport. They made it through security no problem. The boys went to get Dunkin Donuts and the girls took a seat next to each other at their boarding gate. They took a selfie and posted it on Facebook, announcing their exciting adventure they were about to embark on.

Brody and Bennett brought the girls their coffees and sat next to each other across from them. They boarded twenty minutes later and after a two hour flight to Miami they made their connecting flight.

Several hours later they were in paradise. They were met at the airport by their driver who drove them to the all-inclusive resort. Their bags were carried to their rooms and cocktails were placed in their hands.

Toes in the water, ass in the sand, not a worry in the world, was the song Harper was humming to herself as she tapped her well-manicured foot as she sunned herself on the beach. She felt she should pinch herself as she was reminded that she was on a tropical getaway. Her thoughts drifted away remembering how they all had met.

Kara had been her roommate at Boston College. They had liked each other instantly. The two girls were like two peas in a pod. They could look at each other and know exactly what the other was thinking. They had the same sense of humor. They would laugh hysterically at things no one else could fathom why they found it funny, causing them to giggle all the harder. They liked all the same things books, movies, TV shows and loved all the same Hollywood men.

Even though it seemed they shared the same brain and were as similar as two people could be their looks couldn't be farther away. Harper was tall and thin with ivory white skin, jet black silky hair, and crystal blue eyes. Although after having Paige she was having a hard time shedding the final fifteen pounds. Kara was blonde and petite, curves in all the right places and hunter green eyes.

Bennett had come as a package deal with Kara. She had never known one without the other. Kara and Bennett had been high school sweethearts. He was on a football scholarship and studying business. He was a good guy no, two ways about it. He looked after her like he looked after Kara. One time they were at a frat party and she had too much to drink. One of the guys tried dragging her into a room. Bennett was the one that carried her home and put her to bed. They never talked about the incident. It was a mutual understanding it wasn't necessary.

Sophomore year Harper walked into her Chemistry class late. The room was a lab set up with long tables and stools on either side. There was only one seat left and it was right in front of the professor and right next to an arrogant ass. Across from her was another girl and next to her was a cute guy in a baseball cap. He kept giving her looks under the brim of his hat every time the jack ass next to her made an annoying comment. One of those times she giggled out loud and tried to cover it up with a cough. She caught him smirking out of the corner of eye.

The following week she got to class early and the cute guy and not the jackass was sitting in the seat right next to hers. "I'm Brody." He introduced himself as she sat down. Oh my God, that voice was even better than she imagined it. Then she noticed his eyes. They were crystal blue, deep cobalt blue that she could get lost in.

"I'm Harper." She placed her bag on the ground next to her chair.

"That's a beautiful name."

She blushed and looked away. The professor came in along with jackass who glared sending daggers at Brody for taking his seat. She turned around to give Brody a look to see how he was taking it. He shrugged his shoulders nonchalantly then winked at her. That was the day they were assigned lab partners. The professor told them to pair up with the person closest to them.

After the lecture they had a twenty minute break until lab started. Harper went to the restroom and when she came out she was heading back to class. She saw Brody at the end of the hall in a little sitting area. She walked down to the area passing the door to their classroom. It was a circular shaped end of the hallway all windows. Three comfy looking chairs curved around a small circular table.

Brody was sitting in the seat to her right with one foot on the coffee table. He looked so relaxed not a care in the world. She envied him; she was so uptight with school and work.

“Have a seat,” he offered.

“Thanks,” she sat down on the chair across from him and crossed her legs.

He took his foot down and leaned forward, “You should give me your number.”

“What?” she thought that was a little forward of him.

“So we can set up a time to study.” He explained.

Harper felt a little stupid. Of course that’s why he was asking. He pulled out his phone and copied her number into it. She did the same with his number. He leaned back and smiled warmly at her making her insides melt. Does he know what he is doing to me she wondered? She was so glad he was her partner but she didn’t know if she could handle it.

Later that week when Brody called Harper, she was in the shower. Kara picked up the phone for her “Hello?”

“Hey, Harper?” he sounded unsure.

Kara grinned, “No this is her roommate, Kara. She is in the shower right now. Who is this?”

He seemed flustered and she tried hard not to giggle on the other end. “I’m-this is Brody, her chemistry partner.”

"Oh… Brody." Was all she said making him wonder what had been said about him?

"Umm yeah, can you have her call me please?"

"Sure, not problem."

"Thanks, Kara."

She ended the call. Well, he got brownie points for remembering her name. Harper came into the room drying her hair with a towel a few minutes later. Kara looked like a cat that caught the canary. "What happened?" She asked.

"Oh, nothing."

"Yes." She pointed her finger at her, "Yes something absolutely happened. Tell me."

"Okay," she couldn't tease her anymore, "Brody called." She waited to see her friends reaction. She wasn't disappointed.

"He did?" she squealed, "What did he say?" she demanded. She grabbed Kara by the shoulders and shook her. "What. Did. He. Say?" she emphasized each word.

She laughed and handed her the phone. "He wants you to call him."

Harper ripped the phone from her hand and started to call him back but her nosey roommate was watching her. "I'm nervous," she confessed.

"Ah man! I was going to tease you, but I'll give you a minute."

"Thank you." When Kara closed the door behind her she clicked on his number.

"Hey." He answered the phone on the first ring.

"Hey, yourself," she smiled into the phone.

"How are you doing?"

"I'm good. How are you?"

"I can't complain. What's your schedule look like this week? Professor Randall said we can do our homework together. It would be nice if we could get together and work on it."

"That works for me. I'm available now or-"

"Now works for me." He said quickly.

She laughed, "Okay. Well you have to give me a half hour."

"I can give you an hour, how's that? We can meet at the library, on the second floor in one of the study rooms?"

She looked at her watch. "Okay, I'll see you then."

They hung up and she rushed to the door. She had to find Kara to help her get ready. Flinging open the door she ran out into the hallway. Kara was waiting for her.

"I need help!"

"I'm here for you." With that the girls ran back into the room.

They settled on the perfect pair of jeans that hugged her body just right, boots with heels and a cream colored sweater. Kara flat ironed her hair while she applied makeup. They picked out jewelry to accent the look. Kara pulled out her perfume and gave a little spray and she walked through the mist and did a little twirl.

"How do I look?" she asked.

"Beautiful. Honestly and truly" she added when she knew her friend would ask if she was sure.

"Thanks, Kara." She gave her a big hug.

"Knock him dead." Kara wished her luck.

Harper started to leave the room, "Harper?" Kara called out.

"Yeah?" she asked from the door.

"Don't forget your books."

She started laughing, "I don't know how I'm going to concentrate on studying."

"Well it helps to have a book," she joked.

“Very funny.” She grabbed her notebook, Chemistry book and a pen. She made it to the library in fifty minutes and found him waiting for her. He had one of his hands in his jeans pocket. Looking up, Brody’s face lit up causing her heart to skip a beat.

“I was going to suggest we go into one of the study rooms but they all seem occupied at the moment.” He offered up.

She looked over one of his wide shoulders and could see he was right. “We could take one of these tables here or see if there is somewhere a little more private?” he asked.

“Let’s go looking,” she suggested.

He turned and stretched out his arm, “Lead the way.” She walked by him and she felt him lightly touch her back. She weaved around the bookcases and walked the perimeter of the library. They found a small rectangular table near a window on their right with rows of books to their left and no one was around.

She sat down closest to the window and he quickly took the chair right next to her instead of the one across from her. They put their books on the table and pulled out their homework worksheet. They worked well together. It seemed that if she didn’t know the answer he would find it and vice versa. Within the hour they had completed the worksheet and felt confident in their answers.

He had a great sense of humor. He liked to crack jokes, mostly making fun of the serious guy in their class. At one point she was laughing so hard she was crying. She tried to wipe the corners of her eyes praying her mascara and makeup weren't running.

"Are you seeing anybody?" he asked as they were packing up their stuff to go.

"I am not."

"How come," he inquired?

"Well I was but he went to Penn State and didn't feel we could make the long distance thing work. I agreed and we broke up. What about you?"

"I'm not seeing anyone."

"How come," she threw the question right back to him.

"She found someone else."

Their bodies had gotten close. He was facing her and she had turned towards him one of her knees was wedged in between his thighs though none of their body parts were touching. She put her hand over his, "I'm sorry."

"Are you?" he asked.

"Not really." They were looking directly into each other's eyes. Her thumb caressed the top of his hand. He had the most amazing blue eyes. His free hand came up; he brushed her hair aside his knuckles softly grazing the side of her neck. His hand curved around her throat his thumb resting on her collar bone.

"Me neither," he whispered as he leaned forward his hand ever so slightly pulling her towards him. He was a breath away from her lips their noses grazed slightly. Then his lips were on hers. She gave him no resistance. The world melted away; nothing else existed in this moment. There was nothing outside of this kiss.

His lips were soft and sweet-not in taste but in the gentle way he coaxed her to open up to him. She did so happily giving in and getting lost. She didn't even remember she was in the library. His lips were soft and urging her on. She opened her mouth and touched her tongue to his. When she did and their tongues glided together it was electrifying taking her breath away. He groaned and deepened the kiss, his hand combed through her hair.

He was slow and methodical, his thumb rubbed softly on her neck. Her pulse beat wildly against his hand. Her one free hand worked its way up his thigh. He changed the position of the kiss her tongue tingled along with her nipples tightening. Brody sucked gently on her lower lip then captured her mouth again. Her hands came up to cup his face her arms circling up and around his shoulders as she angled to get closer.

"Ah-hem!" was said from somewhere from behind them. A clearing of the throat and an "Excuse me." Finally broke the magic of their kiss.

They looked up to see a very prim and proper librarian standing behind them looking stern and dissatisfied. Her arms were crossed across her chest and her bifocals were sitting dangerously close to the edge of her nose.

"You can't do that in here," she informed them.

"Sorry." Harper gathered her things and stood up. Brody was a little slower to stand up. He picked up his book and led the way. They walked out of the library and when he got outside he turned to her.

"Can I walk you to your dorm?"

"Sure." She smiled but she was a little shy after the kiss they had just shared and been caught in. She turned to walk away and he slipped his hand into hers. It felt… perfect. Her heart flip flopped inside her chest. She couldn't wait to tell Kara about her little study date.

He walked her all the way to her door. "Thanks for walking me home." She had stopped and turned towards him. She was leaning up against the wall not sure how much longer her legs would keep her up.

His arm rested casually up against the door jam and leaned in towards her, "Thank you for meeting me for a study date." His other hand brushed her hair aside.

“Was that a date?” she asked.

“Not a proper one. Can I take you out for a real date this weekend?”

“I’m going to the football game with Kara on Saturday to watch Bennett, her boyfriend, play. But after that…I’m available.”

“Perfect, I’ll pick you up here, around seven?”

“Sure, sounds good.”

He leaned in for another kiss. He barely had his lips on hers when her door opened wide and Kara came out.

“Whoa!” she threw her hands up in surprise and circled around then turned back around when she heard Harper speak.

“Kara, it’s okay, this is Brody.”

Kara had a radiant smile as she turned to meet Brody. “Well hello there, Brody. It’s nice to meet you.”

He shook her hand, “Nice to meet you too Kara. Thank you for giving Harper the message to call me back.” He turned to look at Harper as he said it causing her to blush.

“You are more than welcome.” Kara beamed as she looked back and forth between Brody and her best friend Harper, whom she had never seen look so happy.

"Well I need to get going," Brody had not let go of Harper's hand. He leaned in and whispered in her ear, "I can't wait until there is a time we don't get interrupted," then grazed her cheek with his lips.

She actually giggled, "Good night ladies," and then he was gone. They watched him walk down the hall.

"Oh. My. God!" Kara was not good at whispering. She grabbed her friend and hauled her into their dorm room. "What happened?!"

They flopped down on their beds facing each other as Harper proceeded to tell her every minute detail. Kara squealing and clapping her hands in excitement the whole time.

That weekend she barely made it back to her dorm just in time to meet Brody. "Sorry," she apologized as she saw him waiting for her at the door. "The game went into overtime. We won!" she announced excitedly.

"God your beautiful," was all he could say. She was wearing a gold t-shirt that all the students wore to the games and she had Eagle stickers on her face on both cheekbones. She laughed as she looked down at herself.

"Just give me a minute to change," she was unlocking the door.

"You look fine."

She turned around to look at him, “You’re sweet.” She gave him a quick kiss, “but honestly I already have an outfit picked out. So I will be one minute.” And with that she was inside her room and shut the door on him.

She pulled her shirt over her head and flung it in the hamper. She grabbed her red sweater off her bed and pulled it on over her head. Peeling the stickers off of her face she tossed them into the trash. She pulled her hair tie out releasing her ponytail and shook her hair into place. She slung her purse over her shoulder as she pulled the door open to find Brody waiting for her.

“Wow” came out of his mouth.

She beamed at his approval. “See! Was it worth the minute?”

“It was most definitely worth it. Where would you like to go? Pizza or Chinese?”

“Oh, Chinese. No question.”

“Done.” He held his hand out to her and she took it. He walked her out to his car, it was ten years old but he kept it clean. He opened the door for her and closed it after she had climbed in. What a gentleman she thought.

He drove her through the streets of Boston until he pulled alongside a brick building with gold dragon painted on the red door. “We’re here.”

She looked around she had never been here before. She mostly stuck close to campus. They went inside and he escorted her over to a booth where a pretty Chinese girl came to greet them. Harper ordered her favorite Peking Ravioli.

"Do you want to split a Pu-Pu platter for two?" he asked her.

"Sure." She readily agreed because Chinese food was her absolute favorite. They talked as they waited for dinner. She found out about his family. He was the oldest son and had a younger brother, who was still in high school. His parents were still happily married.

She told him that her parents had divorced when she was five and her dad had a new family and she didn't see him much but he sent presents and cash whenever his guilt struck him. Her mom had remarried when she was eight and she had been included in the wedding. Her stepdad Frank was amazing. Frank treated her like she was his own daughter.

Frank was a good man and loved her mom. They were never able to have kids of their own. She never asked them about it. They seemed content just to love her and she was fine with that.

They talked about what type of music they liked to listen to. They told stories from their childhood. She told him stories about her and Kara and Bennett. Brody told her he was from Ohio and she told him she grew up in Connecticut.

"I like them already," he was laughing at one of her stories.

"I can't wait until you meet Bennett. He is a great guy."

"I don't have to worry about being jealous do I?"

"Oh, God, no, Bennett is like the big brother I never had. You should be worried that he will kick your ass if you're not nice to me." She warned him playfully.

"I can't ever see that happening." He was serious as he made the statement.

She smiled warmly at him, "Neither can I."

Dinner came and they split the food up and polished off the entire order of food.

"That was so good." She practically purred, "This place is great, I've never been here before."

"Do you have room for dessert?"

"Always."

"Do you want to take a walk? There is a place up the street that has amazing cannoli."

"Ready." She jumped up from the table. He had already paid the bill, so off they went.

They held hands and strolled down the busy streets of Boston until they came across the Sweet

Treats dessert bar. It was on a corner with all glass windows and tables inside and a bar along the outer glass wall. People were coming and going from the place. Brody held the door open for her and she walked into the delicious smell of a fresh bakery.

"I think this is heaven," she whispered to him in line.

He had slipped his arm around her in line. He felt so comfortable like she belonged there. She cozied up to him as they talked about what they were going to order. Because they couldn't decide they ended up getting Crème Brule, Chocolate covered strawberries, a chocolate chip cannoli and a pistachio cannoli, and German Chocolate Danish.

She laughed as she helped carry the order to the stools along the glass wall bar. "You are going to think I'm such a pig."

"I think it's great to see a girl eat what she wants and not worry about what anyone thinks of her. Honestly I don't know where you put it." He looked her slender figure up and down. "Do you have a wooden leg you forgot to mention?"

She giggled, "No, but I will have to get on the treadmill for days after this, but it's totally worth it."

They had sat down and he leaned in close and whispered, "You're totally worth it." They kissed a sweet lingering kiss until she finally pulled away. They were in a public place after all. They would have to keep it in check.

Later when he brought her back to her dorm they made out for quite some time in his car in the parking lot under a street light. Not that anyone could see in the car because it was embarrassingly fogged up from their heavy breathing. She was glad he didn't push for more because she wasn't ready for that yet

He walked her to her door and kissed her good bye again. They made plans for another date and a study date the following week. She knew then that the chemistry they shared wasn't just in the class room. Later he confessed he had moved on purpose hoping they would be paired together.

When she introduced Brody to Bennett they hit it off just like she knew they would. It was like they had always been best friends. Kara loved him too. She was ecstatic her friend was happy and she liked that he made her happy. They were quite the foursome after that.

Brody convinced Bennett to minor in finance which was his major and together they started their own company as Investment Bankers after graduation. Kara studied law and after college joined the largest law firm in Boston, who had recruited her intensely. She was on the fast track to make partner.

Harper had gone into college not really sure what she wanted to be. After taking liberal art courses for a year and taking different classes she decided she wanted to do Event Planning. So she switched her major to business. She went to work for a company she had done her internship for and after four years started her own company. They all had busy lives but they always made time for each other.

Two weddings and five kids between the four of them later, they lived next door to each other. They found a great neighborhood where everyone got along for the most part. The guys played golf together, and were in the same football fantasy league, they played poker and watched UFC fights together. The girls went to the gym and got pedicures together and had girls night out or in. The neighborhood had cook outs at each other's homes and celebrated birthdays, anniversaries and anything else that came up. Their kids were all friends, some got on the bus for the first time together, and other's had their first communion with each other.

"What are you day dreaming about?" Kara asked Harper trying to bring her friend back to present day.

"Huh?" was her reply.

"Huh?" Kara mocked her playfully. She was always saying she was going to buy her a cochlear implant to help her hear well, because she was sick of repeating herself.

Harper who was so used to this banter didn't even respond to the retort but instead answered the question she had actually heard but hadn't processed yet. "I was just thinking about how lucky we are."

"Yeah, we are." Kara agreed whole heartedly. She raised her pink plastic cup full of Pina colada with pineapples and cherries sticking off to the side with a blue paper umbrella.

Harper picked up the same pink cup filled with her margarita on the rocks. They bumped the plastic together and took a sip. They were seated in lounge chairs under a wide umbrella. There was a slight breeze of warm air caressing their bodies clad only in bathing suits. Harper was wearing a blue full piece and Kara was in a teal bikini.

A man with no shirt on that looked like a Greek God came up to them, "Can I get you ladies anything else, another drink or something to eat perhaps?"

"No thank you we are good for now." Kara let him know. When he was out of ear shot she whispered, "I wish we could bring him home as our souvenir. He would be great to have around the house" she said with a grin.

"Yes!" Harper exclaimed, "He could do our laundry and dishes!

"And windows!"

Both women giggled and knew that in reality that would not be an option. They both were in love with their husbands. Their kids were happy and healthy. Life was good.

Just then their husbands came running up to them, dripping wet from the ocean. Bennett leaned both hands on either side of Kara and dripping wet planted a kiss on her mouth. She squealed as she got wet and put her hands to his face to accept the kiss. Brody wiped off with a towel before giving Harper a kiss, which she appreciated because she wasn't in the mood to get wet.

Every once in a while she would get a twinge of jealously that her husband wasn't climbing on top of her soaking wet. Then she realized he didn't because he knew her, knew she wouldn't like that, it would potentially mess up her hair or get her wet when she didn't want to be wet. She got that and she loved him for it. She felt sometimes they had a more mature relationship. Maybe it was because they had they started dating in college verses high school, she wasn't sure.

Bennett grabbed Kara's hand and pulled her up from the lounge chair. "We'll see you guys at dinner." He winked at them.

"You bet." Brody called out, because they were half running back to the hotel. Brody rolled into the lounge chair vacated by her friend. "You having fun?" he asked as he ran his now dry hand from her raised knee down her thigh. See, now that's what she liked. She turned towards him causing his hand to dip in between her thighs and further down. "Oh, yes."

Chapter Two

It had been raining steadily since last night. They were in the little island airport waiting to board their flight. The airport was so small they didn't have terminals with boarding ramps. There was one gate and it opened out onto the tarmac. There the airplanes sat with the long stairs folded out for people to climb inside. From the time the door would open to the time they boarded they were bound to be drenched.

"May I have your attention, please?" The overhead announcer paused before continuing on, "The incoming flight has been delayed due to inclement weather. Flight 924 is fueled and ready to go. We will just need to reroute your plane and it may take longer than anticipated. You have the option of staying an additional night for a discounted price. Again Flight 924-"

The announcer continued to repeat the announcement as the group of four turned to face each other. "I'm ready to be home," Kara confessed to the group.

"I need to see my babies." Harper agreed.

"We might not make our connecting flight." Brody forewarned them.

"We can always find a new connecting flight. Let's get these girls home." Bennett winked at them.

Brody easily gave in, "I miss the kids."

"Done!" Bennett marched up to the counter and slapped his plane ticket down on the counter. The group followed in close succession. "We are going home." He announced.

"Yes, sir," the attendant agreed enthusiastically. She scanned the group's tickets then held the door open for them. A gust of wind blew through the doors. They braced themselves but were not prepared for the big fat cold rain drops that pelted down on them during their mad dash across the tarmac.

The couples were laughing as they made it inside the airplane. It took a carefree week to not allow a little thing like rain to disturb them. The flight attendants were handing out blankets at the door for them to dry off with. They gladly took them and found their seats. Harper and Brody were close to the back on the left. Bennett and Kara were another three rows further back from them and on the right side of the plane.

The plane filled up with passengers in the next twenty minutes. Not many people must have chosen to wait out the storm.

The turbulence was a little rough on the ride back. Rain was coming down hard on the window panes of the airplane. It just reminded Harper she needed to pee again.

"Hey, I need to go to the bathroom again." She tapped Brody on the knee.

He was reading, well actually flipping through the airline magazine. "Again?" he asked closing the magazine and folding it into the back of the seat in front of him. He unbuckled his seat belt and stood up to let her go past him.

"Well it's technically your fault," she said as she moved past him running her hand across his chest.

"How do you figure that?"

"Well since having your babies I have no bladder control." She grinned at him.

He smiled warmly at her, "Small price to pay."

"Says the man with the bladder of steel." She kissed him quickly on the lips and his hand skimmed down her back. "I'm glad we got this week to ourselves."

She smiled her eyes sparkling as she met his with the same sparkle, "Me too." She kissed him one more time.

"You wanna try the mile high club?" he whispered in her ear.

She slapped him lightly on the shoulder. "You wish. I'll be right back." He sat back down in his chair and she made the walk back several rows to the back of the plane to go to the bathroom. The two bathrooms were occupied and she found Bennett standing outside one of the doors.

"Are you waiting?" she asked.

"No. No, just stretching for a little while."

Harper leaned against the opening to wait. "Did you guys have fun?" she asked.

"The best time ever. Thanks for inviting us, after all these years of talking about doing a vacation, I'm so glad we able to make it work. We had tons of fun. What about you guys?"

"We did too. We were just talking; we should make this an annual thing."

"Absolutely."

One of the bathroom stalls opened up Bennett made a big show of sweeping his arm towards the open door. She smiled. "Thank you." Harper walked past him and closed the door sliding the lock into place. She looked in the mirror and grinned widely at herself. She loved her life. Things were good. She had the best husband, beautiful kids, the perfect family and the best friends in the world. Yes life was good.

She went to the bathroom and washed her hands. Suddenly she was slammed into the door of the bathroom. Her shoulder hit hard. She gasped as she felt the plane dip; she was thrown backwards into the wall her head hit with force. Harper was pinned against the wall as the plane seemed to be in a downward decent.

This is not happening she thought as she heard the Captain's voice come across the intercom. "Please return to your seats and remain buckled. It appears we were struck by lightning. We are preparing for an emergency landing. Please remember you may use your seat as a floatation device. We are still over the ocean at this point. We have notified-"-

The transmission broke off as she heard a noise that did not sound normal and she could hear passengers screaming. She had slumped to the floor when she heard banging on the door of her bathroom stall. It was Bennett.

"Harper, Are you ok!? Come on we need to get back to our seats."

She managed to reach up and unlatch the lock. The door flew open and Bennett went flying backwards he crashed into the food cart. His body crumpled to the ground. She fell out but was able to grab the door jam. The plane was in a severe decent.

"Bennett!" she screamed to be heard over the noise of the plane and everyone screaming. "Oh my God!" she cried. Brody, she thought. He was up there alone and he was worrying about her she knew. They were going to crash and she couldn't get to him and he couldn't get to her. Was this the end? Was she never going to see her babies again? Her Mom? Brody? Kara? She could feel tears start to well up.

The plane leaned to the left towards Bennett. He slid further away from her towards the emergency door.

"Bennett!" she heard Kara scream from her seat.

"He's okay!" Harper lied to her.

She thought she heard her say "Oh thank God."

"Harper!" Brody bellowed.

"I'm here. I'm okay."

"I love you."

She choked out a sob, "I love you too!"

Then there was impact. The left wing grazed the water and caused them to go into a cartwheel across the water. She lost her grip on the door and hit the roof with Bennett by her side then they were thrown around like rag dolls to the opposite side of the cabin and against the emergency door.

When the plane flipped back to the tail end of the plane, it severed from the rest of the plane. She and Bennett were catapulted into the ocean. The plane continued to flip further away from them.

Emerging from under water she was pelted in the face by the driving rain. The freezing cold water luckily was a rude awakening for Bennett who had regained consciousness. He started to tread water about twenty feet away from her. The tail end of the plane was about fifty feet away from the both of them. It was still floating, for now. She began to swim towards it. The swells of the ocean were huge possibly because of the recent disturbance of an airplane crashing into its water. Or maybe it was the storm they were in, or the combination of the both.

She reached the plane about the same time as he did. It was going down. She could see the bubbles around it.

Her mind began to race this was an urgent situation. “What do we do?” she demanded. She had full confidence he would know what to do.

“I think there might be rafts in the door panels.”

“Really?”

“Yeah, you ever see them have to land on the tarmac and they open the door and that slide comes out? I think if we get the doors open we may get a raft.”

"Great. Let's do it." The door was half under water.

"You stay here. I mean it." He looked directly at her when he could tell she wanted to protest.

He swam over to the door and went inside the open end of the plane. She looked in the direction the rest of the plane had gone. She couldn't see it anymore. She saw lots of debris. She looked for anything that could be useful. She saw water bottles floating nearby. She went to get them. She stuffed one in each of her shorts pockets. She had a zippered pocket she opened and she maneuvered it into place and zipped up the pocket as best she could.

She realized then she had lost her flip flops in the crash. Harper turned back to the plane and realized much more of the plane had submerged under water. She quickly swam back to it.

"Bennett! How's it going in there?"

"I almost have it," she heard him say and she breathed a sigh of relief. A suit case popped up next to her. She held on to it. It had a hard plastic shell that was purple with yellow polka dots and was buoyant in the water. She stopped treading for a while. Even the short time they had been in the water she was tired. She placed her head on the suitcase and took a deep breath.

Big bubbles welled up around her. Harper couldn't see the door anymore. "Oh my God, Bennett!"

He didn't respond. She left the suitcase and started towards the plane. The door burst forth from under the water. No raft and no Bennett. She dove under the water but it was dark and murky. She came back up for air. Still nothing.

"No, no, no" she started to panic. The raft emerged out of the water like a phoenix rising from the ashes. Yet still no Bennett. She could feel her heart racing inside her chest, and had she had stopped breathing? Tears welled up in her eyes, this could not be happening!

"Ahhh," Bennett gasped as he surfaced.

She let out a strangled cry of relief. She turned around and grabbed the suitcase and started swimming towards the raft. Bennett had already made it on board. She flung the suitcase over the side. Bennett reached his hand out which she took and he pulled her inside. They heard the bubbling of the ocean water as the last of the plane submerged under water.

"Ka-Boom!" They both whipped their heads towards the sound. They both had a gut wrenching feeling as they saw the explosion in the direction of where the rest of the plane had gone. A huge black cloud lifted in the sky that seemed like miles away.

Neither one said what the other was thinking. Neither one wanted to admit to that fact that this was happening. It felt like a dream-correction nightmare. Harper prayed that she would just wake up. They collapsed into stunned silence. The giant waves were rocking them back and forth, away from where the tail end of the plane had been and away from the black billowing cloud in the distance.

Bennett passed out about a half hour later. "Oh my God," she rushed to him. He was still breathing, shallow breaths but still breathing. She noticed a gash on the side of his head. Because of the rain the blood from his head wound was washing away almost instantly. She needed to stop the bleeding.

She looked behind her and saw the suitcase. Scooting over to it she flipped it over and tried to open it but found it was locked.

"Damn it!" she swore. She looked around. There was nothing on the raft she could use. She looked down on herself, she could use her shirt. She saw the water bottles she had pulled out of the ocean then later out of her pockets on the bottom of the raft. She peeled the plastic wrapper off one of them and placed it to the side of his temple. It stuck to his head. Okay this could work she thought. She applied pressure and after about ten minutes, well maybe five, her knees started to ache.

She needed to reposition herself. She sat down and put his head in her lap then reapplied pressure. She leaned her back and side against the wall of the raft. The rain continued to pelt down on the two of them. It was a driving cold rain. She started to shiver. Her clothes were plastered to her body, which began to ache.

Hours later the grey of the day began to turn darker and darker. It was turning into night. She saw no rescue helicopters. The waves were still powerful and they had a continuous motion of up and down. It was mesmerizing. Her eye lids became heavy she awkwardly scooted her body down next to him and tried to keep pressure applied to his forehead.

The following day Harper woke up staring at the raft wall. She could hear the slapping of the water up against the sides and she could feel gentle sway of the waves. At first she was wondering where she was at. Was this part of a dream? She rolled over, Bennett was lying behind her and he was still unconscious. She tried waking him but he just groaned. She checked to see if he had a fever. He felt warm but she couldn't tell if it was from the sun or if he had a fever. She prayed it was from the sun.

She looked up at the sun it was high overhead which meant she had slept until almost noon. This day looked nothing like the day before. It was like nothing happened but she knew better. Her and Bennett's whole world had turned upside down yesterday. They had each lost the love of their life. How was she going to tell the kids, Daddy wasn't coming home? How was she going to live without Brody and her best friend?

In the light of day she noticed Bennett had suffered an injury on his right leg as well as his head. There was a large gash across his calf that had been bleeding all night but the blood had dried up in the sun.

She scooped some ocean water in her hands and tried to rinse off the wound to get a better look. It wasn't good but at least it was clean. She had to make sure no infection set in.

She had three water bottles. She opened one and took a sip. She had to conserve what she could she had no idea how long they would be out here. She lifted Bennett's head and tried to feed him a sip of water too. He coughed and managed to swallow some but did not regain consciousness.

She laid him back down. She looked around on the horizon there was nothing but sea out before them. Wow this sun was hot. Her drenched clothes from the night before were now bone dry. She was starting to sweat. She looked for something to do. She took the bottles of water and put them in the shade of the suitcase and pushed it up the side of the raft to keep them from rolling around.

She moved Bennett closer to the side wall of the raft to get him out of the sun and into what little shade she could get him into. Well now that she was done there was nothing to do but think and that was a dangerous thing to do.

We need to survive this she thought. She began to replay every survival T.V. show she had ever seen trying to think of things she could do. She hated seafood with a passion. They had better be rescued before she was forced to eat things she didn't even want to touch.

She began to pray for rescue. None came. She prayed Bennett would be okay. She would have to wait and see on that one.

When the sun started to set she allowed herself another drink of water and gave one to Bennett who hadn't done much other than groan every once and a while. The night came and went. She struggled to sleep tossing and turning. She eventually cried herself to sleep leaving herself exhausted.

Chapter Three

While Bennett was unconscious his life was replaying in his head. He had a volatile childhood growing up. His mom had suffered with bouts of deep depression and his dad was an alcoholic.

One day when he was eleven he came home from school to find his mom had committed suicide. She was sitting in the kitchen, her head down on the table. Her pill bottles were lined up meticulously, all empty; with the caps put carefully back in place. At first he thought she was sleeping until he saw her note that simply stated, "I'm sorry."

His dad who was a functioning alcoholic began to lose his battle with staying sober. Most nights he would drink himself into a stupor in front of the television. The only thing he was thankful for was his dad was not a mean drunk, just an uninvolved parent.

Bennett had to learn to take care of both of them. One night he almost burnt the house down cooking on the stove top. A hand towel had gotten to close to the flame and caught fire. His dad woke up long enough to put out the fire and eat a half cooked hot dog before lying back down on the couch and dozing off.

Bennett tried not to have too many friends in school. It wasn't hard, he just didn't communicate with anyone. He never invited anyone over and in return was never invited to anyone else's house. If he was he just declined. One day in his freshman year of high school he had a science project to do and was assigned a lab partner, John.

John was a year older than him as were most of the kids in his class because it was an AP Biology class. Bennett was really smart and got good grades in school. It thankfully came naturally to him. He offered to just do it for John but he wouldn't hear of it. He also never had anyone decline his offer to do their homework. It was a win/win, he didn't need to interact with them and the other person didn't need to do anything and came out of it with an A.

"Why don't you come over after school and we can work on it?" When he saw his hesitation he persisted, "My mom picks me up after school and I'm sure she can drive you home."

He had never caved in before and he wasn't sure why he did this time but he agreed.

After school they waited side by side and his mom pulled up in a minivan. "Lame, I know." John apologized for the mode of transport.

"No problem," Bennett said quickly.

John slid open the van door, "Mom, this is Bennett. We were assigned a project that he is going to come over and help me work on."

She smiled warmly, "Nice to meet you, Bennett." She offered her hand and he shook it.

"You too, Mrs. Marshall."

"Oh, manners!" she appeared extremely pleased by this, "You will be joining us for dinner?" she really didn't ask a question, it was more of a statement.

"Yes, ma'am."

She smiled satisfied and put the car into drive. They drove through the center of town past businesses and then past older homes, then neighborhoods. A little further out of town she pulled into a newer development with stone pillars on either side with the name, Emerald Estates. Everyone had well-manicured lawns and nice cars parked in the driveways. They pulled into a circular driveway at the end of the cul-de-sac.

John gave him the tour of the house. "This is my sister's room," he mentioned nonchalantly as he passed a room on the right at the top of the stairs. He glanced in and saw lots of pinks and purples, fluffy things and sparkly things. The room scared him. He knew nothing of girls. He stayed clear of them. "She is at soccer practice she will be home for dinner with my dad."

John had kept walking, "That's the spare bedroom, but my mom uses it as a sewing room." He waved his hand in the general direction of the room. "And this is my room." He walked across the hallway. John sat at his desk and turned his computer on. Bennett didn't have a computer, let alone one in his room. He had also seen one in John's sister's room at her desk.

He put his backpack that was three years old at this point on the floor and plopped down on the edge of the bed. He pulled out his book while John booted up his computer. Mrs. Marshall came up a half hour later with milk and fresh baked cookies. "Don't spoil your dinner, boys. I made homemade meatballs. Bennett, do I need to call your parents to let them know you're here? I don't want them to worry."

"No ma'am, my dad doesn't come home until till after seven so I'm fine. Thank you."

She smiled at him. "Okay." And she left the room just as quickly as she had entered it.

"Sorry," John apologized again after his mom left the room; "She tends to be…" he stalled searching for the right word.

"It's fine." Bennett quickly assured him. Truth was he was half in love with John's mom. Not in a romantic way she was just everything he didn't have. She was a woman that loved her family and it showed. She kept a clean house, worried about her kid's well-being, and nurtured them.

He tried not to think about it but it was all the things his mom never was, or ever could be. It made him sad he had missed out on that in his life and he was a little pissed that John couldn't see how lucky he was. Maybe he didn't take his mom for granted but was just trying to act cool in front of a kid from school. He actually hoped that was the case.

A couple hours later they had plenty of research collected and put together when they were called downstairs for dinner. John's mom made both boys wash their hands before sitting at the table. Bennett sat next to John in the extra chair pulled up for him and his parents sat on either end of the rectangular table.

John's little sister bounced into her chair at the table just as they were about to say grace. She was cute. She was still dressed in her soccer gear and her hair was pulled into a high pony tail but she had blonde wispy and frizzes trying to escape on all sides. She looked up at him curiously with intense green eyes. She gave him a dazzling smile with a mouth full of colorful braces that made her all the more adorable.

Introductions were made, her name was Kara. He also shook hands with Mr. Marshall who he learned was their high school football coach. He had a day time job as a bank manager. Bennett waited until everyone else had filled their plates with pasta and meatballs. He didn't even know they had real shredded parmesan cheese he had only seen the fake grated stuff in the plastic bottles and he was lucky if they ever had that. Mrs. Marshall had also made garlic bread and a fresh salad. His mouth was watering so badly.

"Can Bennett come over tomorrow after football practice? We still have some work to do on this project." John inquired of his parents as he took a piece of garlic bread from the basket.

"I can't tomorrow."

"Really, how come?" John asked.

"I have to work."

"How old are you son?" Mr. Marshall asked.

"Fourteen, sir."

"And at fourteen where do you work?"

"I mow lawns sir."

He leaned back from the table. "Well that's awfully admirable. What does your dad do? Do I know him?"

"He's a mechanic at the Ford dealership, his name is Hank Treadwell."

"Good honest hard labor. I don't think I know him though."

"What about your mom?" Mrs. Marshall asked.

Bennett saw Kara's eyes widen. She knew, he thought.

"She died when I was eleven."

Mrs. Marshall reached out and squeezed his hand. "I'm sorry."

He didn't look up but down at his plate when he mumbled, "It was a long time ago." He missed the exchange between the Marshall's.

Mr. Marshall asked Kara how her practice went and she began to tell him. The conversation moved on from there but never circled back to Bennett and he was relieved. When they were done Bennett carried his plate to the sink and helped clear the table.

Mr. Marshall offered to drive him home. Bennett ran upstairs to grab his bag. On his way back downstairs he walked by Kara's bedroom. She was sitting on her bed propped up by a pillow with a history book on her knees. "Goodnight Bennett." She called out without looking up.

He stopped short just outside her bedroom door. "Um, goodnight."

She looked up. "I'll see you at school tomorrow?" she asked.

"Sure." He sounded unsure to his own ears.

"Okay." She gave him another dazzling smile.

"Bennett you ready?" Mr. Marshall called up the stairs.

"Yes, I'll be right there." He looked back at Kara, "I have to go."

"All right."

Bennett quickly made it downstairs where Mr. Marshall was waiting for him. Bennett said goodbye to John and thanked Mrs. Marshall for a wonderful meal. She seemed to blush at the compliment.

Bennett climbed into the front seat of the family sedan. He gave his address and some quick directions.

"So do you play any sports, Bennett?"

"No, sir."

"Well that's a shame. Have you ever tried out for any sports?"

"No sir."

"Would you be interested in trying out for the football team? We have already started for this season but you could practice with us to see if it's something you would be interested in doing next year." He added, "John's on the team," when he sensed his hesitation.

"I'm not sure. I don't want to lose my lawn mowing job."

"Have you thought about your future? Do you plan to go on to college?"

"I would like to. I need to apply for scholarships, I do get good grades."

"That's great, grades are important. Colleges tend to look at more than transcripts though. They like to see a well-rounded student." Bennett considered this as he pondered all Mr. Marshall had said. It was true he knew that colleges liked the whole picture, especially if it came down to a scholarship.

"I'll think about it," he told Mr. Marshall.

"That's good enough for me." He seemed pleased with himself.

The car pulled in front of his modest brick ranch house. "Thanks for the ride, Mr. Marshall."

"You are very welcome. Have a good night."

"Thanks, you too."

The next day Bennett was at the lunch table with his social studies book open reading when Kara slid in next to him her shoulder bumping his; her thigh touching his.

"Hey!" she put her back pack on the table and fished out her lunch bag. Once she had retrieved it she put her bag on the floor.

He looked down at her and she looked up at him a huge smile plastered across her face. He grinned down at her. He shut his book.

"Hey, yourself." She stole one of his French fries off his cafeteria tray and popped it into her mouth. She pulled a pudding cup out of her bag and offered it up to him. "Do you like butterscotch? John does but I don't. Do you want it as a trade for maybe one or two more fries?"

He took up her offering, "Sure."

"Great," she took another fry and swirled it around in his ketchup. She scooted away so they were no longer touching and he missed it. They ate lunch together, she mostly asked questions and he answered them.

"So, are you going to join the football team?"

"I'm going to see what all the fuss is about." He told her.

She lit up and clapped her hands together, "Oh, good. Dad's going to be so happy."

"What about you? Will it make you happy?"

She stole another one of his French fries off his cafeteria tray. She shrugged her shoulders, "If it makes you happy, that's what really matters, right?"

The bell rang and they stood. They walked together as she threw out her trash and he got rid of his tray.

"I'll see you around." She waved good bye and was swallowed up in the crowd of high school students.

He stood there a moment. In the course of twenty four hours his life had completely changed.

Chapter Four

Bennett moaned. He was unsure where he was. All he knew was the sun was bright overhead and he hurt, everywhere! His head was pounding and his leg was throbbing. His back was sore along with his shoulders and knees. His hand came up to his head.

"Bennett, are you okay?"

"Kara?" his voice croaked out.

There was a pause then, "No, it's Harper." She sounded sad. She was right by his side. Why was she sad? Then it hit him all at once, like a ton of bricks, what had happened, the crash, the raft, the explosion of the plane. His beautiful Kara was gone. He squeezed his already shut eyes even tighter shut and his hand came up to rub them.

He took a moment to let the pain wash over him, and then opened his eyes. The sun was blinding. He focused in on Harper's concerned face. He tried to sit up, Harper helped him up.

He looked around and saw nothing but ocean on either side of them. "How long have I been out?"

"Two days."

He was shocked. "Two days?"

"Not including the day we crashed. We are down to one bottle of water left." She offered it up to him. "Just take a sip please."

He gladly took it from her trying to process the information she had given him. He opened the bottle and took a sip even though he could have downed the whole bottle. He put the lid back on and handed the warm water back to her. She tucked it back into the shade of the suitcase.

"What's in the suitcase?" he asked.

She laughed, "I wouldn't know. It's locked."

"Bummer." He looked around for something to say. "Where's the Calvary?" he asked half joking.

"Well, they showed up yesterday, but I told them we were good." She smiled at him.

He cracked a smile, "Good call."

“You have a pretty good bump on your head and a gash on your legs. They are starting to scab over and are black and blue.”

“I can feel it.” He gingerly touched his right temple and felt an egg on his head then inspected his leg. “It hurts like a bastard.”

“I’ll bet. I’m sore all over too but I don’t have nearly the injuries you have. Mine are just a few black and blue marks that I’ve found.”

He noticed and mentioned, “You lost your shoes.”

She looked down at her bare feet, “Yup. You’re lucky your shoes are strapped on. But if we never leave this raft it won’t matter.”

“Don’t say that. We are going to get rescued.”

“I have been praying non-stop. We have kids we need to get home too.” Her voice broke. Her head turned and she angrily swiped away a tear, she thought she had already cried them all out.

“We should have opted for that extra day.” He sounded bitter.

“I’ve already been over this. We obviously had no way of knowing this was going to happen. We can’t change it now and there is no sense in beating ourselves up over it. I’ve already done that.”

“What am I going to do without Kara?”

Tears welled up in her eyes, "I guess we will find out."

"Come here." He held his left arm out. She joined him on his side of the float and his arm went around her shoulder. "I'm sorry I brought it up."

She shook her head. "It's okay. It's not like we can pretend it didn't happen. We need to accept that this is our life now. We no longer have spouses or best friends." She spread her arm towards the raft and the ocean.

"We still have each other." He offered up.

"True, and our kids at home." She responded. He nodded.

They sat in silence for a while. She hadn't gotten much sleep since the crash and she had worried constantly about Bennett waking up that she ended up falling asleep on his shoulder. He let her sleep and his thoughts wondered on to what they were going to do. Not much of a choice. They were somewhere in the middle of the ocean. They needed a rescue or needed to wash up on shore, preferably somewhere with civilization.

A couple of hours later Bennett was shaking her awake. "Harper!" he sounded excited, "I think I see something!"

She rolled away from him slightly embarrassed she had fallen asleep on him. "What?" she asked looking around.

"There," he pointed to the right of him, "I see something."

Squinting her eyes, she scanned the horizon. She didn't see anything on the first sweep but on the second time back around she did notice something that was a dark form.

"Oh my God!" she squealed. "I see it! I see it! What do you think it is? Do you think it's an island or a boat?"

"I'm not sure, but I think we should start paddling in that direction. Just in case this current has us going in another direction. I don't see it moving but if it's a boat it could be coming straight at us."

They wasted no time getting a system in place to start using their arms to paddle in the direction of what they weren't quite sure of yet.

After about an hour they were exhausted and closer but not much. They had determined it was more than likely was not a ship. Bennett told Harper she could take a break. She massaged her shoulders while she lay on the floor of the raft.

Then she took over and Bennett took a ten minute break. Then they worked together again for awhile. This continued on for quite some time. They took a water break. Two hours later they could definitely tell it was an island. Now they had picked up the current of the island and were able to let the raft do the work and draw them in.

Exhausted but excited they sat in the raft and waited. The sun was low on the horizon and close to setting. Close to shore their raft got snagged on a rock popping the raft. The rock was just under the surface. They scrambled to get the water bottles, suitcase and what was left of the raft collected. They swam to shore.

They hauled their stuff through the sand to the shade of the trees and collapsed. Once they had caught their breath they sat up. They watched the sunset. They spread the raft out to lie down on. They each had one more drink of water. There was just a little left for tomorrow, hopefully they could find fresh water on the island.

Even though they were no longer on the boat her body still felt like it was rocking back and forth. Harper felt like she was swaying up and down with the swells of the waves. She finally curled up and dozed off.

The next morning Bennett was awake before her.

"I found coconuts, but haven't been able to crack them open yet."

"We will have to look for something to bust them open."

"I've tried throwing them at trees. I'm surprised I didn't wake you. I also tried using these rocks to bash them in but it didn't work."

"I think you need to peel the outer layer off first."

He turned the coconut over in his hand. "I think a sledge hammer would be good right about now."

"There are a lot of things that would be good right about now."

"We should make a sign on the beach that can be seen from the water and the air. So it needs to be big."

"We can use those rocks," Harper suggested.

"Sounds good."

They worked together until Harper noticed how much he was dragging his leg behind him. "Why don't you go sit down?" When he wanted to protest she continued, "We are going to need to find fresh water and I don't know how long that is going to take. I could always go without you and bring you back water I may or not find…" she left it at that.

He held up his hands in defeat. "Alright, alright I'll go rest." He hobbled over to the tree line and took a seat.

Harper was worried about Bennett he had suffered a serious head injury. He also had a severe gash on his leg that was causing him to limp. She was concerned his leg may get infected and didn't want to have to think about what that meant if they didn't get off this island quickly.

She was hauling out rocks as big as she could carry and trying to create large, letters spelling out HELP as large as she could make them. She was sweating and tired and hungry and her mouth felt like it was full of cotton. Her muscles ached from yesterday's paddle to the island. This hard labor was not helping them recover. This was not like an air conditioned gym workout by any stretch of the imagination.

She struggled through the hot sand and into the shade where Bennett was rubbing his calf. She was shaky and light headed and in desperate need of food.

"Are you sure you want to come with me? I could go and come back?"

Stubbornly he struggled to get up, sighing she helped him. Then went and found him a big stick he could use to support himself. They had determined that if they headed in land it would be their best bet rather than walking the perimeter. It was a dense long trek; but at least it felt several degrees cooler under the cover of the trees. She had to stop several times to wait for him to catch up but he never asked to stop. After what seemed like an hour they made it to the other side. They had not found any fresh water.

"Well this sucks," Harper sank down to the sand. Bennett collapsed next to her. "How are you doing?"

"I feel like I've been in a plane crash," he replied dead pan.

She laughed a quick short laugh, and then it bubbled up inside her. It wasn't funny, it really wasn't but if she wasn't laughing she would be crying. Once she composed herself she asked, "Okay what do you think? Right or left?"

He looked up and down the beach seriously contemplating her question. "I say we go left."

"Okay, left it is! Are you ready?"

"Ready as I'll ever be." They sat for another minute unmoving, neither one of them really ready to get up. Bennett moved first and Harper followed. Staying in the shade as much as they could, they walked down the beach. About halfway down the stretch of beach that they could see they decided to cut inland. Bennett took the lead. That was where they found bananas.

"Awesome!" Harper sang it out loud. They each ate one banana after another until they almost felt sick. She had three empty water bottles in her pockets so Bennett put as many bananas as he could in his carpenter short pockets. She picked up two bundles to carry.

About twenty minutes later Bennett stopped and cocked his ear to the right.

"What?" she asked.

"I hear something."

She cocked her head to the side listening. It was rushing water. Her head whipped back around to Bennett. Her eyes were alight with excitement. They both picked up the pace and made their way towards the sound.

When they made it through the clearing they stopped to stare. There was a twenty foot waterfall that came down into a large body of water. Rock walls surrounded the area. It started about ten feet to the right of the waterfall then the majority of the wall curved around to the left of them. Large flat rocks went from shore into the water.

Harper dropped the bananas she had been carrying on the ground and they both ran/limped out onto a big rock and lay down on their stomachs. They scooped large handfuls of fresh water past their chapped lips into their dry mouths. They drank until their bellies were full.

Bennett groaned and they both rolled over onto their backs, their bodies at least content for now. "I think I have some squished bananas in my pocket," Bennett remembered their existence.

"Oh yeah," Harper laughed as she pulled out two squished water bottles from her pockets. She opened the lids and blew air into them popping them back into shape. "What are we going to do now?"

“We need to make a shelter.”

Harper laughed, “That’s not really what I meant.” She pushed herself into a sitting position and looked around. “This place is really nice.” She surveyed the area a little more. The sun was shining into the little alcove and as she was studying the rock walls she noticed some vines covering what looked like a cave. She jumped up to go investigate.

Bennett sat up, “What do you see?” he asked.

“I think there might be a cave over there. She walked back down the rock and onto land that ran around the pool of water. She circled around until she had to climb back up onto the rocks. The opening in the rock was a little higher than her head but she was able to scale the rocks easily to get inside past some vines that only covered a portion of the opening.

“Be careful,” he hollered up to her.

“This is great!” she exclaimed once she was inside. “It’s flat and it’s about ten feet wide and about twelve feet deep. The ceiling slopes towards the back. You can stand up fully in the front and you could sit in the back. On the right side there is a rock jutting out you could use as a seat” She described the area to him.

She walked back to the opening of the cave and sat down on the edge then jumped out, “I think that’s the perfect place to camp out. But we will need to find something to pad the rock with because that would be uncomfortable to sleep. I didn't see any signs of wildlife in there. I don't think an animal has already laid claim to it."

He got up and hobbled over to her. "Great, but we should go back to the beach to see if there are any signs of rescue. We can get that suitcase and try and open it to see if there is anything of use in there."

She assessed his condition and suggested, "How about I go back for the suitcase and you try and start a fire for tonight?" She could tell he didn't want to be separated from her and saw the internal struggle he was having with himself. They both knew she would be faster on her own and they might not get back in time to get a fire started if they both went.

Finally he asked, "Are you going to be able to find your way back?"

"Yes," she answered instantly hoping this would reassure him.

It didn't but he wasn't up for the argument. "If you are not back in two hours I am coming looking for you."

"Deal."

He sighed, "Well you better get going." He watched her leave fearful of the unknown. As soon as she was out of sight he got to work on collecting dried palm tree branches and twigs to have kindling for the fire then he went in search of larger pieces of wood. When he had an adequate pile of wood he then scouted out a place to start this fire. He decided to try and start a fire on one of the flat boulder near the water. It would be safe there, nothing that shouldn't catch on fire would and it would be close to water if and when it came time to douse the flame.

Harper made her way through the jungle once more still plenty of daylight in her mind, but she knew she only had a two hour window to get back. When she finally reached the beach she took a left. She didn't walk long before she made it back to where they had started this morning. "Oh, no!" she cried out when she realized her large, HELP sign she had spent a good deal of time on this morning on was half covered in the high tide.

She ran over to see the water coming over the rocks and washing back over them. Her sadness became joy when she realized that she had inadvertently caught fish! The high tide had brought the fish in but as the water began to roll out the fish were caught behind the rocks she had placed.

She did a little happy dance on the beach. Then she began to wonder how on Earth she planned on carrying fish back to their new campsite. She walked up to the polka dotted suitcase. They hadn't tried breaking the lock yet. It was a little lock it shouldn't be that hard she prayed.

She set the suitcase up right so the lock was pointed in the right direction. She picked up one of the boulders and brought it down hard on the lock. The suitcase tipped over but the lock remained intact.

She tried again and again. Her lips puckered up and she jammed her fists into her hips. She picked up the suitcase and flung it as hard as she could. It hit a palm tree with a solid thwack and the suitcase burst open and all of its contents spilled out on to the ground.

With a squeal she ran to retrieve them. She flipped over the suitcase and the first thing she found was a hairbrush with colorful hairbands wrapped around the base of the brush. She kissed it. She found a beach towel which would come in handy. When she began to realize the clothes in the suitcase were that of a little girl's big fat tears began welling up in her eyes. Her hands found a stuffed animal. She could no longer make out the rest of the contents in the suitcase, just shapes and sizes as her vision was blurry with tears.

She hadn't taken a moment to grieve since she had come to the island. It all came rushing in at once. Sobs wracked her body. She cried and cried and cried some more. Harper clung to the stuffed animal she had her hands on and brought it to her chest. She rocked her body back and forth like she was trying to comfort a child when she was really trying to comfort herself. It wasn't working.

This suitcase contents were what was left of someone's little girl. Tears streaked freely down her face. It could have been one of her girls. She had babies waiting at home for her that she couldn't get back to. She began to imagine how they were reacting to the news that both their parents were dead or best case scenario missing. They were as good as orphans now as far as the world was concerned.

Once she was spent she decided she was going to make it off this damn island if it was the last thing she did and she was going to see her babies again. She collected herself and put all the items back in the suit case. She pulled two fish out of the water and released the rest of them hoping she could repeat the process the following day.

Her kids needed her and they needed her alive. She was bound and determined to make that happen. She realized the tarp was still there so she rolled up the two fish in the tarp with a couple of coconuts. She threw the tarp over her shoulder and picked up the suitcase by its busted up handle. She followed her foot prints in the sand until it turned into the trees and started on her journey back to camp.

She made it back to camp before dark to find Bennett had been successful in starting a fire. She also noticed he had taken a dip in the water. His hair was wet and his wounds were cleaned up. She would need to find a time to bathe as well. He jumped up when he saw her coming. He rushed to her. "What happened? Are you okay?"

She gave him a weak smile, “I brought dinner and I managed to get the suitcase open.” She dropped both on the ground. He lifted the suitcase lid looked inside then dropped it. He pulled her into his arms and held her tight. She didn’t think she had anymore tears left in her but she was wrong. She clung to him and cried some more. It took her less time to recover this time. She backed away and he turned away from her and she suspected he may not have been ready to let go either. He was trying to be strong for both of them.

Bennett grabbed some sticks and speared the fish. He handed one to her, “Can you help me rotate them? I’ll have to try and build something to use to cook these.”

She took it thankful for something to do. He found two sticks with forks on the end and made them the same height. He wedged them between the rocks on either side of the fire. They combined the fish on the one stick and laid it across the forked sticks. They each sat on either side and turned the handmade spit. It didn’t work well but they made it happen.

She hated seafood but after not eating a real meal for three days she was starving. Surprisingly enough her mouth began to water. It still took her a few minutes to get over the idea of just biting into it, but once she saw Bennett do it she gave in. It didn’t have much taste because she just inhaled the fish. They had filled their water bottles and drank out of them to wash down their dinner.

Later they took inventory of the suitcase. The name on the label said, "Daphne" Her home address was in Austin, Texas. They guessed the girl to be around the age of ten. The stuffed animal she had held was a grey bunny with long floppy ears. There was a pair of pink flip flops that Harper could just barely squeeze into. One fluffy beach towel that was multi-colored cheetah print would come in handy. There was the hairbrush with six hair ties, two headbands, one was black and stretchy and the other was a hard plastic blue one with rhinestones.

Inside a quart sized Ziploc baggie were shampoo and conditioner, sunscreen and along with that a toothbrush with stars and toothpaste. Inside a zebra print makeup bag were nail clippers, a ring, and bracelets, Q-tips in a separate plastic container, Chap Stick and purple nail polish. A yellow hand mirror, a pair of black sun glasses, a couple of sundresses, four pairs of shorts, four tee shirts, a couple of tank tops, a skirt and a pair of jeans, one sweatshirt, five pairs of panties and a pair of socks filled the rest of the suitcase. At the bottom she found a coloring book and crayons.

"Wow, there is a lot in here we can use." Harper tried to think survival and getting home to her kids.

"The clothes aren't going to be much help. Nothing fits us."

"Oh I can do something with the clothes. I think I can make them into blankets and pillows."

He seemed impressed, “Okay MacGyver I will be anxious to see what you come up with.”

She loved being able to prove people wrong. She held out her hand, “Challenge accepted.” He shook her hand firmly.

They decided on a game plan for the following day.

“I want to keep track of how long we are on this island.” Harper informed him, “I can use the coloring book and crayons.”

“That’s a good idea. We need to go back to the beach and remake the HELP sign further away from the tide. We should probably do one for the other side of the island, just in case. We can hunt and gather, To do that we need to explore more of the island. Hopefully we can find more than bananas and fish, but if not it’s a good source of protein and potassium.”

“I want to see what I can make out of these clothes. Also I have been noticing lots of downed palm branches. I think I can weave them together to make mats for the cave. We are going to need to add a little cushion to the floor in there before it’s a comfortable sleep. But seeing as we are getting rescued tomorrow it will just be something to keep me busy.” She smiled at him in exaggerated hopefulness.

“Should we divide and conquer? Bennett asked.

"It might be faster, but I also feel I don't want you to have to do all that on your own. If we get up early we can have a banana for breakfast. We can start on the opposite side of the island and work our way back to where hopefully we will have caught fish. We'll come back here have lunch or dinner depending on what time we get back. Then I'll work on my stuff and you can scout out the interior of the island."

"Deal," he sounded pleased with the solid plan.

"How's your leg doing?" she inquired.

Bennett looked down at the injured limb, a deep gouge, six inches across his calf. "It felt better after the dip in the pool," he was referring to the body of water next to them, "but it's starting to ache again. Really wishing we had Advil right about now. My head is pounding."

"I'm glad you got it cleaned up. We really need to be careful you don't get an infection." She didn't have to add that would be extremely bad.

"That reminds me, I am going to take a long walk so you can freshen up."

She contemplated, "I think I will tonight especially since we found shampoo AND conditioner but I'm worried about this being our drinking water.

"I hear you, but I did find a run off stream over there," he pointed in the general direction, "so the water does filter out. After tonight we can go down to the beach to wash up."

She agreed feeling better. He got up to leave, "Take your time." And he hobbled off.

She gathered up the towel, flip flops, shampoo and conditioner and placed them on the rock near the water. She waited five minutes until she didn't hear him anymore then quickly removed her short sleeved button up blouse, under spaghetti strap tank, and shorts. She paused to look around. She debated keeping her bra and panties on but realized they would still be wet to sleep in and get her clothes wet.

She didn't like being naked and even if she knew there wasn't a possibility of being seen. She removed them quickly then sat down on the rock to put her feet in. She was trying to judge the distance to the bottom. She didn't have to guess, her legs slipped into the cool water up to her knees.

Harper was worried she would be grossed out by a slimy bottom but was pleasantly surprised to find a smooth sandy bottom. She stood up and found herself in about three feet of water. She waded in further down the gradual slope to get to her hips, then her shoulders. From there it dropped off and was over her head.

She dove under water and swam a little further out. This felt nice. She wadded in the water for a little while. She forced herself to relax. She leaned back and floated her arms and legs resting comfortably away from her body.

Eventually she swam back shampooed her hair and used the suds of the bubbles to wash the rest of her body including her feet she lifted out of the water. She swam out to dunk under water and rinse off then came back to apply conditioner.

She was thankful she had such a short haircut. She only used the smallest dollop of conditioner. She swam back out keeping her head above water and made it to the waterfall. She swam under the waterfall and the strength of the pounding water pushed her under. She swam down and out and repeated the process.

She liked the noise of the falls and she felt like it drowns everything else out. She let the water push her under once more. Then she tried floating nearby and allowed her feet go into the water. It took her a couple of tries but if she didn't get too close it gave her a great massage on her aching feet. If that worked she wondered about her back. If she only got partially in the falls she got a wonderful pounding back massage.

On the swim back she saw the stream Bennett had mentioned. She climbed out of the water and toweled off quickly and redressed. She put on the flip flops and returned the shampoo and conditioner to the suitcase and removed the brush. She laid the towel out to dry and added another log to the fire. She sat down on the flat boulder next to the fire to brush her hair and wait for Bennett to return.

The sun had started to set when she heard Bennett return.

"Are you decent?" he called out.

"I'm good," she responded, "You can come back."

He joined her by the fire. He sat down on the rock on the opposite side of the fire. Darkness began to close in around them. They sat in silence for a while both in their own thoughts. She pulled the bunny out of the suitcase and set it on the rock behind her. She lay down on her back with her knees bent and rested her head on the bunny.

He saw her and followed suit using his own arm as a pillow bent behind his head. They watched the stars and listened to the steady rhythm of the waterfall and the crackling of the fire. That's how they fell asleep.

Chapter Five

They woke up stiff and sore the next morning and discovered the fire had gone out in the night and was smoldering. They stood up and stretched their tired muscles. They each took a banana on the go. They made it out to the East Beach that's what they were calling it because it was the opposite side of the island from where they had first landed. They knew the other side was the west side because that's where they had watched the sun set so this is where the sun must rise.

There weren't as many rocks on this side of the island so they used downed tree branches as big as they could find and dragged them out of the jungle. They loaded up on more bananas and walked down the island towards the South Side.

On the South Side there was just a small half-moon shaped beach set back in a deep cove. They used a combo of rocks and logs to create their HELP sign. Bennett was wondering if they should put SOS instead.

"Or…we could put FREE. People have a hard time passing up the word free."

Harper laughed, "Yeah, especially Kara. She stopped at every yard sale, side of the road stand. It didn't matter."

"It's not like we couldn't afford anything she wanted."

"She just loved a bargain. She liked anything she could get for a steal and transform it into something useful or a conversation piece."

He smiled warmly, "She was good at it."

Harper pointed towards the trees, "Is that?" she asked but didn't finish her sentence as she walked towards her point of interest, "It is. It is!" She exclaimed excitedly.

He hobbled up behind her, "What did you find?"

She bent down and broke off a piece of a plant and turned around a huge grin on her face. "Do you know what this is?"

He shook his head.

"This is an aloe plant. This is awesome for healing. This will be really good for your leg. It's also great for sunburns."

“I’ve heard of Aloe lotion.”

“Yeah, this is what that’s made of. We can take this with us and once we are back to camp we will clean your leg up, apply this and wrap it so it can heal.”

“Good deal.”

She put the aloe filled pointy leaf in her pocket and on second thought took an extra one with her.

They were done the West Beach around noon. They hadn’t caught anymore fish because the rocks and begun to sink into the sand. They pulled them up and created a bunch of V shaped rocks to try and catch more fish. Then they made a large HELP sign further up the beach away from high tide.

“Well I guess its bananas for lunch.”

“My favorite,” Harper pulled one out and started peeling it. “Well this wasn’t the “crash” diet I was looking for.” She did air quotes.

He smiled as he peeled one of his bananas and ate it quickly then pulled out another one and ate it a little slower.

“I’ll go to the North Side with you before heading back to camp.”

“Alright.” They headed in that direction. What they found on the North Side was a whole lot of rock. It was the opposite of the South Side, it jutted out into the sea rather than the concave cove of the South Side. The waves were crashing up against the rocks. They climbed up the rocks. There were a lot of nooks and crannies where the water pooled in places.

They were excited to find crabs hanging out in the pools of water. They contemplated how to get them back to the camp. How did they kill them without getting pinched?

Realizing there wasn't a good option here to make a sign they climbed to higher ground. There was slate rock everywhere. Some were really sharp.

"This we can use," Bennett picked up some pieces of slate. "I can try to make tools from this and we can maybe use this to split open the coconuts." He held up a piece that looked like the top part of an axe.

"Good call. I would love to eat something other than bananas. Not only that but we could use the open coconuts as bowls once they are scraped out." Harper looked around they were at the highest vantage point of the island. This was also the narrowest part of the island.

She realized this was the top of their waterfall. She looked over the edge and could see the pool of water below and their make shift camp. She could see the ocean all the way around, no ships on the horizon. She looked up no planes in the sky. There were trees up here that lined the ridge on either side of the waterfall.

"Well maybe we can build a bonfire up here as a signal, in case-when we see someone going by." She corrected.

He was nodding his agreement with her as he did his own assessment of the area. "Okay, I'll get on that either later today or tomorrow." He put some of the rocks in his short pockets and carried the large axe looking one. "I can come back for the crabs later and that's what we can have for dinner."

"Alright, are you ready to head back?"

"Sure, lead the way."

Careful not to fall down the hill she held her hands out to steady herself. Bennett scaled past her on the slate rocks. He gave her an apologetic look. They circled back around to the waterfall.

When they got back to camp she washed her hands then opened up the aloe plant. Bennett stood still while she smeared the aloe over his wound. Then she tied Daphne's socks together and wrapped it around his calf.

Before Bennett left he tried one more time to bust open the coconuts they had lying around. He wedged the coconut in one of the crevices in the large boulders. He slammed the axe slate rock into the top of the coconut. It made a slight indentation. Picking up a rock he used it as a hammer and split the coconut wide open.

"Success!" Harper who had been watching him exclaimed.

He handed her a half. There was a drop of the coconut milk inside, she sipped it. "Not bad." She tried scrapping out the coconut flesh inside. "Oh this is good." She managed between bites.

He scooped out his fruit and ate it. "Well we can add coconut to the list of edibles on the island."

"I'm hoping we can use the open coconuts as bowls. If only we had silverware…" she gave him a look willing him to promise her that was happening next.

He laughed at her puppy dog eyed look she was giving him. "I'll see what I can do. Well, I better get going if I want to be back before dinner."

"Good luck." She called out. He waved and started for the woods. "Hey, Bennett," she called out. He turned around to look at her, "Be careful." She cautioned.

"Will do." He gave her a salute.

Harper gathered as many palm branches as she could find and stacked them up next to one of the big rocks. With her back up against the rock she began stripping the palms off the branch and making a separate pile. When she had a good pile started she began laying the pieces out to see if she could get them to weave together. It was hard at first to get them to stay together but once she got a rhythm going she got in the zone. She made sure she made it as tight as she could so hopefully none of it would unravel.

She had to get up twice to gather more palm branches but she managed to complete one mat the size of a queen sized mattress. She tried to get fancy and managed to create a border so it wouldn't come apart.

She assessed the clothes she had. She needed to find something soft she could stuff them with. Looking over the coconut she realized they had fine threads in the outer shell. Peeling it off, she pulled apart the threads. This could work she thought, but she would need a lot more. She made a separate pile of the coconuts strands. She could also strip the palm branches down to use to stuff the clothes.

She took one of the t-shirts and tied off the neck and one of the arms. She tied the other arm to another t-shirt arm. Then she began stuffing the inside of the shirt with the coconut hairs and the shredded palm branches. She tested the cushiness and was pleased. She had to get up and get more stuffing. She finished one by the time Bennett returned. Well at least he would have a pillow for tonight.

Bennett strode towards her, "You're going to be happy with me." He promised.

"Oh really?" she asked.

"Yup, hold your hands out and close your eyes."

She gave him a look.

"You don't trust me? I'm hurt."

She laughed he didn't sound hurt. "Does it move?" she asked.

"Nope."

"Okay," she closed her eyes then peeked one eye open.

"Hey!"

She squeezed them shut and held her hands out. She felt something being dropped into her hands. It wasn't wet. It didn't move. It was light weight.

"Okay you can open."

She did and was ecstatic to see what her prize was, "Almonds?! No way! This is awesome! Did you try any yet?"

"No. I needed to use the tool I had made to get them out of their outer shell. He brought them over to the rock and proceeded to crush the shell so they could get to the delicious morsel inside.

Quickly she popped a few in her mouth and crunched down on them. She thought she was in heaven. She loved almonds and they were a great source of protein. She was happy with this find.

"I didn't know what they were at first. They looked so weird on the tree. There was a green outer layer that curled out to expose the light brown shell. I picked some off the tree before I figured out what they were."

She put more in her mouth and tried to savor them. "I made a mat for the cave. I'm still working on the blanket." She informed him.

When she noticed him looking around she pointed towards the cave, "I put it in there already. He walked over to the entrance of the cave and looked in. He ran his hand over the tightly woven mat.

"Nice work, good job."

"Thanks, but it's not nearly as cushy as I would like it to be. I will have to make more. I started the blanket but for tonight it can be your pillow." She held up the one shirt she had managed to stuff.

"Nice," he took it from her and squeezed it, "Not bad, not bad at all. I can't wait to try it out tonight."

Bennett got the fire going and he cooked up the crabs he had brought back. He also had more nuts in his pocket that he shared with her after cracking them open with his rock tool. After dinner she worked on her calendar in Daphne's coloring book. She opened it to the inside cover.

She wrote down June 12th that was the day the plane went down. Then she made two marks after that and wrote above that out to sea. Then she made another two marks and wrote above that island.

Flipping to the back of the coloring book she drew a map of the island just the outer edges. She drew the waterfall nestled in between the North and East Beach. She marked each side with North, South, East and West. They knew which side was which because of where the sun rose and set. She named them, Sunset Beach, Sunrise Beach, South Cove and the other end North Pointe.

Harper looked at her drawing and was pleased with herself. She closed the coloring book and put it in the suitcase. She picked up the suitcase and took it to the cave. Inside she lined up the shampoo and conditioner on the rock ledge along with the brush. She closed the suitcase and put it in the far back corner.

Pulling out the cheetah towel she laid it on the mat. The bunny and stuffed shirt made it to the top of the mat as pillows. Laying down on it to try it out she settled in. Well it was better than the rock she slept on last night but not by much.

Meanwhile Bennett worked on making tools with the slate rocks. He used sticks with palm branches to wrap around the edges and tied them into place.

Harper hopped out of the cave and he wrapped it up for the night because it had started to get dark. They sat in front of the fire and recapped the day and tried coming up with a plan for the next day.

"Well we don't know how long we are going to be here. We are losing weight for two reasons. One we don't have much of a menu to choose from and two at least it's healthy and no junk food. We should try to get in shape while we are at it. It will be something to keep us busy and keep us strong." Bennett offered.

"I totally agree with you. We have plenty we can do, running, swimming, sit ups, push-ups, jumping jacks."

"We can start with a run tomorrow morning. Then we can work more on our projects."

"Sounds good."

They retired to the cave and lay down on the mat. "Do you want to share the towel?" she asked.

"No, it's okay you can have it. Thanks for the pillow though, it's pretty good," he said as he fluffed it up under his head.

"Good night," she rolled onto her side facing out of the cave.

"Good night," he lay on his back and eventually fell asleep.

Chapter Six

The next morning they woke up Harper asked Bennett to show her where he had found the almonds. He agreed but told her they should plan on running back.

"How's your leg doing?" she asked concerned.

"Much better, it's still a little sore but not bad"

They each took a banana for the walk through the woods. The almond trees were not far from their camp they were towards Sunrise Beach.

Once they got there they picked and ate almonds to their hearts content. They put their collection in the zippered or button portions of their shorts. Bennett weaved his way through the woods and they came out on the beach. As far as she could tell their rescue sign was still intact it was further up the beach, closer to camp.

“We should stretch so we don’t cramp up,” he suggested. He put his hands against a palm tree and stretched his legs one at a time behind him. She followed his lead. Then she picked up one of her legs from behind folding it in half, one followed by the other.

They both stretched out their arms folding an arm across their chest then pulling it tight with the other arm. She twisted at the waist. Bennett thought it would be best if they took off their shoes to run. Agreeing they left them there and decided to come back for them later.

Once he felt they were fully stretched he walked down to the waves and started out on a slow jog. She was having a hard time running next to him because his slow jog with his long stride was no match for her shorter legs. Only making it about half way down the beach Harper was begging for mercy.

Holding up one hand and clutching the other hand to her side gasping for breath she called out, “Stop!”

He had already gone several paces in front of her. He turned around maintaining his jog he came back to her.

“My side is killing me, and I can’t breathe!” she gasped out.

"Okay, here we go," he said as he raised her arms above her head. "We can walk for a bit if you like?"

"Yes, please."

"We should have brought water with us."

She looked up at him wide eyed just now realizing the gravitation of his words, no water. "Amateur," she accused.

He just laughed at her. "We will get better at this you'll see."

"I don't want to get better at this. I want to get rescued. I want to see my kids again. I want to stay fat." She stomped her foot into the ground.

He laughed again at her outburst. "How about we do this until we are rescued then you can go home never exercise again and eat anything you want."

"Promise?"

He grinned at her, "Promise."

"Okay," she huffed out. Standing up straight putting her arms down she fell into step with him.

"Griffin has a crush on Chloe." Bennett was referring to his youngest son and her oldest daughter.

"What?!" Harper exploded. This was news to her. "When? How did you find out?"

"He told me."

"He told you? Just told you? Like, hey Dad I like Chloe?"

Bennett laughed, "I wasn't going to say anything but yeah he told me a couple of weeks ago. After a cook out he was grumpy and he was mumbling under his breath. I asked him what was wrong and he said he wanted to punch Chris Tompkins in the face. I said, that's not nice, buddy. And he said, well he is being mean to Chloe. Long story short, he confessed to having a crush on her."

"Awe… that's cute! Do you think they will date?" she gasped and grabbed his arm, "Get married!?"

"Whoa, whoa, whoa, calm down. See this is why I wasn't going to tell you."

"Oh, I'm so glad you did. That's really sweet. I love Griffin, he's a great kid, Lucas too."

"Yeah, Kara and I lucked out to have two great boys. So do you and Brody, you made beautiful children."

"Thanks." She sobered up though, "They have to be so devastated right now. I can't imagine what they are going through."

"I know. It's tough knowing that they are suffering thinking both their parents are dead and we are here unable to get to them."

"Poor Paige, she is so little. The others, it will be hard on them but they will somewhat understand it. I'm afraid she won't even know what's going on."

Continuing on down the beach they contemplated their situation. They had made it down to South Cove. Her breathing had started to become normal when he asked her, "Ready to run some more?"

"Oh, sure, what the hell?" she gestured with one of her hands out in front of her.

"I'll go easy on you," he vowed.

She smiled. He jogged slower next to her and didn't leave her side. They made it thought South Cove and onto Sunset Beach when she demanded another break.

"Enough!" she gasped out.

He stopped instantly. And they fell into step walking. "I want to talk to you about something," he began.

"More family confessions?" she asked.

He smiled, "No. I was thinking…" he paused.

She waited for him.

"I want to make a burial site, no, a memorial site for Kara and Brody."

She reached out and grasped his forearm. "Bennett, that's a really good idea." She looked at him, "Were you afraid I was going to say no?"

"I wasn't sure what you would say. I was thinking about it last night while I tried to fall asleep. I would like a nice spot to go and reflect and I thought I could make markers for them with their names on them and we would have a place to be with them."

"Thank you for asking me. I love it. Where were you thinking we should put it?"

"I don't know, I was going to ask you the same thing."

Harper pondered the question. She looked around. "How about here? This is where the sunsets, and it's a really pretty spot."

"Done," Bennett agreed, "I'll work on their crosses tonight. Ready to run?" he asked.

"Seriously?" she asked but started running anyway. This time she made it to the opening they had been using to get back to camp, but just barely. As they were walking through the woods she said, "Lesson number two carry your shoes with you while you run so you don't have to go bare foot through the woods. Ouch!" she called out as she stepped on another tree branch that stabbed her in the bottom of her foot.

"Good thinking, Lincoln."

They made it back to camp and Harper filled two water bottles, handing one to Bennett who gulped his down. Sitting down on the edge of the rocks she put her blistering feet in the water, "Ah…" she sighed in relief, "They better find us tomorrow, because I do not want to do that again."

"We can swim tomorrow, or sit ups?"

"I hate sit ups," she said quickly.

"Good then swimming it is."

"I don't have a bathing suit though."

"You can stay in your underwear."

She gave him a look.

"Or…not. I can turn around so I don't see anything," he offered.

She contemplated. "Fine."

"I'm going to go get our shoes, do you want to come?"

"No thank you. I want to get working on another mat. My back is killing me from two nights sleeping on big hard cold rocks."

"Okay, I'll be back."

"See ya,"

When her feet stopped aching, or aching less she got up and went to the cave. She dug through Daphne's luggage to find what she was looking for. It was the Ziploc baggy. She opened it up and pulled out all her almonds and put them in sealing it for freshness. She left it on the ledge next to the bananas and shampoo and conditioner.

Crawling back out of the cave she gathered as many palm branches as she could find and sat down to start a new mat. This time the mat went much quicker and she was done half a mat by the time Bennett came back.

"Where were you?" she asked, "I was starting to worry. It shouldn't have taken you that long."

"Sorry, mom." He tried to sound contrite but completely failed.

She looked up to see him holding something behind his back. She scrambled to her feet and ran to him. "What did you find?!" she knew even to her own ears she sounded like a little girl Christmas morning but she didn't care. She had to know what he was holding behind his back.

He tried teasing her, "I don't know what you are talking about," and he made evasive maneuvers when she tried to run around behind him.

"Gig is up pal I know you have something."

"What's in it for me?" he continued to tease her.

"I don't beat you?" she asked dead pan.

He threw back his head and laughed. "Nope, not good enough,"

She growled in frustration, even though she wasn't really frustrated she just liked playing the part in their little game.

"How about an extra mat to sleep on tonight?" she tried bribing him.

"How about two extra mats?" he countered.

"Done. Deal. Let me see!" she was jumping up and down in front of him clapping her hands together trying and not succeeding in her attempts to see what he was hiding.

"And..." he added, "You have to run with me four days a week."

"Four!?" she cried. "Three!" she countered.

He seemed to be thinking about it.

"Bennett!" she whined.

"Okay, fine." And with a grand display he swept both arms out at the same time and produced the most beautiful pineapples she had ever seen.

She screeched in excitement and flew into his outstretched arms. He hugged her pineapples and all.

“I would have settled for four,” she said.

“I would have accepted two.” He laughed.

She let go of him sounding indignant she pushed him away from her.

“Do you want to try them?”

“Ah…yes please!”

He went over to the tools he had been working on yesterday and used one to cut off the ends of one of the pineapples. He cut it in half then trimmed the outer edges off. Then cut the half in half and handed her one of the pieces.

The juices dripped from the pineapple. She tried a bite and moaned in pleasure at the taste. “Oh my god so good,” she was wiping the juice from her chin and she looked up to see him staring at her. Embarrassed she ducked her head, “Sorry.”

“You have nothing to be sorry about. Was it worth the running and extra mats?”

“Totally worth it.” She took another bite. “This is delicious.”

That night Bennett worked on the crosses for Kara and Brody. He used two good sized sticks and formed them in the shape of a cross then used palm branches to crisscross at the junction to get it to hold. Next he cut off sheets of bark from a tree and used the inside as paper. He used a burnt stick he kept sticking in the fire to burn their names into each piece of bark. Using one of the sharp pieces of slate he ground out a hole in each corner of the bark. Then he threaded palm branches through each of the holes and tied them to the crosses.

He showed her the finished project. She looked up from her second almost completed mat. "Oh, Bennett they are beautiful. What a nice job you did." She stood up and came over to admire them. She ran her hands reverently over Brody's name. "Do you want to go put them in now?" she looked at him pleadingly.

"I wouldn't have it any other way," he told her.

"Just give me a sec." she went and finished up the mat quickly and put it in the cave.

Then she took Brody's cross and carried it while Bennett held Kara's. They walked through the woods and made their way to the end of Sunset Beach close to South Cove. They picked out an exact spot and buried the crosses in the sand. They sat down and reflected as the sun set behind them.

They didn't talk just got up and made their way back to camp. They crawled into bed that night on top of three mats. "Getting better," he commented.

"Yup, I'm making more tomorrow," she promised.

"Good deal," he yawned, "Good night Harper."

"Good night Bennett."

Chapter Seven

The next day they walked down to Sunrise Beach. He kept his back to her as she stripped down to her underwear. She carefully folded her clothes on top of her flip flops next to the beach towel. She tip toed into the water. She let out a screech. He whipped around to see what the matter was. She held out her hand and tried to cover herself with the other hand. "Sorry, sorry, the water is cold." He quickly turned back around.

"Sorry." He called out to her.

"My bad, the water just took me by surprise. It's already getting better." She waded out past the waves. Once she was hip deep she dove under the waves.

"Okay I'm in," she called out.

He started stripping down and she turned around and waded in the water. He joined her shortly with a game plan, "Okay, we stay this distance away from shore. We swim down and back."

Harper turned out to be a much better swimmer than runner. He had her beat at first but she had much more endurance for the long haul. She waited for him when she reached the end of the island.

"Wow, you did really well," he seemed impressed which made her feel good.

The swim back was much tougher. They were swimming against the current. Her muscles ached by the time they got back. This time they finished side by side. He let her get out of the water first and turned around so she could have her privacy.

Harper took off her tank top and wrung it out. Taking the towel she wiped down as best she could then tried to dry her short hair. She quickly put on her shirt, shorts and flip-flops. "You can come out now."

He swam out and when she saw his chest coming out of the water when he had gained his footing she quickly turned around. She held the towel they needed to share out at arm's length.

He took the towel from her. With her back still to him she started talking, "I liked the swim, much better than running."

"Yeah, you did great," he said as he toweled himself off. "You want to alternate? Run, swim, run?"

"I was thinking, run, swim, swim, run."

He laughed, "Okay, with me. As long as we are doing something it should be good." She could hear him getting dressed behind her. "Good to go," he said as he zipped up his shorts. "Do you want to try exploring the island with me?" he asked her.

"Sure, you seem to find something new and wonderful every time you go out so why not. Maybe you could show me where the pineapples came from?"

"Sure. It's this way." He walked down the beach away from camp then cut into the woods. There were actually several pineapple trees along the way. He showed her his method. He walked from one beach to the other then would walk about ten feet down the beach then cut back through woods. He explained he was trying to get the lay of the land without missing anything. She asked if he could fill in her map back at camp.

"Sure. I'll even make a key to show where certain foods can be found."

"Good idea."

They walked through the woods three times and didn't find anything new just a lot of the same. "I guess it's you that's the good luck charm." She pouted slightly.

"You never know," he told her, "I've probably found everything there is to find on this island."

They walked back to camp. She gave him the coloring book and he began filling it out.

She worked on making more mats. They worked in comfortable silence until he pointed out, "It's been a week since the plane crashed?!"

She looked up "I know it feels twice as long." She looked around at their camp. "We have done pretty well for ourselves though. We have food, shelter and fresh water. Now if we could just get somebody to rescue us we can brag about all we've done and get home to our kids."

"That would be nice. They are probably at our funeral now."

"Did you and Kara have a will?"

"Yeah, her parents will get the boys. They will liquidate what they can and we have college savings accounts set up for both of them. What about you?"

"Brody took care of all that. I do know that we asked his brother and his wife to take the kids but now that he is getting a divorce, I don't know. Maybe my mom and Frank or Brody's parents can take them. I would like to hope that they would move into our house so the kids will be able to stay in a familiar place and not have to change schools. Did you guys have a burial spot picked out?"

"No. Did you?"

"No, Brody didn't like talking about things like that. I was lucky we had a will made out. Do you think we will have combined services? We have so many similar friends and our families all know each other."

"Probably."

"I want to be buried on a hill, under a tree," she told him, "with a nice view."

"Well hopefully when we get back you will get to see where your parents picked for you and Brody."

"I hope you and Kara are right next to us." She started to get choked up talking about it. When they got home it will be weird to see all of their graves.

"Me, too," sensing she was done with the topic he dropped it. "I'm done with the map." He stood up, "Where do you want me to put it?"

"In Daphne's suitcase please."

"I'm going to go get some food."

"Okay, can you make sure you bring back some coconuts I need more stuffing for the blanket. The palm branches are okay but the smaller fibers of the coconut work better."

"Will do." And with that he was gone.

She finished up the mat and tied the mats she had already finished together so they wouldn't shift which they had been.

They continued with their exercise routine and she finished up the mats so they were thick enough to have a decent night sleep on. They ate a lot of coconuts trying to get the clothes stuffed.

Bennett came rushing into camp. "I have two surprises for you!"

She jumped up and ran to him. He tossed her something in the air and she caught it. It was about the size of a softball. It was green and red on the outside. She turned it over in her hand, "Is this a mango?"

"I think so."

"Let's open it up."

He followed her over to the tools and she quickly spliced it open. Inside was a yellow fruit. She handed him a piece and ate the piece in her hand. "Yup this is absolutely mango. Great find. Hey, what's your other surprise?"

"You are going to need your towel."

"Okay!" she ran to the cave and grabbed the towel and slipped on her flip flops. She was so excited, "It's like we are going on a field trip." She grinned at him and he grinned right back at her. He led the way through the jungle. They ate their mango as they traipsed through the woods.

After a while Harper was having a hard time keeping up with Bennett, "Slow down," she called out.

Bennett turned around to wait for her. "Where are we going anyway?" she asked.

"It's a surprise," was all he would allow. They were headed through the jungle towards South Cove. All he had told her was to bring her towel. They came to a small clearing and she could see the cove beach about fifty feet away through the trees.

Bennett stepped aside and she noticed a pool of water. It was oval in shape about six feet wide and four feet across. She could see steam coming up from the water. She looked at Bennett, "A hot spring?"

"Yup."

"Oh my God! I could kiss you!" she threw her arms around him. He was taken by surprise but returned her embrace laughing. "Did you try it yet?" she asked as she released him.

"No I found it and came to get you."

"This is awesome. Are you going in?"

"Um, I was going to let you go in by yourself."

"Don't be silly. You turn around I'll get in then I won't look and you can get in. The water is cloudy we won't see anything. This is a luxury we should both enjoy it together."

"Alright." He seemed pleased she was including him in this.

“Okay, turn around.” She twirled her finger.

“Oh right.” He quickly turned around.

She stripped out of her clothes but left her bra and panties on. She left her stuff including her towel right next to the edge. She sat on one of the rocks surrounding the hot spring she slipped her legs in the water. It felt incredible. It was piping hot like a hot tub unfortunately no bubbles which were her favorite part. She slid in and sat on one of the rocks the water came up to her neck. She sighed and leaned her head back against the rock and closed her eyes.

“Can I come in yet?”

She laughed, “Don’t take this the wrong way but I totally forgot you were here.”

“Ouch,” his hand went to his heart, “Why would I take offense? It’s not like I have feelings or anything.”

She looked up at him, “I’m really sorry.” She was sincere, “Come in and see for yourself and you will know exactly what I’m talking about. I’ll close my eyes.”

Bennett stripped down to his boxer briefs and lowered himself into the opposite side of the hot spring. “Ohhhh…” he groaned.

“You see what I mean?”

“What? I’m sorry were you talking to me?” he grinned at her when she looked at him.

"Touché." She smiled back. Their eyes held for a minute longer than was comfortable. She broke contact first and put her head back and closed her eyes again. What was that all about, she wondered? Her heart was racing just a little bit.

They soaked relaxing in the heat. "We should name the island." Harper suggested.

He sat forward, "I like it. Hmm…" he pondered the gauntlet she had thrown down. "How about…Desert Island? I don't know I'm no good at this."

"Not a bad try, how about combining our names like, Harnett Island or Benner Island."

"Survivor Island?"

"Oh, good one."

A couple of days later they found some washed up driftwood and decided to carry it back to camp to use as seats. They carried a log and set in down in front of the spot they used to have their campfires.

They stood back and admired their bench. Bennett's hands splayed out to the log, "We have furniture!" he proclaimed.

She smiled, "I've never been so excited to have a log to sit on."

Chapter Eight

About a month after being on the island Bennett broached the subject he had been dreading. “I think we should consider making a raft and getting off this island.”

Harper looked up at him over the fire. “I don’t know if that’s a good idea,” she said slowly.

“What if no one ever comes for us and we never leave this island. We would never see our kids again.”

“Okay what if we get killed out at sea!? We will never see our kids then either!”

“But what if there is civilization right around the corner?”

“Then we would have seen a plane or boat or something. Listen I’ve always been told if you get lost stay put and someone will eventually find you. If we leave they could miss us."

"Harper, no one is looking for us anymore. They are assuming we are dead. No one is coming." He let the gravity of his words settle over her.

"That may be true but we can live here. We have food, water and shelter. Out there how long will it last? What if we run into a storm? What if the boat sinks? What if we get eaten by sharks?"

"What if we die here?" he asked.

"I have to believe that I will see my kids again and I have to stay strong and healthy for them here."

"I plan on making a raft and you can choose to come with me or stay here the choice is up to you."

"What?! You would leave me here by myself?"

"You just said you can survive here." He pointed out. He leaned forward. "Harper, I have to try. It will kill me not to try. This way here I get rescued then we can come find you."

"And what happens if you die out there and I never know what happened to you?"

"Then you tell my kids I died trying to get to them."

Tears welled up in her eyes. "I can't lose you too." She got up and ran from him and the fire and everything she didn't want to hear. She made it to the beach before she collapsed letting out a gut wrenching sob. She knew he was right but that didn't make it any less scary.

Yes, she would love for him to be rescued and come save the day but that's not what her gut was telling her would happen. She knew if she went with him it would mean less supplies he could pack and the supplies would go twice as fast.

She was already having a hard enough time only having one person to talk to. To be by herself she just might go insane. Yes she had the substance to keep herself alive but would she have the mental capacity to keep it together. She sure hoped so because she couldn't see herself going. It was too scary out there. She felt safe here. And soon she would feel alone.

She wondered how long it would take him to make a raft. Maybe he would fail at that and she wouldn't have to worry about it. Did she want him to fail? She wasn't sure. Maybe, maybe not? She growled in frustration.

Bennett didn't come for her. She was almost wishing he would. That he would tell her he was stupid and he didn't really mean it and he would stay here with her as long as it took to be rescued. That didn't happen and when she was done crying and feeling sorry for herself she walked back to camp.

He was still sitting up next to the fire when she returned. He seemed like he was contemplating all the problems of the world which in a way he was. "I'm going to bed." She announced and she headed straight for the cave.

He didn't respond with his normal, good night like he did every night since they had been here. Feeling even sorrier for herself she crawled in the cave and threw herself down on the mattress she had created.

She was still stewing hours later when he finally crawled into bed. Neither one spoke to each other and it was a long while before either one drifted off to sleep. The next morning she woke up to find he wasn't there. She got up and realized he wasn't in camp either.

She went to the bathroom and when she got back she found he still wasn't back. So much for their run this morning she thought, it's a nice day off. Then she heard some noise off in the distance.

Bam, bam, bam. What the hell was that she thought? She began following the noise into the woods. The noise just got louder and louder. She came across Bennett in the woods with his shirt off swinging his man made axe over his head chopping down trees.

"What the hell are you doing," she demanded.

"What the hell does it look like? I'm making a boat."

She covered her face with her hands, "Oh my God, are you serious? I thought ..." she trailed off. What? What did she think? That because she said no he would listen to her? Of course not. He didn't have to listen to her.

She was exasperated and she could tell he was too. He stood there looking at her waiting for her to finish her sentence. "Fine!" she threw her hands up in the air. "I'll help you but I'm not going with you." She pointed a finger at him.

He grinned at her. Of course he was grinning, he had won. She hated losing. "What do you need me to do?"

"Can you make me rope?"

"Can I make you rope?"

"Yeah, I saw the way you weaved our mattress. I'll bet you could make rope out of the coconut shavings."

She groaned, "Do you know how many coconuts we had to eat to make that blanket?"

"We don't necessarily need to eat them all just pre skin them." He suggested.

"Do you know how long that's going to take me?"

"Months, I'm guessing."

"Oh goodie," she said with false excitement. She looked up at the sky in frustration, "Where's a freaking helicopter when you need one?" She threw her hands up in the air before walking away.

Bennett grinned as he watched her walk away. He wiped the sweat off his forehead that had already accumulated. He hadn't needed his morning run, he was getting quite a workout swinging this axe.

This island living was the best diet and exercise plan he had ever been on. His beer belly seemed to be melting away. He could tell Harper's face had slimed down, not that it needed to but was more angular now not the soft curves she once had.

His arms were starting to get toned along with his calf muscles from running. He was also getting quite the beard growth. Thankfully it wasn't scratchy anymore. He was starting to get used to it. In his line of work he was used to shaving every day. It was a nice break, but he would take it all back to be home. He would take back his beer gut, his shaving daily, all the stresses of life to be home with his kids.

Bennett got back to chopping away at the trees thinking about what it would be like to see his kids again. He fantasized about the reunion he would have with them, they would be so excited their dad was alive. He was excited to think about them realizing they weren't orphans.

Meanwhile, Harper was taking the shells off of the coconuts swearing under her breath. Not that there was anyone around to hear it. Her rumbles and rants were just that, it was just making her feel better to have something to gripe about.

This was going to be so labor intensive and who knew if it would be worth it or not. It's not like she had anything better to do but still. She was not happy about this. She was worried she wasn't exactly sure about what yet but it wasn't sitting well with her.

She stripped all the coconuts they had gathered and sat down to try and figure out how she would possibly make rope. She thought of friendship bracelets she had made as a kid that she would braid. She took a bunch of the strings and tied the ends in a knot, then began braiding them together. Before getting to the end she tried adding extra string to keep the braid going.

It was messy but it was working. She wasn't sure how thick he would need this rope but she kept going. Worst case scenario she would have to braid the braids together to make it thicker. She got a smile on her face as she started to compare this to braiding her girl's hair. She wondered if she would ever be able to do that again. She really believed she would.

Her fingers and hands were getting calloused with all this labor and without any lotion to rejuvenate her skin. She really wished she had music she could listen to while she worked like when was at home. She used to get so much accomplished when she could rock out to music while she was at home. It inspired her to keep going.

Her kids kept her going. She pictured Chloe's beautiful face, Colton's sense of humor and Paige dancing around the house. She needed to get home for them and everything she did was for them.

Two weeks later Bennett noticed that Harper was oddly quiet all day. At dinner he asked "Is everything okay?"

She shook her head and started to cry. He went to her side immediately he put his arm around her shoulder. "Are you still mad at me? Is it the rope? You don't have to do it if you don't want to."

She was shaking her head as he talked. Wiping her nose she explained, "It's not that."

"Then what is it? Can I help you with something?"

"It's Paige's birthday today!" she wailed, "I'm not there for her. She's this many today." She held up her hand showing five fingers. Kids that age did that when asked how old they were. "She is missing me and I'm missing her. I can't get this time back that we are losing here."

Understanding registered "Oh Harper, I'm sorry. I had no idea. We should do something to celebrate."

He jumped up and put a hand down for her. She looked up at him with a tear stained face. "What are you doing?"

"We are going to a birthday party."

"What?"

"Just follow me." He still had his hand outstretched to her. She didn't take it immediately and he almost though she wouldn't. Surprising them both she reached up and gave him her hand. He hoisted her up quickly bringing her to her feet.

He let go of her hand and started walking. "Where are you going?" she asked.

"Come on you'll see." And he kept walking.

Hurrying she caught up to him. Conversation was non-existent as they walked out to Sunset Beach and down to Kara and Brody's memorial site. "Have a seat," he instructed her.

Doing so, she watched him walk around the beach collecting sticks. Then he came to kneel down in front of her with his back turned to her. She couldn't see what he was doing and she was curious.

After a couple of minutes he sat back and said, "Walla!" with a grand gesture sweep of his hands. In front of her was a beautiful rounded three layered sand cake with five twigs sticking out of the top representing candles.

Smiling warmly at the gesture she looked to Bennett who was anxiously awaiting her approval. He handed her a branch, "Do you want to do the honors of decorating the cake? I'm no good at such things." He told her.

"I don't know about that. You seemed to do pretty well." She took the stick anyway and began to draw flowers and swirl patterns in the sides of the layers. She picked up sea shells and placed them at intervals around the cake. Then she got up and walked to the edge of the jungle where some wild flowers were in bloom.

She plucked a red one that had a bright yellow center which reminded her of her daughter's fiery red hair and her sunshine personality. She rearranged the candles on top to circle the circumference rather than going straight across then placed the flower in the center.

She sat back on her haunches and admired her creation, with Bennett's help.

"See, you're much better at it than I am. I think Paige would love this cake."

Smiling a sad smile she nodded her head, "She would have loved it."

"Do you want to sing her happy birthday?"

"Okay." And they did that too. Harper sang in a much gentler tone, while Bennett sang loudly and with a lot of flair adding "Cha, cha, cha" in between lines of the song. Something their boys would have done. She was laughing at his antics by the end of the song. She was still sad she was missing her daughter's birthday, but Bennett had taken a lot of the sting out of it.

Doing something, helped. She knew it would never be enough for her or Paige but it was something she could tell her daughter she did for her. That she was loved and missed and thought of.

"What would you have gotten her for her birthday?"

She laughed, "A flashlight."

It was his turn to laugh, "Really, a flashlight?"

"I know it sounds crazy but that's what she wants. She was always taking our emergency flash light and burning out the batteries. That's another thing we would have to get her is plenty of batteries. I'm sure Brody would have bought her the latest and greatest toy as well but I'm pretty sure the flashlight would have been a big hit."

Pausing she thought of how her daughter's birthday party would have gone. Everyone from the neighborhood would have been there. They would have sent out invitations to all her classmates. They may have had it at the house or one of the birthday party venues.

Looking over at him she expressed her gratitude, "Bennett, thank you so much for this. You always know what to do."

"I try," he grinned sheepishly at her.

Chapter Nine

One night in the cave Harper was having a nightmare. She was crying out in her sleep.

Bennett awoke and saw Harper tossing and turning. He scooted over to her and tried shaking her shoulder to wake her. She rolled over and her arm went around his hip. Her head snuggled under his chin on his chest. She was crying in her sleep.

"Shhh…Its okay." He rubbed her back and tried to comfort her.

"I was having a bad dream," she offered up.

"I figured. Do you want to talk about it?"

She sniffed into his chest. "Sorry."

"Nothing to be sorry about," he reassured her.

"I was dreaming the kids were in the ocean after the crash and I couldn't reach them."

"Harper, I'm sorry. Thankfully it was just a nightmare. They are safe at home in their beds." He was methodically rubbing her back. She eventually began to calm down and he could feel her muscles relax. Once she was fully back to sleep and resting comfortably he tried to pull away but she only tightened her grip.

He sighed and tried to fall back asleep. They had been on this damn island too long. Eventually he fell asleep as well.

When Harper was coming too in the morning for a split second she thought she was home in Brody's arms. Her head was on his chest one leg thrown over one of his. His arm was around her back and resting on her shoulder. She realized quickly this was not her husband; it was her best friend's husband. She sat up quickly and rolled away.

Bennett stretched and opened his eyes. "You okay?" he asked.

"Yup, I'm just fine. You?" she asked briskly not turning around to look at him.

He sat up next to her. "I'm good. You ready for breakfast?"

"I think I'm going for a walk. I will just take a banana with me."

He thought about asking her if she wanted company but didn't want her to have to tell him no. She put on the flip flops then slid out of the cave and didn't look back. She hustled through the woods.

When she got to the beach she went to the right and around the corner. She made it to the rocky area where the tide was coming in strong. She climbed up to the high point and found a spot to sit under a tree. Her back rested up against the tree trunk as she stared out at the sea and tried to think.

She had always loved Bennett but as a friend, big brother type. She wasn't sure when it happened but it was no longer that way. He was different, she was different. This whole experience had changed them both. They were all they had. She didn't want to mess with that and he was almost ready to leave. They could be off this island shortly and she didn't want to jeopardize that.

If she confessed feelings for him would he stay? Would he confess the same feelings? She wasn't sure and didn't want to find out the answer was no. She sat a little while longer then got up to help him finish packing for his voyage.

Bennett was ready. The boat was finally finished. He had built a box to put his supplies in. That had been Harper's idea. They had already filled it she insisted he take all three water bottles. She claimed she would be fine without them. She had wanted him to have as much as he could carry.

She had stock piled it with fruits and used the Ziploc baggy and filled it full of almonds. She also cooked him so fish to take. She gave him strict instructions to keep his rations to a minimum. He had promised her.

They had also used the old raft/tarp as a sail. They had also thought of making paddles just in case. It had taken them four months to complete.

He was about to set sail and he needed to say his goodbyes. They had built the raft on the Sunset side of Survivor Island. He eventually determined that that was not the direction he wanted to head. He knew that's where they had come from and it had taken them over two days to get here and they had been flying for hours before that so finding anything that way seemed unlikely.

He was going to push off here but sail around to the other side and start heading north. That was the plan. He was excited and nervous, not necessarily for himself but for Harper. He didn't like that she was staying here. He would have also worried about the unknowns of her coming with him as well.

She was standing behind him nervously wringing her hands. He hadn't seen her do that in a really long time.

"Well, it's time to go."

She nodded her head and whispered, "I know."

He opened his arms wide for her. She ran to him and threw herself into his arms. “Don’t die.” She instructed him.

“I promise.”

“Come back for me.”

“I promise.” He squeezed her tight. They held on to each other for a moment longer before they broke away.

She swiped a tear off her check but pretended she was pushing her hair back but that wasn’t the case as she attempted a smile. It was a pitiful smile at best. She clapped her hands together, “Okay, let’s get this show on the road.”

They strode over to the corners of the raft. They looked at each other their hands poised on the edge ready to push. “One, two, three.” With that they shoved off the shore. Harper was thigh high in the water when Bennett jumped up on the raft and started paddling out to sea.

She already felt alone. The separation between them already felt like an ocean apart. She prayed he would be alright and he would succeed and come back to find her. Her heart clenched inside her chest. She missed him immediately even though she could still see him she felt like she had already lost him. She didn’t want to think that this could be the last time she could be seeing him.

She waded out of the water and meandered down the beach following his progress. Heading to North Pointe she climbed the hill as she watched him sail off. He waved to her on his way by and she waved back.

"Hurry back," she said to herself. She contemplated his voyage in front of him. She hoped he had enough food and found help. She found a tree on the edge of the cliff sitting down her legs dangled over the edge and she leaned back up against the tree.

It took hours before she couldn't see him anymore yet she stayed. Her butt started to get numb. She stood slowly and dusted herself off not taking her eyes off the horizon. Carefully she scaled her way down the hill and made her way to Kara and Brody.

"He left." She told them. She looked at the crosses almost as if she was waiting for a response. She had a surge of excitement and she grinned, "I could be going home soon. What do you think? A week tops?" She clapped her hands together when she got excited about something. She started to daydream about being home. "I could have the kids in my arms soon. Oh, that will feel so good.

I wonder if my house was sold. We could always move into a smaller house. Maybe a fresh start somewhere else would help everyone."

She stopped talking and pondered all the questions she had about her future. She eventually started to get hungry and headed back to camp. She had a mango and some almonds. She took the coloring book out of Daphne's suitcase. She wanted to mark today as the day Bennett had left. She wrote the tick mark and circled the day and wrote above it. "Bennett set sail" She counted back; they had been on Survivor Island over five months.

She flipped through the book. In the back they had a now complete map of Survivor Island which they had written as the heading. She was ready to close the book when she saw some writing through the pages. Flipping the pages she saw a letter written across the coloring page.

"Dear Harper,

If you are reading this I have probably already left our Survivor Island. I call it ours because it is ours and only ours, no one else's." She smiled at that and continued reading, "I write this now as you are sleeping. I leave tomorrow. I want to thank you for all the help you have given me. Not only with the building of the raft and all your input and great ideas but you kept me going. You nursed me back to health when we crashed. You have more than pulled your weight making us a comfortable bed and making our cave a home. You have helped me heal with the loss of Kara and I hope I helped you as well otherwise Kara will kill me in the afterlife."

She was crying as she read but laughed out loud as she read that last part. She wiped her tears and continued reading.

"Harper, I want to ask you something serious and I wanted to ask you in person, but I couldn't bring myself to do it. If I don't return and you get rescued I would like it if you could take my kids in. I know I'm asking a lot being a single mom and having five kids, two of which are not your own to look out for and support. But I will make this my last will and testament and confirm that I am of sound mind.

I know you can do it and love my boys as if they were your own. I think Kara would really love it if they were with you too. Her parents would always be there to help you too. Kara and I also had a fund in place to help with their college tuition. Please make sure my boys go to college.

I really hope I am writing this letter for nothing and I will see you soon bringing the cavalry. If not I'm so glad we met. You were a great friend to Kara. She loved you as a true friend and thought of you as a sister. Thank you for being my friend and introducing me to Brody. I wish you all the best.

Love,

Bennett Paul Treadwell"

Tears streaked her face and more tears clouded her vision as she finished reading the letter. He damn well better come back she thought. Her stomach was in knots as she thought of all the terrible things that could happen to him out there. Please find help, please find help she pleaded. She reread the letter over and over again.

Of course she would take care of his kids. She was honored he had asked her. She put the coloring book back and decided to take a walk. She made her way through the woods and out to Sunrise Beach.

Nothing on the horizon, not that she expected there to be anything. She walked down the beach and in the long run did the perimeter of the island. She picked up some fish for dinner and walked it back to camp.

She built a fire and started it. She cooked her fish and had some pineapple with it. She was bored, like really bored. She did some jumping jacks, sit ups and push-ups followed by squats. She let the fire burn down then went to bed.

It took her awhile to fall asleep but eventually staring at the rock wall of the cave her eye lids became heavy and she fell asleep. It was weird falling asleep without Bennett at her side.

Meanwhile Bennett was eating his dinner sitting in silence on his raft. It was dark the island was long gone behind him. This better work he thought. He wondered if Harper had found the letter he had left for her. She probably had she usually did her daily entry at night.

Did she accept his proposal to take care of his kids if he was no longer around to do so? He hoped she would, he was actually pretty confidant she would.

Days later he was not so confident that he had made the right decision to leave. There had been no signs of anyone. He was running low on water and supplies were depleting rapidly. Even if he turned around now the chances of finding Survivor Island was slim to none.

His heart stopped as he realized what he was seeing. A dorsal fin of a shark was circling his raft. Where once there was one now two circled his raft. He stood in the middle of the raft feeling barely secure at his advantage point being out of the water.

That was until one of the sharks bumped the raft causing the boat to rock. The motion took him so off guard that he fell sideways nearly falling off the raft. His arm grazed the edge of the raft and fell briefly into the water. The slippery body of the shark bumped up against his arm. He quickly retrieved his still attached arm out of the water and made his way back into the center of the boat.

He realized too late that he was bleeding. Shit, sharks could smell blood from a mile away, if not more. One of the sharks came out of the water and took a large bite out of the corner where his arm had scuffed the side. He fell down on his back side and started sliding towards the sharp teeth of the shark attacking his boat.

He scrambled backwards as the other shark was rocking the boat from the other side. He reached the supply box and pulled out one of the oars. He used it to hit at shark number two that wasn't eating his raft. He didn't know if this would scare them off or piss them off. He guessed he was about to find out.

The one he hit swam away for now. Shark number one had stopped eating his raft and was still circling. Much to his relief he swam away but it was only to get a head start as he lined himself up to charge the raft. Bennett raised the paddle over his head and struck the shark in the head as hard as he could. This broke the paddle in two.

It left the end jagged and sharp. He used the end as a spear. He barely made a dent in the shark but it did draw blood. Shark number two came back and they started fighting amongst themselves. They left him alone after that.

That night he ran into a strong storm. The wind was whipping and the waves were enormous. He was worried the raft might tip over. He pulled the sail down and tucked it away in the supply box. That's when a wave crashed over pushing him forward. His head slammed against the edge of box knocking him unconscious. His body slumped and fell awkwardly into the box.

Chapter Ten

Harper tried to keep up with the routine on the island as much as she could without Bennett. She got up every morning and exercised either running or swimming. It was lonely without him. She missed him, a lot.

There wasn't much to do on the island but think when you had no one to talk to. She talked to Kara and Brody but they obviously weren't as responsive as Bennett had been. There had been a tropical storm two nights ago and she worried about Bennett. Had he missed the storm or was he caught in it?

She hoped he was on a boat somewhere making his way back to the island. She searched the horizon for any signs of life and was disheartened to see none. She kept running, her lung capacity had much improved since arriving to the island. She was able to make it all the way around the island without walking.

That night she crawled into bed alone again and sent up a prayer that she would be found and Bennett was okay. She curled under the blanket and fell asleep. Sometime in the middle of the night she was startled awake. She heard a noise and strained to listen to hear anything else.

She screamed the most blood curdling scream when she saw a shadow at the entrance to the cave. Suddenly the shadow was gone but she heard a swear word. That was a person. She scrambled to the edge of the cave and looked out. In the moonlight she could see Bennett lying on the ground.

"Holy crap, Harper, you scared the living shit out of me! Where did you learn to scream like that?" he asked seriously as he rubbed his ear as if he was trying to remove her scream from it.

"You!" she sounded incredulous. "I scared you? You have to be freaking kidding me? I have been alone on this island for five days and you show up in the middle of the night creeping into the cave and I scared you!?"

He sat up and groaned, "Point taken. Did you miss me?" he asked as he stood up.

She flung herself out of the cave and into his arms. He caught her, "Of course I missed you. You did it? You really did it? The cavalry is here? Are they waiting for us on the beach?"

He set her back from him the look on his face said it all but he told her anyway. "I'm sorry Harper. The cavalry isn't here."

"You can't leave me again. It's not allowed." She warned him.

"I promise." He swore to her.

She hugged him again and he hugged her back. "Are you hungry?" she asked.

"Starving." He confessed.

She started a fire and handed him some fruit and gave him some almonds.

"Do you want me to go get some fish or crabs?" she asked.

He was already eating a banana shaking his head, "No thank you this is good enough for tonight but I would love some for breakfast."

"Okay. Sit down, tell me what happened." He obeyed and sat eating almonds. He told her all about the storm and getting knocked unconscious but skipped the part about the sharks. She sat listening to him.

"I know you are disappointed that you didn't find help and don't get me wrong I am too, but at the same time I can't tell you how happy I am to have you back safe and sound."

He gave a huge grin but didn't respond.

"So a lot has happened since you've been gone," she told him.

He looked up surprised, "Really?"

She laughed and tossed a mango at him which he caught. "Of course not, nothing has changed here, same old, same old."

As the fire roared to life she noticed how haggard he looked. There were dark circles under his eyes and his cheekbones looked a little sunken in. That's when she noticed a gash on his forehead.

She gasped at the nasty cut and reached her hand out to him.

"What?" he asked as he pulled away from her touch.

She got up and knelt in front of him, not looking directly at him but at all the blood she could now see caked in his hair and down his face.

This time he didn't move and he allowed her to examine him. Her touch was gentle as she assessed the damage. She got up and went inside the cave. She returned with a pair of Daphne's socks. She dunked them into the cool water of the pool and proceeded to wash the dried blood off of him.

He winced when she got too close to the wound. Bennett was observing Harper as she worked. She was taking care of him again and he didn't mind the fuss. When had she gotten so beautiful? She had always been drop dead gorgeous but he guessed he had never considered her beauty.

Her blue eyes sparkled in the light of the fire and her lips were full and looked totally, indisputably kissable. He realized then that he had been thinking of her like this since the night in the cave when he had held her after a bad dream.

After the morning when she had taken off from the cave he realized it was not the time, place or person he should be getting involved with. It was almost too bad they had so much history together. He noticed her hands as she cleaned him up they were soft and she had long thin hands, that still wore the engagement ring he had helped Brody pick out and her wedding band.

She looked up at him and he lost his breath for a moment. Maybe it was the adventures out at sea that had him fantasizing about her but it needed to stop.

"I'm glad you're back."

Did he want to get off this island? Damn straight he did, but was he glad to be back by her side? The answer was a resolute, yes. “I am too, thanks, Jones.” He told her, and he was.

Her heart stopped at the use of his nickname for her. One night when they were in college they were sitting around in her and Kara’s dorm room getting to know each other and their full names came up. Harper had complained that for as pretty as her name, Harper Grace was she was bummed her last name was boring, Jones.

“I don’t know,” Bennett had said, “I like it. It’s a good strong name.”

After that he called her Jones. After she started dating Brody he called her Jones less often. On her wedding day in her reception line Bennett had hugged her and whispered in her ear, “Guess I can’t call you Jones anymore.”

She had laughed and joked, “Thank God.” But deep down she was a little sad he wouldn’t be calling her Jones anymore. She had gotten used to it and had actually started to like her last name.

She wondered now why he had decided to bring it back. Whatever it was it brought a smile to her face.

The next day he asked that they not run but take a walk, he was still a little sore from his adventures out at sea. She readily agreed and they walked around the island. What she was unprepared for was the sight of his marooned boat.

“What the hell is this?” she asked when she saw the chunk of the boat that was missing.

“Oh, that…” he stalled.

She gave him a look. “Bennett that looks like a shark tried to eat your boat.”

“Hmm…” he pondered her intuition.

“Bennett!” she slapped him on the arm, “You tell me right now that isn’t what I think it is.” She pointed to the boat.

“It isn’t what you think it is.” He said without much conviction.

“Are you lying to me?” she had her hands on her hips now, she was getting serious.

“Yes.”

She hit him again, “Bennett Paul Treadwell!”

Oh boy she was pulling out all three of his names.

“I can’t believe you left this part out of your story.”

“Sorry,” he said even though he wasn’t, “I knew if I told you, you would be up all night worrying about something that already happened. I’m fine, look at me. I’m good. I’m back and I’m not going to try and go anywhere.”

She snorted. He was right. She sure as hell wasn't going to admit it to him, but she would have tossed and turned all night worrying about the what ifs.

"Tell me what happened."

He proceeded to tell her in detail his shark attack story and how he managed to get out of it. They had taken a seat on the boat as she listened to him retell the story. She noticed that the mast they had made had broken in the wind and they were no longer in possession of the deflated raft he was using as a sail.

After his story and answering her questions they continued on their walk. When they passed Kara and Brody she called out to them. "He's back!"

He gave the crosses a salute, "Hey guys." He called out to them.

When they got back she cooked him up a big breakfast with everything she could scrounge up. He ate every last morsel licking his fingers afterwards.

"That was delicious, my complements to the chef."

She giggled at his praise. It was so good to have him back.

They fell back into step with each other over the next couple of weeks and it was like he had never left. They didn't have the big project of building a raft but he disassembled the raft and brought the supply box back to camp so they could store their supplies out of the elements.

One night they were getting ready for dinner. He was starting the fire and she was preparing the fish.

"I miss double stuffed Oreos," Harper announced.

"I miss Chinese food," Bennett countered.

"Oh, that's a good one. I miss bathrooms and toilet paper!"

"Touché. I miss football."

"I love Sundays. I miss furniture, beds, tables, chairs. I would love a couch to lie down and watch a football game on T.V. OH! I miss T.V. all my shows," she pouted.

"I miss beer and chicken wings."

"Cherry pull twizzles and Cheezits." She declared.

"I would love a steak."

"I miss grocery shopping."

"Seriously, grocery shopping?"

"What? It was my down time away from everything, although when I get home I don't want any down time from anything."

"You'll change your mind after about a month of that."

She laughed, "Probably, but as of right now I miss everything."

"I miss my phone."

"I miss wardrobe options."

"Good one. I miss music."

"I could sing for you," she offered.

He actually laughed out loud, "No offense Harper but I've heard you sing."

She gasped and fringed hurt feelings her hand on her heart, "Well I never," she sang in her false southern accent then switched back to her regular voice. "Well, I miss electricity.

"I miss the fall, the changing of all the leaves."

"What and leave all this? I would love mascara. Oh, and lip gloss!"

"Why? You look fine. I would kill for a coffee."

"Oh, my God, Yes!" She paused to day dream about coffee, "Sex!"

"What?!"

"Sex. I miss sex."

"Me too!" Bennett full heartedly agreed.

And then, there was awkward silence after that. They continued getting ready for dinner.

That night there was a tropical storm. They moved quickly into the cave, moving the mattress as far back in the cave as they could. Lightning flashed in the sky and thunder cracked loudly causing Harper to jump.

"I hate storms she confessed."

"I know. It's okay. You can have the back wall if you want."

"Um, no I think that will make me more nervous being cooped up where I can't see over you."

"Okay." He lay down and pulled the blanket over him and held it open for her. She lay down next to him and let him wrap her up in the blanket. She rolled onto her side to watch the storm raging outside their cave home.

Thunder and lightning happened simultaneously outside. She squealed, "Okay bad idea. I don't want to see what is happening outside. You need to change places with me."

She started to climb over him but he was still on his side and with the ceiling so close she was half straddling him. She lay back down because he was trying to go over her. He was hovering over her and he looked down. He was trying not to make contact with her but in doing so the process was much slower.

Her hands were on his sides trying to help guide him over her but it felt intimate when he made contact with her. Bennett settled himself on the other side of her. She was turned to face him her back was pressed up against the wall and his body was turned in towards her. His hand was still resting above her on the wall.

She realized her hand was still resting on his side. She could feel his warmth through his shirt. She didn't remove it. Slowly his hand came down off the wall and rested on her hip. Her heart began to race a little and her mouth went dry. It felt good to have contact. She missed being touched. And she supposed he probably did too.

They didn't move for a long time both afraid to move forward and afraid to stop. A rumble of thunder so loud and so close felt like it shook their little cave. She moved closer and he scooped her up into his embrace. Her arm curled up his back the other went around his neck. Her head was resting on his shoulder and his other arm curved around her back. His leg shifted and she slipped one of her thighs in between his. His thigh rested heavy on top of hers but she felt safe and protected.

Her face snuggled warmly against the crook of his neck. She breathed in the scent of him. She missed her husband, she missed her kids, she missed her life and she had told this man today she missed sex, which she did. But was she ready to move on, and with him? He was also the widow of her best friend. Why hadn't they been rescued yet? It had been a long time.

She honestly didn't think anyone was coming for them. They could survive on this island they had already proven that. They had food, shelter, water and each other that was, it. What if this was it forever? What if they never saw their kids again? They had already been told their parents were dead. What if no one ever found them? Would it have mattered if they found comfort in each other?

These were the thoughts running through her head as she eventually fell asleep in his arms. Neither one made a move, but they didn't let go either.

Chapter Eleven

The next morning she woke up to find she was alone in the cave. She lay there thinking about what could have happened last night. It was probably for the best she thought. She stretched and rolled off the mat. She scooted to the edge of the cave and assessed the damage of the storm. Palm tree branches were everywhere, what a mess. Bennett was outside picking them up and making a pile. She slid out of the cave and went to help him.

"Good morning," she called. Like every morning, like nothing had happened between them in the middle of the night even though both of them knew it had.

He stopped what he was doing and looked at her. Oh no, she thought something is wrong, something's off. He dropped the branches he was holding and started striding towards her. What was he doing? Her heart picked up pace and started beating wildly. She took a step back before he reached her. But he caught her anyway.

His arm went around her back and pulled her solidly against his body his other hand slipped through her hair and held her head firmly tipping her face up towards his. She looked up at him in surprise and saw in his eyes what he wanted from her before his lips descended on hers. It was a crushing kiss, nothing sweet or innocent about it.

She had gasped a second before it happened so her mouth was already open for his tongue to plunge into her mouth and it did. She was so shocked, this was Bennett. But all her thoughts began to melt away as the kiss took over her body. Oh, my, God, as Kara would say.

Harper's arms came up and wove around his neck, and became an active participant in the kiss. She met him with his force and pent up frustration at this situation. His hand on her head roamed down her back and both hands grasped her behind. Instinctively she knew he was picking her up. She jumped when he did and wound her legs around his waist.

He never broke the intense kiss they were sharing as he walked her back to the cave. He pinned her up against the outside wall and held her there. Her fingers were in his now longer hair, twirling it in her fingers and getting a firm grip. His hands were holding her thighs for support.

This went on like this for what seemed like an eternity. Then Bennett broke off the kiss he had started. He put his forehead down on her shoulder and she knew that it was over. She held him for a long minute.

"I'm sorry," he choked out in a whisper.

"It's okay," she whispered back.

He gently lowered her to the ground and walked away, away from her, away from their camp, and through the woods. She stood there for a long time letting it all soak in. She crawled back into the cave curled up in the back corner and cried.

This time she cried for her. Now what she thought? This couldn't happen she realized. He was Bennett for Christ sake. He was Kara's Bennett. But Kara was gone and so was Brody. They were all they had left on this island. They may never see their kids again or anyone else for that matter. They could very well end up dying on this island together.

She rolled over in anger and frustration. She began to think of that kiss. She replayed it over again in her mind. That kiss was intense. It had rocked her to her core, and that's what she was afraid of. This could be a dangerous game to play.

Once she had cried until there was nothing left she sat up wiped the tears away and composed herself. She got up and started to finish the clean-up job Bennett had started. She was really starting to worry about him when he returned. She was almost done. He didn't say anything and neither did she as he helped her finish up.

He handed her a banana but he wouldn't meet her eyes. Was this how it was going to be she thought, because this was awful?

"No thanks, I'm not hungry."

"Do you want to go for a run?" he asked.

"Sure," it couldn't hurt to try and work off this frustration. Bennett filled a water bottle for them. They walked through the woods to Sunrise Beach. She took off her flip flops and they stretched.

They walked down to where the sand was hard packed and the waves came in. She took the lead. She pushed herself running hard. He kept up behind her never trying to pass her. She made it to South Cove then she just stopped. He slammed into her back totally unprepared for her abrupt stop.

They tumbled through the sand. His arms wound around her trying to protect her from the fall. They rolled and he came to rest on top of her their legs were tangled together. He looked down at her, "Are you okay? I didn't know you were stopping. I'm sorry I kissed you this morning." He was rambling.

She reached up and pulled him down to her. He didn't resist her which she was afraid he would. She didn't know what she was trying to prove with this kiss but she got her point across. He returned her kiss with the same kind of fever.

Bennett rolled one more time so she was on top of him. She pulled away and looked down at him. He reached up and tucked her hair behind her ears. It was growing out and getting longer. "I feel guilty," he confessed.

Tears welled up in her eyes, "I know." She looked down at his chest then back up at him, "I do too." Then she rolled off of him and sat down. He sat up next to her and put his arm around her shoulder.

"What should we do?" she asked.

"I don't know. I've asked myself that question a million times. Every time I ask I receive a different answer."

She laughed not because it was funny but because she knew exactly how he felt.

"I respect you, you know?"

"I do know." She responded.

"I don't want to jeopardize our friendship."

"Okay." She let him talk it out.

"I miss Kara."

"I miss her too, and I miss Brody tons."

He hung his head, "I miss him so much. He was such a funny guy, a great friend."

"He really was," she agreed. "Do you think they are looking down on us in heaven and are really happy or super pissed if we end up together?"

"See? I think that's what's really hanging me up on this. I don't want to make the wrong decision. I don't want to feel guilty. I really enjoy kissing you."

"You do?" she asked looking up at him. He was close.

"I really do." He leaned down and kissed her again. This time it was a gentler kiss. She sighed into his mouth. His knuckles brushed her chin. She sucked on his lower lip gliding her teeth gently over his lower lip.

She made the decision to take over. She got to her knees still maintaining the kiss and she straddled him. She was cradled in his lap facing him. His knees were bent up against her back. She pulled back to look at him. He was sitting up she was in his lap facing him her thighs hugging him on either side of his hips.

"Let's just make out for a while. No thinking, no talking, just kissing."

"Deal," he agreed before his hand came up and pulled her to him. This time they took their time. No rushing, no urgency, but there was passion. Their hands explored each other, but they were still shy and didn't take it too far.

Harper's lips would meet his then pull back for a single breath less than an inch from him then do it again. Her hands roamed down his back and pressed her breast to his chest. He allowed her sweet torturous game to continue until he couldn't stand it any longer.

Bennett's strong hands roamed down her back past her waist and pulled her harder against him. She gasped when she felt his arousal between her thighs. He took advantage of her surprise and deepened the kiss.

She moaned into his mouth and she felt him grow even more. God help her she was not going to be able to keep up her promise of just making out if this continued. One of his hands came up and grasped a handful of her hair and twisted it around in his long fingers then gave a tug.

This exposed her throat to him. Her neck was assaulted by his lips his teeth gently grazing her throat. This sent all new feelings coursing through her body. She felt like Jell-O and surprisingly alive and tingling all at once.

She broke away from his spell and took his earlobe into her warm mouth and sucked on it. His fingers dug into her back and she was encouraged on. Gliding her tongue up around the rim of his ear then blowing ever so slightly on it sent a wave pleasure through the both of them.

Without warning she was flipped onto her back, Bennett hovered above her. Her thighs were still wrapped around his hips and he was nestled comfortably between her legs. He looked down at her his eyes were half closed with how aroused he was. She was pretty sure she had close to the same look on her face.

"We should stop soon," he rasped out but didn't sound completely convincing.

"Soon," she promised and he lowered himself down on her. She met him in an open mouth kiss. Their tongues rubbed together their jaws working together to find the perfect rhythm. They found it together. His arm came under her head cradling her.

Her right arm curved up and her hand curved around the strong bicep muscle through his shirt. Her left hand traveled down his back and came to rest on the curve of his waist. He came up for air they were both panting. Softly his lips came to rest on her forehead, then her nose, both her eyelids, chin then a sweet kiss on her lips.

They lay there for a while trying to regain their composure. Eventually he stood up and held his hand down to help her up. She took it and he easily pulled her to her feet. She realized she was no longer in possession of her flip flops due to the collision and his water bottle had flown a good distance as well.

"Let's go back the way we came," he suggested. She knew why he suggested it. Because he didn't want to walk by the empty graves they had made when they had first gotten here.

"Okay," she readily agreed because she wasn't ready to face those two. They gathered the flip flops and water bottle and began their walk back to camp. He handed her the water bottle. Grateful she took it opening the top taking a long couple of gulps. She handed it back to him with the lid undone to offer him a drink. Taking it he too took a long drink. She passed him back the cap and he screwed it on top.

"Why don't you hold your flip flops in your other hand?" he asked.

Puzzled she gave him a look as they meandered back down the beach. "Why?" she question his reasoning.

"So I can hold your hand." He replied.

"Oh," was all she could manage to get out. Switching which hands had the flip flops she placed her small hand into his much larger one.

Taking their time they made their way back. While they were still on the beach he stopped her abruptly pulling her around to face him.

"What?" she asked.

"I would like another kiss," he grinned.

"I think I can handle that request," and tipped her face towards him.

"You're really beautiful." He whispered before his lips descended upon hers. Their hands stayed clasped as they shared a kiss. This kiss was much briefer than the ones preceding it. Afterwards they fell into step and made it back to the path they had worn through the woods.

Walking through the woods was harder to do holding hands because in most places it was single file. She was ahead of him when she stopped and turned around. They were under a large tree that, surprisingly enough hadn't suffered much damage from the storm.

"I need another kiss." Was all she had gotten out and he was on her. Sweeping her up into his arms he walked her back up against the tree. The rough bark bit at her back but she didn't care. His right hand lifted her left leg to settle on his hip and he pressed himself to her.

The kiss was intense and satisfying, her lips were starting to feel bruised from their day of kissing but it was so worth it. He bit her lip and it shocked and aroused her. Her fingers ran though his hair and pulled him closer crushing him to her. It took them longer this time to break apart.

He didn't move his body away from her as they tried to catch their breath. "I fear we have ventured down a path we may not be able to turn away from."

Harper turned and kissed his wrist then sent him a look, “I think maybe you are right.”

The way she looked up at him through her lashes demanded he kiss her again.

Then he stepped away from her and they walked back to camp. They had a hard time getting any work done. They were stopping to steal kisses throughout the day.

Chapter Twelve

Bennett woke up in the middle of the night and found Harper wasn't by his side. Rolling onto his back he threw his arm over his forehead and contemplated his situation. He had loved Kara with all his being and before June twelfth he had never pictured his life without her. Now she was gone and he missed her every day.

Harper came to his mind. She was beautiful, and funny and brave and Kara's best friend and Brody's wife. He growled in frustration. She was his only connection to the outside world. She was his whole world now. Beside this island she was it.

His boys came to mind. They were growing up without him and Kara. They were experiencing puberty and with who's guidance? He wondered if they had girlfriends or were still playing sports.

Realizing Harper hadn't returned he guessed she wasn't taking a bathroom break. He crawled out of the cave. It was a little cool tonight so he brought the blanket with him. Weaving through the woods he was able to see because of the moon was shining down brightly. The beach was isolated but he kept walking.

He found her where he thought she would be. Harper was sitting on the beach her knees pulled up to her chest. She was staring at the makeshift crosses they had made to honor their loved ones.

She saw him coming and didn't look at all surprised he had found her here. "I've been talking to them," she explained waving a hand in the general direction of the crosses.

Bennett sat down next to her and wrapped them up in the blanket she had made. His arm wound around her shoulders. She cuddled up next to him winding her arms around his waist. "Have they given you any answers?"

"Nope! This is where I wish I had a really big glass-no bottle of wine."

He smiled and kissed her on the temple. They sat in silence looking at the make shift graves that housed no bodies. Suddenly the silence was broken. At first they didn't know what or where the sound came from, but they scrambled to their feet instantly.

Looking overhead a small plane flew over the island. "Hey!" Harper shouted. Bennett started sprinting faster than she had ever seen him move before. "Hey!" she screamed as loud as humanly possible. She began doing jumping jacks waving her arms madly back and forth. Their blanket forgotten she dashed after Bennett.

The plane didn't seem at all affected by the island or its stranded occupants. Harper knew exactly where he was headed. She found him at North Pointe down on his knees swearing as he attempted to start the fire they had prebuilt.

Turning to see if she could still see the plane she looked off in the distance. She could barely hear it anymore. Spotting lights flickering in the distance dread began to creep into her heart. What was once excitement and joy was quickly being replaced.

Bennett shouted out when the fire licked up the sides of the tepee of dried wood. Blowing at the base of the fire he tried to spur it on. It caught in seconds, but sadly it was too late.

Both stood on the peak watching in the direction the plane had disappeared, nothing was happening. They stood for a long time while the fire blazed behind them. Neither one spoke, both discouraged.

Harper's eyes strained though the darkness then did a scan around them, nothing else lit up the sky. She was heartbroken. They hadn't seen anything remotely close to civilization in the months since they had been on the island. That was it. It may have been their only hope.

After her legs started to ache she sat down. After about an hour of Bennett still fueling the fire she announced, “I’m going to bed. Are you coming?”

“No.” was all he said. He didn’t glance her way and his jaw was set in stone. He had not sat down but instead paced.

Oh boy she thought, “Alright, you don’t mind if I go do you?”

“No.”

Okay then. She went to go but turned around one more time. He wouldn’t look her way. She felt dejected. She had to walk all the way back down the beach to get the blanket they had abandoned.

She crawled into the cave feeling numb. They could have been rescued tonight. They could be going home. They could be seeing their kids. None of those things were going to happen. She tossed and turned, Bennett never came back to bed.

Waking up alone in the cave she felt rotten. She scooted to the edge of the cave. She brushed her hair and put it up. Bennett was pacing outside. She went to him but he kept her at a distance.

“We’ve been so stupid,” he continued to pace. “We should have been taking shifts. We could have missed dozens of planes flying at night." He waved his hand in the air as if to point out a plane, "I thought to myself, how come we couldn't hear it? And I realized we are sleeping on top of a fucking waterfall! Of course we wouldn't be able to hear it."

"So what do you suggest we do?"

"I am going to stay up at night and keep the fire going so hopefully we can flag down anyone flying by or sailing by. I will need you to take care of our food and chores during the day. Can you do that?" he was almost like a drill sergeant barking out orders.

"Yes," she stammered out.

"Good. It's settled. I'm going to bed."

He strode to the cave and climbed inside. She looked around where to start. She took a walk. She collected bananas, almonds, pineapples, mangos and coconuts. Bringing them all back to the camp she stacked them. After cracking the almonds she put them in the Ziploc bag. She gathered fire wood and stacked that too.

She walked to South Cove, took off her clothes except her under garments. She went for a swim in the ocean. She swam until her arms and legs didn't want to move anymore. Coming out of the water she picked up her clothes and walked into the woods to the hot spring. She climbed in and tried to relax.

Afterwards she went to visit Kara and Brody. She lay down on her back and looked up at the sky. "Bennett's acting weird. He wants to take shifts. I won't see him for god knows how long. He won't look at me. I don't know if he thinks this is a sign or what but this could be rough going. We are the only two people on Survivor Island and incase he hasn't noticed it is going to be a very lonely existence. I mean at the same time I hope he's right. Maybe he is on to something. We could be missing planes while we sleep. We could get off this island and go home to our babies. God I hope that's the case." She rolled over, "Well I have to go, food duty." She smiled and got up. She kissed her fingers then touched each one of their crosses.

Gathering up the trapped fish she brought them back to the campsite. She started a fire and cooked up the fish. She ate one and cut up the other two for Bennett. She cracked open a coconut and filled one side with fish the other with almonds. She took a bushel of bananas and with the coconuts walked them up to the peak. She remade the fire tepee then went to gather more wood to stack next to it.

She headed back to camp. There she snuck the coloring book out the cave and the purple crayon which was this month's color. She tried to be organized in her recording of their time spent on the island. She marked the days with tick marks and only went a week at a time so she could easily count the weeks, then switched colors when they were on to the next month. She circled last night's tick mark and wrote above it, "Airplane."

Chapter Thirteen

Harper was relaxing in the hot spring she was still in her bra and panties even though she knew Bennett was sleeping. You never knew when someone could fly or sail by she would need to chase down. The towel was rolled up and near the edge where she rested her head. Her arms were outstretched on the rocks on either side of her.

Waves crashed behind her soothing her into letting go. This had been the worst month since reaching the island. Bennett spent every night manning the campfire. She barely saw him and when she did he wasn't himself. He hardly spoke to her. She felt isolated and tired. She had soon realized that she had a hard time sleeping without Bennett.

She had grown accustomed to his presence and missed him. "Can I join you?" That sentence startled her out of her musing. Gasping she sat up right and crossed her arms over her chest even though he would be unable to see through the cloudy water.

"You scared the crap out of me, Bennett!"

"Sorry," he gave her a crooked smile.

Cocking her head to the side she contemplated him. Something had changed. He was different, back to his old self. She wasn't complaining. Letting out a long breath she laughed, "Sure." She gave him a weak smile.

She had missed him so much and even though she knew that, it really hit her seeing him smiling at her. He wasted no time stripping down. He unbuttoned his shirt and she couldn't help but watch him and he didn't ask her to look away. He looked good. Since being on the island they had both lost a lot of weight and because of their diet and exercise they had both firmed up quite a bit. His body was chiseled his stomach was like a washboard. His arms were tan and firm and she could see his entire muscular physic move and accentuate each movement.

His long fingers moved to the button on his shorts and she didn't even realize she was staring. Stripping out of his shorts he kicked off his sandals. He was standing in his red boxer briefs. He sank into the hot spring across from her and she finally looked into his eyes.

"I want to apologize." He started. "I know I haven't been the easiest to deal with lately."

She gave a curt laugh, "Ha!"

"I know, I know." He held his hands up. "It's been a month-"

"I know." She tried not to sound exacerbated, but she was unsuccessful.

"I'm sorry. I really am. I-"

"I forgive you."

"Stop interrupting me. Oh," he said when he realized what she had said. "I thought maybe we were missing something, some kind of flight pattern at night, and they weren't seeing our signs because it was dark. But at this point I think it was a fluke. I don't think there is anyone coming."

She didn't say anything she was looking off in the distance.

"I missed you," he confessed.

That got her attention she looked up her vision was blurry. She hadn't realized she had tears in her eyes. He was kneeling in front of her. "Don't cry." Bennett reached up and wiped away her tears, "I didn't mean to hurt you. You are too precious to me."

"Why? Because I'm the only one here?" she asked frustrated.

"No, it's because you are, Jones. You're funny, and smart. You're a brave strong willed woman surviving out here like nobody's business." He hadn't called her Jones since the night he had returned to the island and she was happy to have the nickname back.

She laughed at that. He grinned at her making her knees go weak, "Not to mention sexy as hell," he admitted.

She smiled at him. Her hands came up to cup his face. She started into his green eyes that were genuine. "I missed you too."

Then they were kissing, it happened so fast she wasn't sure who made the first move or if it was simultaneous. Her arms slipped around his neck and his went around her waist. It was shocking so much bare skin touching.

It felt so good being in his arms again. All of the pent up frustration and loneliness went into this kiss. It felt like they couldn't get close enough. Their tongues rubbed together their jaws opening and closing in quick succession. One of his hands slipped down to grasp her hip the other glided through the water under her thigh. Her legs opened and he slid between them. Her back was up against the rock wall of the hot spring and her front was up against the solid wall of Bennett.

Bennett kissed each one of her cheeks where the tears had been. He pulled back to look at her, assessing if she was okay with this. She responded by kissing his neck. His hands didn't stop roaming her body. One of his hands came up and cupped her breast.

"Bennett," she gasped into his ear.

His hand instantly came off her breast. "Don't stop." She breathed.

With the green light he reached around and unhooked her bra. He pulled off her bra and flung it in the woods. Neither one bothered to see where it landed. His hands glided down her back and when he reached her butt he hoisted her up.

Naked wet breasts were in front of his face. "Perfect," he whispered. His warm mouth clasped over one of her nipples. Throwing her head back her hands gripped his hair. He moved on to her other breast bringing her nipples to taunt peaks.

Deep inside her pressure began to build. Her hips were starting to rock against him. He eased her back down into the hot water. Harper's lips sought out his and he met her greedily. Her panties were the next thing being discarded out of the hot springs.

Her hands slipped under the water and helped him strip out of his underwear which joined her under things. She felt his hard erection against the entrance of her. He wasn't moving forward she looked at him. He was staring intensely at her.

"Are you sure?" he wanted to be absolutely positive. There was no going back after this.

She nodded, "Are you?"

"Hell yeah," and he thrust deep inside her.

"Ah," she gasped out. Oh this feels good, better than good, amazing. He didn't move for a minute just filled her. Then he glided almost all the way out of her then rammed back into her. She couldn't help but moan. He did it again.

"You feel incredible," he rasped out.

"I can't even tell you how good you feel," she managed as he glided out then slammed back into her pushing her up against the rock behind her.

His arms went past her, his hands gripping the edge of the rocks using them to pump inside her. Her hands curled up to grip his upper arms his muscles were flexed, it was so sexy to see. She watched him as he continued his sweet torture of her. He returned her stare as he pulled back then pushed up to the hilt inside her. Water sloshed around their bodies.

She used one of her hands around the nape of his neck to pull him in for a kiss. He came closer and met her lips. She kept breaking off the kiss to release a sigh or a moan. Her hand roamed down his back cupping his ass. Not that he needed any help with his rhythm but she just wanted to touch him so she pulled him in closer with each thrust.

Her head fell forward her cheek resting next to his. He lowered his head and kissed her neck and nibbled on it in between kisses. Her body quivered in response. She could feel her climax coming on, it was building deep inside her.

"Bennett," she called out his name.

"Yes, Harper?" she melted to hear her name on his lips.

"I need you," she told him.

"You have me," he promised.

"I'm coming."

"Come for me," he encouraged her. He kissed her collarbone.

He increased his rhythm pumping into her harder and faster. Each time she moaned or cried out with the volume building getting louder and more urgent. "Yes, Yes, Yes, Yesssss," Until finally she broke, the waves of pleasure consuming her body. She clung to him. She clenched around him, convulsing, squeezing him tight as she reached her climax.

Bennett held her while she came and when she was floating back down to Earth he began to move inside her again. Her sensitivity was heightened and she began to build again. Sliding in and out of her until his own climax hit him and hit him hard. He shuttered and came inside her. Her body cradled him and caressed him.

He slowly eased out of her but didn't let go. Sitting back on the opposite side he pulled her onto his lap. She circled her arms around his neck and rested her head in the crook of his shoulder. He ran a hand over her hair and kissed her gently on the top of her head. One of his arms draped across her lap and held her hip while his other hand caressed up and down her back.

Eventually when they both had recovered and their breathing had regained a normal rhythm he suggested they get out. She crawled off his lap and stood.

"Holy shit, Harper," was out of Bennett's mouth before he could stop it.

"What?" she asked looking down at him. Realizing he was staring at her body she immediately covered it. He came to his feet in front of her.

He covered her hands and gently pulled them away from her body. "Don't hide from me," he told her. "I'm sorry you just took me by surprise. Your body is magnificent. I had no idea that's what was hiding under your baggy clothes. You're perfect."

Blushing by the compliments she began to feel confident in her body. She knew she had lost a significant amount of weight and with the exercising they had done and she knew her body was changing but without a mirror she hadn't given it much thought, until now.

"What about you?" she accused her hand waving up and down his new sculpted body, "You look like a Greek God statue."

He grinned at her, "Why thank you." He slipped his arm around her and pulled her up against said body. "I'm," he leaned down and kissed her neck, "going to," he sucked on her ear lobe then breathed into it, "enjoy," his hands came up and cupped both breasts in his hands, "getting," he bent over and sucked on one nipple, "to" he sucked on the other nipple. His hands grazed down across her now flat stomach and he leaned down and moved his lips across her belly button, "explore," he licked her left hip while his hands held firmly to her hips. He glided her to the edge of the hot spring and sat her down on the edge. He leaned over her and kissed her inner thigh, "your" she inhaled sharply as he kissed the center core of her. He looked up at her, "body."

Quivering by the assault he had raged on her body she thought she was going to explode right here and now. Then he licked her and she knew she was done for. She was resting back on her elbows he circled her legs around his shoulders and he gave her a long slow deep lick.

Holy shit, she thought. He would tease her and tickle the insides of her thighs with kisses and licks in between sucking on her womanhood. She had been watching him devour her sweetly but it was too much. The sensations were taking her away. Letting her head fall back and her eyes close she realized too late that this made the sensations stronger and she could concentrate fully on his gentle attack.

Rocking her hips back and forth rubbing his tongue against her she began to pant, short little breaths trying desperately to get where he was trying to take her. "Oh my God, oh my God."

He lifted his head, "Do you want me to stop?" he breathed.

"No!" she cried out, "Don't stop. Don't ever stop." Her body was convulsing with her need for him to finish what he had started.

He didn't stop. His licks intensified to quick little flicks of his tongue lashing out at her. When she didn't think she could take it anymore she was practically whimpering from pure pleasure he stood up out of the water. Her legs were still wrapped around his shoulder and he was fully erected aroused by the pleasure she was getting from him.

He drove deep inside her. He almost came instantly the sensation was so overpowering. He had her pinned to the rock her legs were bent up to her chest and her ankles were wound around his head. He was so deep inside her. He drew back and slammed home, again and again building faster and faster. They both cried out this time, sharing the orgasm. Their bodies jerked and spasmed together, he collapsed on top of her.

Their breaths were ragged and their hearts were pounding fiercely. “Holy fuck.” He whispered in her ear.

She laughed, a joyful pure sound. A sound he had not heard in a really long time. “You can say that again.”

He did and she laughed some more. He kissed her and pulled out of her. He helped her up and he crawled out of the hot spring. He gave her a gentle tap on the ass as she walked by. They located all their clothes and they laughed together when she found her panties in a nearby tree limb.

He shrugged his shoulders at her. Once they were dried and dressed they headed back for camp.

“Are you hungry?”

“Starving,” she confessed.

“How about I whip you up something from the kitchen?” he asked.

She smiled, their hands were clasped together and they were swinging them back and forth. She felt alive, exhilarated. “Sounds wonderful.”

When they got back she found he had brought some crab home with him this morning after his shift on the Pointe. She had learned that she preferred the taste of them over most of the fish they caught. She tolerated all of it. She was lucky there was fruit and nuts on the island even though she was quite sick of eating the same thing day after day it could be worse. They could be trying to live off of bugs or something grosser.

He built a fire with the wood she had stacked earlier and got a fire going in no time. He chopped open a coconut and made her a mini fruit salad inside. She ate it while he cooked the crabs.

Chapter Fourteen

They were sitting in front of the fire she was sitting in front of him. Her back rested up against his chest with his arms around her. The fire was warm and the stars seemed to shine brighter tonight. She was enjoying being in his arms and listening to the crackle of the fire.

Leaning down he brushed her hair aside and brushed a kiss on her neck. "I have an idea," he whispered to her.

She turned her head and upper body towards him. "Oh yeah?" she asked.

He bent his head and captured her mouth. Her hands slipped up around his neck, his hand grazed her belly and drifted up under her shirt. Her heart began to race as his hand cupped her breast and his thumb grazed over her nipple.

He pulled his hand back out of her shirt and broke off the kiss, "Before we get too carried away." He gave her another kiss then jumped up leaving her on the ground. She watched him go into their cave. She was surprised to see him haul their mattress she had made out.

She laughed, "I like your thinking."

He hauled their bed in front of the fire and she stood up brushing the dirt off her backside. They met standing in between the bed and fire. She placed her hands on his chest feeling the strength and warmth beneath his shirt. She tipped her face up towards him his hands rested on her hips. They gazed into each other's eyes the fire light dancing in their reflection.

She watched him as she began to unbutton his shirt. Taking her sweet time she allowed her fingers to graze his chest as she did it. She leaned her head forward and kissed his chest through his springy chest hairs. One of his hands came up to caress her hair as she did it. Once she had all the buttons undone she ran her hands softly down his chest starting from his collar bone to the top of his shorts. He sucked in his breath and she grinned at the power she held over him.

She had felt that the last time, last two times, they had made love he had been in control and now she wanted her turn to be in charge. She reversed her hands and this time came up over his shoulders sliding his shirt off his body and it floated to the ground. She looked up to him and licked her lips. He swallowed hard as he watched her.

Her gazed held his as she undid his belt then his button to his shorts. Her hand cupped him through his shorts and she could feel his need for her grow. Slowly she undid his zipper her hands slid into the top band of his shorts and slid them down over his legs.

He stood in front of her with nothing but his underwear. She stood a foot away from him as she undressed herself. She unbuttoned her shirt to reveal her breast clad in a pale pink bra with lace covering the front. She dropped her shirt to the ground and wiggled out of her shorts next. Luckily since she had been on vacation she had matching pink lace panties to match.

She appraised his body and decided to walk around him. He stood still letting her assess him. She ran her hands down his back that had just as many muscles as his front. She removed his underwear from behind him and liked what she saw. She pressed herself up against him and reached her hand around in front of him taking his arousal in her hand.

Gritting his teeth he tried not to move as she stroked him up and down, up and down. The tip became wet with his excitement and she used his natural lubricant to glide over the tip, his head becoming slick. Without letting go she came back out in front of him and led him to their bed. Kneeling down on the edge of the bed with him still standing in front of her she took him into her mouth. Her sweet warm mouth caressed him. One hand came out and cradled his balls in her hand. The other hand remained on his shaft working together with her mouth in sweet harmony as they worked back and forth on him.

Her tongue swirled around the tip of him causing him to jump. "Harper." He ground out. She looked up at him but continued her assault on him, "Jesus," he said as one of his hands gripped her hair. He wanted to thrust his hips towards her, he wanted to fuck her mouth but he restrained. Until both her hands came around to grasp his ass and began rocking his hips towards her.

Both hands held her hair firmly in his grasp as she took him further into her mouth. She didn't pull away but moaned deeply as he pulled her forward meeting the thrusts of his hips. "I'm going to explode," he warned her, but she just encouraged him on sucking harder and faster. He threw his head back and yelled as his orgasm shook him to the core.

He collapsed on the bed taking her with him. He wrapped her up tightly in his arms. "You didn't have to do that." He told her as he kissed the top of her head.

"You're welcome," she responded.

He laughed, "I'm sorry, the correct response was thank you very much." He hugged her closer to him. She smiled and hugged him back. "You know that's not what my plan was."

She giggled, “I know, but it felt so good when you did it to me earlier today I wanted to repay the favor.”

He sat up on his elbow and looked down at her, “You don’t owe me anything,” he told her.

“I know,” She said as she ran her hand down his body, “but wouldn’t it be a fun game of pay back.”

Understanding registered in his eyes, “I like where your head is at, Jones.” His hand grazed down her midsection and under the band of her panties. His long middle finger slipped between her curls and found her wet for him. He thrust his finger inside her and her hips met his thrust. His cupped her to him his eyes never leaving her face as he watched her get aroused.

His finger came out and removed her panties. She lifted her hips to help him discard them. She threw one leg over his thighs and spread her legs for him her other leg bent at the knee. His fingers searched her out and found her clit. He started in a slow circular motion to build the suspense.

He watched himself bring her pleasure, her hips bucking under him. He liked hearing the sounds she was making. The sounds he was bringing out of her, like he was playing a musical instrument. He looked back to her she was cupping and rubbing her own breasts which instantly made him hard again. This woman was going to kill him he though and damned if he cared.

She pulled the fabric holding each breast in their confines down and her gloriously beautiful breast spilled out. They were rocking up and down with the motion of her body. He bowed his head and took one of her nipples in his mouth using his teeth he grazed the nipple making it taunt in his mouth. He swirled his tongue around it then sucked hard.

She bucked impatiently underneath him crying out in ecstasy. Her hands pulled on his hair and dragged his mouth to hers. She groaned into his mouth as she desperately sought to bring him where she was headed. She took charge and pushed him on his back. She straddled him and his hands guided her hips down as he thrust his hips up. His shaft filled her. She sat there feeling him her hands resting on his rigid stomach.

His thumb slipped into her curls and found her sweet spot again. This brought her hips to move. She pushed herself up, then down slowly bringing herself back down. He increased his pressure and pace and she followed suit.

The glow of the fire, with them surrounded in darkness, made all the valleys and curves of their body seem even more sensual. She lay on top of his chest and kissed him. He reached around and unclasped her bra. Then his hands roamed down her backside. He helped her by picking her up and pulling her back down hard, ramming himself back inside her. Her chin rested on his shoulder as he picked up the tempo of hard and fast. He could hear it in her voice as she got close.

Then he stopped. She pushed herself up on her elbows. “Are you alright?”

He grinned at her. “Don’t you worry. I’m not done with you yet.” He rolled her onto her back with him on top of her. “I want to take my time with you.” He kissed her on her neck and the bristles of his beard sent shivers down her body. He slowed his pace way down gliding almost out then a deep thrust then held the position while he kissed, fondled and caressed her bare skin.

Her hands stroked down his back while her thighs cradled him. He hovered above her and sucked on her lower lip and thrust again her breast rubbing up against his chest. He leaned on one elbow and cupped her breast in his other hand. She used one of her hands to bring his hand closer to her lips. Looking up at him she took his finger into her mouth. He thrust into her again.

She sucked on his finger and swirled her tongue around it making him think back to when she had sucked a different part of his body not that long ago. It was also one of the fingers that had pleasured her. She opened her mouth and raked his finger across her lower teeth and over her full lower lip. Down her chin, across her neck and back across her breast she guided him. He thrust into her again. She brought his hand all the way down to her smooth butt.

Taking the hint he held her firmly and pulled her to him with his next thrust. His lips sought out her breast and teased them with his tongue swirling around each nipple then blowing air against the sensitive area. Another thrust.

She began sucking on his neck. She increased her intensity to see how much he could take. She used her teeth to rake across his skin and she felt him tense. She licked him there and gently blew on the area. "Do it again," he growled as he thrust again. She smiled even though he couldn't see and obliged.

His hand next to her head wound her hair in his fist and twisted her hair tight against her scalp. She gasped and bit him. He thrust harder. He pulled on her hair lifting her chin in the air exposing her neck to him and began sucking on her neck like she had done to him. She pulled his hair and crushed his lips to hers. It was a rough, hard intense kiss.

He thrust again and again in quick succession. He let go of her hair and grabbed her other ass cheek and pumped into her more. His full weight was resting on her, his chin on her shoulder. Her fingernails raked down his back then held onto his shoulders pushing him down as he pulled her up. Her hips mashed with his grinding into him and him into her.

Their breathing was becoming ragged they both encouraged the other one on until they exploded. One after the other they both shouted out their release. He pushed into her one more time for good measure before collapsing onto her. She held him stroking up and down his back.

As their breathing became more normal he rolled off her and she rolled with him resting her head on his chest. They lay there still panting her leg thrown over his. He rubbed her arm. "I didn't mean to be so rough with you. Are you okay? I didn't hurt you did I?"

She giggled, "That felt amazing, I'm more than okay. I didn't hurt you did I?"

It was his turn to laugh, "No, you didn't hurt me." They lay there content in each other's arms before he added, "Brody was one lucky bastard."

She laughed, "Kara was a pretty lucky lady herself. She used to brag, you know? Now I know she wasn't bragging just telling the truth."

"Really?"

"Oh yeah, she talked about your sex life all the time."

"She did?" he seemed surprised. "What did she tell you?"

"Oh, no, I can't tell you. Best friend code and all."

"Humph," was all he said to that. "Do you want to go swimming tomorrow?"

"You're thinking about exercise?" she asked incredulous.

"I'm thinking about a naked swim," he informed her.

"That, I can handle."

Chapter Fifteen

One afternoon they decided to jump off the cliff into the pool of water. What once seemed like a good idea turned her nerves to mush as she leaned her head over the cliff to see the jump distance. They had stripped out of their clothes and were in their underwear.

"You go first," she folded her arms across her chest.

"Why don't we go together?" he suggested.

She was already shaking her head no.

"You sure?" he asked but when he could see she wasn't going to budge he put his hand on her hip and leaned forward, "Kiss for good luck? In case I don't make it?"

She slapped at his shoulder as he pulled her into his embrace. “You shouldn’t even joke about that.” She kissed him anyway. What started out as an innocent kiss deepened as she lifted up on her toes with her hands around his neck pressing her body to his.

He pulled away, “See you down there,” then he slapped her backside. Then he was gone over the side. With his hands up in the air he let out an excited, “Woo!” all the way down.

Disappearing under the water she waited for him to resurface. Five seconds go by then ten seconds, “Bennett!” she called down to him. Nothing happened. The splash from his jump settled and there was nothing but smooth water. She couldn’t see the bottom of the water.

What if he hit his head on something? What if he was stuck underwater on something? It would take her too long to run around. She was going to have to jump. Taking a deep breath she jumped.

She screamed all the way down. The water rushed up to meet her. The coolness of the water enveloped her in its depths. She surfaced looking around, he was right behind her with a huge grin on his face, “I knew I could get you down here.”

She was indignant; she splashed him while he laughed at her. Putting her hands on the top of his head she tried to dunk him under water. She did so easily so she was sure he let her. He disappeared under the water.

Treading water she circled around waiting for him to resurface.

Suddenly she was pulled underwater by her ankle. She came back up sputtering. He wrapped her up in a big bear hug as she tried wiping the water out of her eyes.

"I'm sorry, forgive me?"

Her arms wrapped around his broad bare shoulders as they tread water together. She looked into his handsome face that was filled with amusement. She couldn't stay mad at him. She wanted him to work for it though.

"I don't know. You scared me pretty good. Why should I let you off so easily?"

"Maybe, because I'm a good guy?"

"Buzz, wrong answer." She said but she was smiling at him.

"Here, maybe I can show you something. I have found something new on the island."

Her eyes twinkled, "Really?"

"Would I lie to you?" he asked her.

No she didn't think he would. "Where is it?"

"How long can you hold your breath?"

She gave him a skeptical look.

"You don't trust me?" he asked fringing hurt.

Trust him? Of course she trusted him. "Okay, lead the way." He pulled out of her embrace but took her hand. They swam towards the rock wall on the right side of the waterfall.

"Ready?"

She took a deep breath and nodded her head. They dove under water he pulled her forwards towards the rock wall. With her eyes wide open she could see lightness through the water. They swam under rocks and into the lightness.

Surfacing she found herself inside a large cavern. In the ceiling was a round opening letting the light in. To the right was little beach. Swimming to the beach they pulled themselves up and looked around.

"Wow, this is great." Her voice echoed off the walls surrounding them. Looking towards him with her legs swinging in the water with her hands holding on to the edges.

"God you're beautiful."

She gave him a seductive look. "You're not so bad yourself." She looked around at their little hiding place. "I'm surprised you found this and at the same time I'm surprised you didn't find this sooner."

"Crazy it's been sitting here all this time and we didn't know it."

Her eyes lit up as she looked at him, "Hey, do you think there is buried treasure here?"

"You never know."

She got excited at the prospect and he enjoyed watching her clap her hands together.

"It's not like we could do anything with it here."

"No but when we get home… Hey and you never know, there could be jewels I could wear." She grinned at him.

"You are a jewel all on your own."

"Awe, thank you." She leaned over and kissed him. "Do you want to christen this new cave?"

"I thought you would never ask."

They made love, the sounds of their pleasure reverberating off the walls. Afterwards they lay together satisfied. "I never get tired of that." She sighed.

He rolled onto his side and looked down at her, his hand moved lightly down her sternum across her belly over her hip and curved her towards him. She threw a leg over him. "Good," he told her, "because I plan on never stopping."

"Never?" she asked with a smile, her hand reaching up to push his hair that had fallen forward back.

He looked into her eyes and with all seriousness and repeated softly, "Never."

Her heart soared at his promise.

Chapter Sixteen

Harper was blind folded, her hand firmly in Bennett's as he lead her through the woods. He stood behind her and pulled the blindfold off. His hands resting on her shoulders as she took in the view before her. He had made tiki torches and stuck them in the sand. They surrounded a table and two chairs he had made. A blazing fire was near the table. The sun was low on the horizon casting a pinkish glow to the sky.

"Bennett, this is beautiful. Is this what you've been working on?"

"Yes, I wanted to surprise you."

"Well it definitely worked."

"Well I couldn't give you Oreos or Cheezits but I can give you furniture." He seemed pleased she was happy with his gesture.

She wrapped her arms around him and pressed her body to his. "I love it, thank you."

His heart thudded in his chest as he thought maybe for a split second she was going to tell him that she loved him. He took it.

Her hands roamed up his chest and into his hair. She brought his lips down to hers. She kissed him with all the gratitude she felt. She pulled away from his kiss and realized he had picked her up off the ground. She smiled at him and he grinned at her. Kissing the tip of her nose he set her back down on the ground.

Like a gentlemen he pulled her chair out for her. She graciously sat down and he walked around the other side taking his seat. "This is our first date." He announced.

"It is?" she smiled coyly at him. She looked around. "I'm impressed."

He raised his water bottle like he held a flute of champagne. "To us."

She picked up her water bottle and tapped his. "To us."

He had cooked them up crab and fish. He had displayed it beautifully on large green leaves as a plate. In coconut bowls he had cut up fruit and made a delicious fruit salad. They tried to slip into first date mode. It was hard. They had known each other for years and now they had already slept together. They were doing things a little backwards. These were unusual circumstances.

She decided she was going to play the first date game and try to get to know him on a deeper level. "So tell me something that no one else knows."

After taking a drink he put the water bottle down, "Hmm…that's a tough one. I don't know if there is much you don't know about me."

"Do you remember that party we went to in college?"

"We went to a lot of parties in college."

"The one Kara couldn't make it to, and I had too much to drink…"

Recognition registered on his face, "I carried you home that night."

"Yes you did. Why? You could have let me go into that room. I was a big girl."

He leaned forward, "You and I both know Kara would have killed me."

"Yeah, but if that wasn't the case would you still have done it?"

He didn't hesitate, "Yes."

She smiled and leaned back in her chair, "Hmm…I find that interesting. Why?" Her eyes narrowed as she playfully interrogated him. What he had to say she was not expecting.

"I knew a girl. She was young and pretty had the whole world in front of her and she had a night like yours. She drank too much and frat guy took advantage. She got pregnant and had to drop out of school.

I know you were a big girl and could make your own decisions and you would be able to handle any consequences that may have come from that one night." He paused looking up at her.

"I didn't want for you to have to go through that when you didn't have to. I would stand by my decision every single time."

She smiled and reached across the table and squeezed his hand. "Thank you, I appreciate that."

Watching the sunset they sat and talked for hours after dinner. "Do you know what I am thinking right now?"

"Hard telling, not knowing," she used Frank's favorite saying.

"I was wondering how sturdy this table was?" there was a twinkle in his eye.

His meaning began to dawn on her. "Oh really, should we test it out?"

"I think we should. We want to make sure I don't do shoddy work."

She stood up and leaned forward with her hands firmly on the table she pushed down. "It seems pretty sturdy." She looked up at him. He was looking quite comfortable in his chair watching her. They had already cleared the table earlier throwing their "plates" into the fire. She could tell he was looking down her shirt.

She crawled up on the table on all fours and slinked towards him. He watched her with curiosity enjoying the view she offered up to him. When she reached the end of the table she sat on the edge. She put her feet on either side of him. His hands glided up each one of her calves. She took her right foot and rubbed it against his crotch which was already aroused.

She began unbuttoning her blouse watching him as she did so. He stood up his hands on her thighs wrapping them around his waist. Her hands went for his belt unbuckling it and sliding it out of his pants. He finished unbuttoning her shirt she had abandoned and removed it. Her bra covered her breasts. He undid her bra and tossed it to the side. She unzipped his shorts and made quick work removing them and his underwear. His hand pressed against her chest with his arm circling around her he gently laid her down across the table.

His hand tickled her as it skimmed her belly. The button and zipper of the shorts came undone easily. She lifted her hips as he helped her wiggle out of her shorts and panties. His thumb slipped through her curls and rubbed against her. Watching her as he brought her pleasure aroused him.

She blossomed under his manipulation of her body. She was moaning and calling his name, "Bennett."

"Yes, Sweetheart, tell me what you need."

"I need you, please."

He flicked his thumb over her clit one more time. She gasped, "I need you inside me."

"You do?"

"Yes! Now, please." She begged him.

He gave into her, giving her exactly what she asked for. She cried out. His hands circled around her thighs bringing her up. She held her own breasts as he rocked her body.

With all the strength in exercising and crunches she was able to easily sit up to meet him chest to chest.

"Well hello there," he kissed her. She wrapped her arms around his neck.

"I think you made yourself a mighty fine table here sir. What do you say we try out your chair?"

He ran his hands down her back and kissed her neck. Picking her up he backed up to the chair and sat down with her on his lap. They kissed, running their hands over each other's bodies she rolled her hips against his. She kissed his neck and down his shoulder her hands ran down his shoulders and arms. Reaching his hands she slipped her fingers in his and they held each other.

They had learned to slow down their lovemaking. Time was no object. They had nothing waiting for them to do, no one to interrupt them. One at a time she put her legs up on his shoulders. Leaning over his kissed her calves his hands ran down her legs and down to her bottom. Fingers gripped her hips and with his muscles in his arms flexed he lifted her up and set her down on his manhood.

It turned her on to see his strength at how he so easily manipulated her body. "Jones." He breathed.

She kissed him, "Bennett."

"I-" he broke off and gave her a crushing kiss causing her to tingle from her tongue down to her toes. Was he going to confess his love to her she wondered? She was actually excited at the prospect. He broke off the kiss and looked into her eyes. "I need you." He told her with sincere emotion.

"You have me." She said the words back to him he had told her and she meant it. He did have her. Anything he wanted from her she was willing to give him.

Looking satisfied with her response for now he pulled her close to him in his embrace. Afterwards with their bodies satisfied she continued to sit on his lap facing him, her legs no longer wrapped around his head but on either side of his thighs.

She leaned her head forward resting her ear on his shoulder trying to catch her breath, "That was some first date."

His hands never stopped running up and down her back in slow light movements. "You can say that again."

She sat up, "Once we get rescued, do you think you will take me on a date?"

"Of course. Why do you ask?"

"Well, what do you think our friends will say?"

"Who cares what our friends say? If they can't be happy for us than they aren't our friends."

"What would a date with you look like?"

"Oh you know pretty much the same thing. Five star restaurant with us having sex on the table afterwards."

She giggled.

Chapter Seventeen

Harper had been somewhat lucky she hadn't gotten her period since they had been marooned on the island. She assumed it was stress and slight malnourishment. At one point she had the thought she could be pregnant because of the lack of period but she quickly dismissed that because she would have known if she was pregnant. Her body would have changed.

Now she was scared it could be a reality that she was pregnant! On a deserted island no less! She clearly remembered when Bennett had his vasectomy. There was no way she could be pregnant but all the signs were there. She was having morning sickness. She felt her body changing, her lower abdomen felt tight. Her breasts were so sensitive she had been avoiding Bennett's touch there.

She had been pregnant three times before. She began sweating at what this would mean for them? How was she going to have a baby on an island!?How was she going to tell Bennett? Um, you remember that vasectomy you had several years ago? Well it didn't work!

That was half the reason she wasn't concerned about unprotected sex with him. She knew he had only ever been with Kara. The fact that he had a vasectomy baffled her that this could happen!

She hunched over, her hand on the tree, as she threw up again. "Hey, you okay?" Bennett came up behind her and pulled her hair off her face and neck. He gently rubbed her back and made soothing noises. "You haven't been feeling good for a while now, have you?" he asked because he knew she had been hiding it from him.

She nodded her head. She wiped her mouth then slipped her arms around his waist. He took her into his arms and held her. "I don't like to see you sick."

She couldn't tell him this wasn't the common cold and she would feel much better in about nine months. He walked her back to camp. "Can I get you something to eat?"

She gave him a look. She wanted to ask if he had any saltines but thought better of it. He chuckled and held his hands up in surrender, "Okay, do you want lay down?"

Harper gave him a puppy dog look, "Will you lay down with me?"

"Sure." He helped her up into the cave and jumped up in after her. She crawled into bed and he snuggled in behind her putting his arm around her midsection. The nausea was overwhelming.

She tried to swallow to keep it all down. Her head was swimming. She groaned. She tried not to think about the fact that there was no OBGYN on this island. She would get no prenatal care vitamins. She tried to reassure herself that women hundreds of years ago did it all by themselves. Granted death rates were way higher. She squeezed her eyes tight trying not to think about it.

Eventually she fell asleep and when she woke up she was feeling much better. She could tell she had slept half the morning because the sun was high in the sky. Bennett had slipped out after she had fallen asleep. He hadn't gone far though he was sitting out by the pool.

She joined him, sitting next to him he put his hand on her knee and she rested her head against his shoulder. "So, when did you figure out you were pregnant?"

She jumped and pulled away from him. She searched his eyes. He wasn't mad, he seemed concerned? "How did you? What did? How?" she managed to sputter out.

"Well I wasn't sure but I started to suspect. I have had two kids of my own and I've seen you pregnant three times."

"I thought, no I know, you've had a vasectomy."

He shrugged his shoulders, "I did, but I never went back to get checked and Kara never got pregnant again. So I guess I thought we were okay."

"Are you mad?" she asked the question she was dreading but needing to know the answer.

"No. Definitely not mad. Just a little concerned about your health and the baby." He placed his on her belly. "I'm surprised. I never thought I would have more kids."

"Especially not without Kara?" she asked softly.

He gently kissed her lips. "No, I never thought that was possible."

Tears welled up in her eyes. She was having a baby with her best friend's widow. What kind of person was she? "Harper." She looked up at him. "I know I've never said the words, but you know I love you right?"

"You do?"

"Of course I do. Honestly I can't remember a time when I haven't loved you." He pushed her hair back off her face and tucked it behind her ears. "Obviously not in the way I love you now. When we met in college I knew you were Kara's friend but I would like to think that we would have been friends even if that wasn't the case. You are an amazing person. When we get off this island I want to be with you. You are not just someone I'm having fun with or passing the time with. I love you and

I made a decision to be with you because I want a future with you. I want to raise our kids together, all six of them!" He swore with the realization. "Holy shit, that's a lot of kids."

She laughed, "That is a lot of kids."

"But we will get though it together. Me and you and the baby we will get off this island and we will be the freaking Brady Bunch." His large hand spread across her still flat belly.

She sniffed and wiped her eyes and nose as she giggled.

"Okay. I'm still scared."

"I know." He kissed her on the top of the head and wrapped her up in his arms. "We will get through this together."

This pregnancy was different for a lot of reasons. One, was the fact that she was on an island, two she didn't have any access to any chocolate. There was no midnight snacking which in the long run did not lead to swollen ankles.

She had a nice round belly. She felt good. She had made it to her second trimester. She kept track of everything on the calendar. Her hair was growing at a rapid rate it was also getting softer and shiny.

She had been sleeping a lot more. She couldn't help being tired. She slept in, took an afternoon nap and went to bed early. Now that she was in her second trimester she had tons of energy.

Bennett had been great through it all. He would massage her aching feet and back. They still made sweet gentle love. Having no OBGYN on the island they wanted to be careful how much excursion she extruded. She had stopped running but Bennett had continued. She still walked and swam but did not go into the hot springs anymore.

They also talked so much more. They talked in depth about their past. They had been friends for almost 20 years but they had grown closer and learned more about each other in the past year and a half on the island.

One day they were laying in the shade on the beach. Well she was lying down with her head in his lap. He was sitting up with his back against a tree. He had been getting really good at whittling wood. He was working on a chess piece, the castle which was called a rook, she was told.

She was turned on her side watching the waves come in enjoying the gentle breeze caress her. Stretched to the brink her shorts had lost a button. She had sworn a blue streak the morning it had happened. She had to make a rope belt to keep her pants up.

Bennett put his tool and block of wood down next to his hip and stroked her long locks. Smiling she rolled onto her back and looked up at him. His was smiling warmly at her, so much love in his eyes it made her tear up a little. His hand slipped down to her face.

Reaching up she covered his hand with her own. "What are you thinking?"

"That I'm so lucky." His hand slipped past her hand and rested on the mound of her belly carrying their child. "Do you want to talk baby names?"

"Ah…yeah!"

"What do you think we are having?"

"A baby?" she giggled at her own humor.

"Smart ass."

"Hey! The baby can hear you." Her hands held the sides of her belly as if she was covering the baby's ears.

"Yes, the baby can hear me and my voice, but the baby does not know I'm picking on his mom."

"His?" she asked.

"Yeah, I think we are going to have a boy."

"Really?"

"Hmm…or it could be-"

"A girl? They don't make any other kinds."

"I was going to say twins."

She sat upright his hand coming off her belly. She slapped him on the arm, “Don’t even joke about that! Are you freaking kidding me?” her fists landed firmly on both hips.

He put his hands on the each side of her belly like she had done, “Hey easy he can hear you.” He leaned his head down to her belly, “Don’t listen to Mommy getting grumpy, she really is a nice person you’re going to like her.” He looked up at her with a smirk and a wink.

She laughed she couldn’t help herself.

Chapter Eighteen

A week later they were walking through South Cove their clasped hands swinging between them. Suddenly Bennett stopped. She looked around to see what had stopped him.

"I know this is a romance formed out of the worst circumstances," with that, he got down on one knee, "Harper Grace Jones Quinn."

She gasped her hands covering her mouth, tears of joy springing quickly to her eyes. He took her left hand and held it.

"Will you do me the honor of becoming my wife?"

She inhaled sharply as the baby moved awkwardly inside her. She brought both hands to her belly bringing his hands with her. He felt the baby's foot squirm under his palm.

She looked down at him her eyes sparkling.

"The baby says yes." She told him.

He looked up at her seriously, so much love radiating from his eyes. "And what do you say?"

"Yes!" she exclaimed, "One hundred percent!"

He jumped up and kissed her his hands cupping her head, his fingers intertwined through her hair. Then he was twirling her through the air. She laughed and held on.

Setting her gently on the ground, "I forgot the best part." He dug through his pocket, "I got you a ring."

"You did?!" she clapped her hands together in excitement.

He produced a silver ring that had two bands woven together.

"Where did you get this?" She turned it over in her hand.

"Daphne came to the rescue again."

She looked down at her own engagement ring a pear shaped diamond with a diamond encrusted wedding band. She handed him back the ring and he misunderstood her gesture.

"If you're not ready," he began.

She removed her engagement ring and wedding band and placed it on her other hand. She held out her now vacant ring finger.

He slipped the ring on her finger which surprisingly enough fit her. Then he took off his own wedding band and in a show of solidarity switched it to his other hand.

They walked back hand in hand swinging their arms back and forth.

One night in front of the fire as she filled out another day on the calendar she looked up at him. "We need to come up with a birth plan."

He looked up wide eyed, "What?"

"Well we need to figure out where."

"How about in cave on the mattress?"

She looked at him, "Um, gross. There is going to be blood and mess everywhere. I don't want that in the cave or on our mattress."

"Oh," was all he said at first, "Kara had two C-sections in the hospital. I tried really hard not to see what was happening over that curtain."

"Let's just pray we don't need to worry about that. If you have to cut the baby out we don't have sutures. That could be a real problem."

He really didn't want to think about all the worst case possibilities that could happen with a birth outside of a hospital without a doctor present. If she needed a c-section she probably wouldn't make it. What if something was wrong with the baby? He didn't like to think of how much loss he could be facing. What if he lost them both?

"Are you okay?" she asked him when she had noticed he didn't look well.

"Fine," he croaked out. He cleared his throat, "Whatever you decide I'll support."

"I think I may have to make a new mat for the birth. We will need something with warm water to wash the baby down in. You will need to make sure your hands are washed. A blanket for the baby and we are going to need diapers. Uh, that was the worse stage, diapers." She was making a list and writing it all down in the coloring book.

One night she started having contractions. Bennett was by her side immediately. "Are you okay? What do we need to do? Is it time yet?"

She shook her head as she held her belly and squeezed his hand for support. "Not yet. The contractions are irregular. I've been counting and they are not consistently the same time apart."

"Okay….do you want to walk? Or try and lay back down?"

"Let's walk. At least we can get near the springs where there is hot water."

They had packed a to-go bag like they were going to the hospital. It had the fresh mat a towel, and bottled water inside.

As they walked through the moonlight her contractions started getting stronger. They made it to the spring and Bennett laid out the mat for her. She paced for a while then finally lay down.

Labor was hard but they got through it together. He encouraged her and told her he loved her. She did the same.

As the sun started to rise a baby cried, a perfect little baby girl. He had cleaned her up and wrapped her in the towel. He had cut the umbilical cord and handed her over to her mom. Harper was crying as she gathered the little girl to her chest.

Relief filled her. She was still alive, her baby was still alive. Bennett loved her. She rolled onto her side cradling the baby next to her. She was already starting to root around. She offered her breast up to her and she greedily suckled at it.

She laughed, "I think she's got it."

Bennett cleaned up and went to bury the placenta. "I didn't even think about you having to walk back." He told her.

She was cooing to the baby, "It doesn't matter. Does it little girl? No it doesn't, Mommy is happy right here with you."

Bennett sat with his back up against a tree facing them.

"Can I hold my daughter?"

She had just finished drinking. "Of course, she will need to be burped."

He leaned over and picked up his daughter. His heart swelled as it had with each of his kids.

"We have to come up with a name. We only talked about boy names," she reminded him.

"I would like to suggest we name her after my mom."

She sat up on her elbow. Bennett rarely talked about his mom. She didn't even know what her name had been so she asked.

"Bertha."

"Umm…" she managed to get out.

A deep rumbling laugh bubbled up out of him. "I'm kidding." He looked up his eyes glistening. "Ellie, her name was Eleanor but people called her Ellie."

"Ellie." She let the name roll over her tongue. "Ellie, that's pretty." She grinned at him. "Okay, Ellie it is."

He looked down at his daughter. "Ellie." He tried the name out. The name fit her.

Harper crawled over to him and snuggled into his arms. He held his two girls, he would protect them forever. He kissed Harper on the top of her head. "I love you so much. Thank you for giving me such a beautiful daughter."

"It was my pleasure. I love you too." She pulled the blanket aside to get a good look at her daughter. "She really is gorgeous."

They used Daphne's suitcase as a crib because the crib Bennett had started to build wasn't ready yet. They used ripped pieces of the towel as diapers. They washed them as they were soiled.

Ellie grew big and strong. She nursed and when she was five months old they introduced her to mashed bananas which she loved. A month later they tried mashed mangos which she didn't like as much but still ate. When she was seven months old they gave her pineapple which she couldn't get enough of.

They applied aloe as sunscreen to protect her delicate white skin. In spite of their best efforts she bronzed right up. Ellie was an adorable baby, not that they were bias at all. She had Harper's big blue eyes and Bennett's sandy blonde hair which was a mass of curls.

She had recently learned to crawl and she was quick. They couldn't turn their backs for a second and she would instantly head for any body of water. She loved the water. She would splash and play all day in the water if they let her.

Harper was in the ocean playing with Ellie on Sunset Beach when something caught her attention out of the corner of her eye. Bennett was in South Cove catching dinner for them but he did like to sneak up on them sometimes. Ellie giggled hysterically when he would pop out of nowhere.

This wasn't Bennett though. Harper did a double take as she saw a large ship passing the North Pointe of the island. "Oh, my God, Ellie this is it!" She waded through the strong waves as fast as her strong legs would allow her.

Once on shore she sat Ellie down in the sand and started shouting jumping up and down, waving her hands wildly. She turned towards South Cove and screamed at the top of her lung like no one has ever screamed before, "Bennett!" long and loud, her voice carrying.

Turning towards the ship she screamed again, "Help! Help! Over here! Please Help!"

Realizing Ellie was taking off and she was half naked, only dressed in her underwear she grabbed her daughter and set her back down and started dressing. Throwing on clothes in record time she ran to get Ellie from the water's edge.

"Hey, come back!" she shouted at the ship as it continued on. Ellie lower lip stuck out in a pout and big alligator tears started forming as she started crying, not used to her mom's tone of voice. Harper put her in the sling she had designed to transport her around the island.

Holding Ellie close to her chest she ran to the top of North Pointe. Up there they still had the signal fire but she didn't think that would help much during the day. They had put a long stick with a red pair of shorts they had fashioned as a flag. Pulling it out of the ground she raised it above her head yelling wildly.

Ellie continued to wail. She tried soothing her, "Shhh…baby it's okay. Mommy is trying to get us off this island so we can go home." Ellie settle for a minute looking up at her mom. Until she started yelling and waving the flag then the tears came flooding back.

Bennett was in South Cove with the spear he had made tracking a large fish he had it in his sights on when he heard Harper's blood curdling scream. Cold fear and dread crept into his heart. Dropping the spear he ran out of the water and though the woods towards his wife and child.

What if something had happed to Ellie? He didn't want to even think about it but all the most horrible possible situations came to mind. When he reached the beach he didn't see either one of them. What if something had happened to them in the water?

As he was running to the water he stopped dead in his tracks as he saw the ship. He knew then this was why she was screaming and that his girls were okay. He continued on to North Pointe when he saw her running towards him. Their flag was in one hand and with her other she held Ellie to her firmly.

"They're coming! Bennett, they're coming!"

When she reached him he wrapped them both up in his arms and held them tight.

The large ship had turned towards them and set anchor off shore. A couple of men came over on a small rescue boat. "I need to grab some stuff," she told him.

"What? Just leave it. Who cares?"

"I do." She handed Ellie over to him, "I'll be right back!"

"Jones!" he yelled after her but it was too late. He knew he couldn't stop her even if he tried. He turned to greet the men coming towards him.

Harper ran through the woods for the last time towards camp. It seemed so surreal. When she reached the cave she threw in the cloth diapers they had made, all of Daphne's possessions, the blanket she had made and their coloring book diary into her suitcase.

Leaving the mattress she had made and the crib Bennett had made she jumped out of the cave. Looking around for the last time she noticed the crate they had made for the ship, the black spot on the rock where they had countless fires, and the waterfall they had swam in.

This had been her home for three long years and it was a little bitter sweet to leave it but she was more than ready. "Good-bye Survivor Island, see you never," she called out. And with that, she turned and ran.

On the beach she realized that the dark skinned men did not speak any English but were willing to remove them from the island. When they got on board they realized it was a cargo ship carrying large containers of all different colors.

They were shown to a kitchen and were served bowls of soup with rolls. It was beef and vegetable and the most amazing thing they had eaten in years. "This is the first carb I've had in three years," she told Bennett as she ate and broke off pieces for Ellie to chew with her four front teeth.

A young man grinning came into the dining hall. "Hello," he said with an accent.

Bennett stood and shook his hand, "Hello. I'm Bennett and this is my wife, Harper and our daughter, Ellie."

The young man nodded his head up and down in greeting, “My name is Peter.”

“It’s nice to meet you, Peter. Please, have a seat.” He gestured to the seat across from the table from them. Peter kept grinning and nodding his head as he took a seat.

“You live on the island?” he asked.

“We were in a plane crash.” Bennett explained.

“Ohhhh.” Peter’s eyes got large as he looked back and forth to both of them. “That’s not good.”

“No, not good at all,” Bennett agreed. “Where are you guys heading?”

“America.” He said proudly.

“Oh good,” Harper chimed in.

“Yes, good.” Peter agreed. “You live in America?” he asked

“Yes,” they said in unison.

“Ah, good, good. We have found some accommodations for you on the ship. We will be in port tomorrow.”

“That’s great,” Harper exclaimed putting her hand on Bennett’s arm. He patted her hand.

“We will get to see the kids tomorrow.”

"Kids?" Peter seemed confused, pointing to Ellie.

"Yes we have more kids at home." Harper tried to explain.

"Where in America is home?"

"Boston," Bennett responded.

"I'm going to radio ahead to let them know that we have picked you up and they can notify your family."

"That's great! Do you think we can talk to them?" Harper asked hopefully.

Peter's never wavering smile faltered a little. "Sorry, we can't make any phone calls we only have the radio transmission to shore."

"That's okay." Harper assured him. "Tomorrow is good enough."

He seemed relieved, "Good, good." He stood up. "I will show you to your room."

They stood up and followed him through several doorways and hallways. He showed them to a small room with bunk beds. "I'm sorry, this is all we have available."

"It's perfectly fine." Harper assured him.

"Good, good." He said as he backed away. "Oh, before I go what is your last name?"

"I'm Bennett Treadwell and this is Harper Quinn."

Peter seemed puzzled because they had been introduced as husband and wife but was wise enough not to ask.

"Very well. I will see you in the morning. I will take you to breakfast."

Bennett and Harper both shook his hand and thanked him.

Inside they found Daphne's suitcase next to a bolted down dresser. There was also a table and two chairs. Pulling a blanket off the bed she set it down on the floor then let Ellie sit down on the floor.

Harper pulled out the grey bunny that had become her snuggles for bed time. Handing it to Ellie she was content to wave it around in the air before stuffing her fist with a floppy ear into her mouth to gnaw on. Bennett and Harper turned to one another. Harper started jumping up and down excitedly and jumped into Bennett's arms.

"Is this really happening? Ouch!" she was rubbing her arm where Bennett had pinched her. "What was that for?"

"I figured I would beat you to the punch where you asked me to pinch you."

"Ha ha, very funny," then she pinched him back.

Hours later Ellie was fast asleep on the bottom bunk surrounded by pillows so she couldn't roll off. They crawled to the top bunk together and snuggled under the covers. Wrapped in each other's arms they lay there in the darkness. His hands began to roam under her clothes.

Rolling over to face him she reached over for a kiss it was deep and passionate. His tongue swirled intoxicatingly with hers. Her hands went to his belt. They stripped out of their clothes effortlessly. Their naked bodies came together.

Harper had again shed all the baby weight and was in excellent shape. Bennett worshiped her body and she revered his. They kept their moans and groans as silent as possible. Bennett rolled on top of her his body sliding easily between her thighs.

They were having sex in a real bed! They whispered words of love to each other, promises of forever. They climaxed together, sweaty and satisfied. He collapsed on top of her. Laying together they slowly drifted back down to Earth.

He rolled off to one side but kept her in his arms. He kissed her temple as she rubbed his chest hair with her fingertips. They talked in whispers about their future and their kids and how amazing it was going to be.

"I can't wait to see my mom and Frank. They are going to be so excited."

"I really want to see Kara's parents. They were the parents I never had."

"John and Judy are the best."

They talked about their jobs. She wanted to go back to work once they had Ellie settled. They talked about setting up an office in the pool house with a private entrance for clients.

The next morning they were treated to pancakes and bacon with orange juice. It was heaven. Ellie gobbled it all up. Afterwards they were treated to a real shower with soap, shampoo and conditioner. When they landed, Peter escorted them off the ship. They were brought into a brick three story building and taken into a conference room.

"Wait here," Peter instructed them.

They stood with Ellie on Harper's hip and Daphne's suitcase at her side. The door on the opposite side of the room opened. A man and a woman stepped through the door. She was dressed nicely in white skirt and aqua blue top and wedge sandals. The man was in plaid shorts and a short sleeved button up shirt.

Shocked faces met shocked faces. Harper and Bennett were staring at their NOT dead spouses, Kara and Brody. Who in turn were staring at their NOT dead spouses that had a baby with them and doing the math in their head could only mean one thing. Things just got complicated.

Book Two

Chapter Nineteen

Three Years Earlier

Frank and Rachel, Harper's parents were trying to round up their three grandchildren for dinner. After dinner Frank was going to the airport to pick up their daughter Harper and son-in-law Brody. Chloe the oldest was on the computer. Colton was playing a game on his phone and Paige was putting on a performance in her ballet outfit.

"Who wants mac and cheese?" Rachel called out to the group.

"Meeeeee" Paige sang out and skipped to the table.

The other two abandoned their screens and ran to the kitchen table. Rachel gave a huge smile to her husband happy that she was able to get all the kids to the table at once. They loved their grandchildren more than anything, but this past week had been a lot. The kids were rambunctious. She wasn't quite sure how they got their energy.

She was happy her daughter and her husband were able to get away from work for a week and have time to themselves. She was also just as happy they were coming back. She was scooping out huge helpings of her homemade macaroni and cheese with cracker crumb topping when the phone rang.

Frank got up to answer it. "Hello?" Pause, "Hey John how's it-" Longer pause. "No. I haven't…" She watched him walk to the family room and turn on the TV. She put the bowl down and started walking towards him.

Colton started to say something. "Just stay here and eat, I'll be right back." When she got into the family room he was sitting on the arm of the couch as if he couldn't quite make it all the way. He still had the phone to his ear and was staring at the TV.

Rachel stared at the big screen trying to determine what was happening. Their local news girl a blonde woman about thirty was reporting, "We have just received breaking news that an airplane destination, Boston has gone down in the Atlantic Ocean. Flight 924 departed from Barbados in a storm. We do know that the pilot did radio in a distress call that they were struck by lightning. Contact with the aircraft was lost shortly after that. We are unsure at this time if there are any survivors as of yet. We do know that the Turks and Caicos Coast Guard have been dispatched. We will keep you updated as soon as we get word."

They were showing a picture of the southern Caribbean with an X marked in the last known location of the plane out over the Atlantic.

Her hand was resting on Frank's shoulder. "Is that…" she started to ask.

"Yes." He responded.

Paige came running into the room. Frank quickly shut the TV off. "Grandma, can I have some chocolate milk? Please?"

She jumped immediately leaving the room that had revealed the devastating news. "Sure, honey. Come on let's go sit down and finish up your dinner." She placed her hand on her back and ushered her back to the table.

Going into the kitchen she opened the refrigerator door and started to cry. Silent tears streamed down her face blurring her vision. Frank came up behind her and took the milk and chocolate syrup out of the fridge and left the door open for her to hide her grief.

"Who else wants chocolate milk?" he called to the table.

"Me." All three kids called out. He made their milks and brought them to the table.

He ushered Rachel outside and into the guest house past the pool. She collapsed down on the couch and threw her hands up in the air then covered her face with them. "Oh, Frank!" she wailed, "What if my baby is not okay? That would not be okay."

He knelt down in front of her taking her hands in his. "I'm sure she is fine."

"What are we going to tell the kids?"

"Nothing for right now, we wait and see how this plays out."

"They are going to wonder why we are not going to the airport to pick them up."

"We will just tell them their flight was delayed."

"Okay." She tried wiping the tears away. Frank got up and turned on their TV on the wall. All stations were now reporting on the airplane going down.

Atlantic Ocean

Water came rushing in and around the passengers from the rear of the plane. Unbuckling quickly Kara stood up and pulled the seat cushion off and wrapped her arms around it. It was utter chaos around her. People were doing the same thing and getting out of the plane as expediently as possible and by any means possible. Looking up her heart stopped. The back of the plane was gone, just gone. Where were Bennett and Harper?

Tears stung her eyes her heart started beating faster. There was no sign of the back of the plane. The rain was coming down hard and the plane was rocking up and down with the swell of the waves.

"Kara!" she heard her name and had a surge of hope until she turned around and saw Brody climbing over one of the chairs in front of her.

"Oh my God, Brody, you're bleeding."

"I'm fine. Where are Harper and Bennett?"

She started crying "I don't know!" she wailed. Her arms spread out towards the back of the nonexistent plane, "It doesn't look good though!"

"Okay," he grabbed her by her shoulders and turned her towards him. "Listen we need to get out of this plane. Make sure you have a seat cushion to hold on to. I'm going to get mine. I will meet you out there. Do you understand?"

Still crying she nodded her head. People were already ahead of her climbing over chairs and the water was getting higher, now up to her knees as she sloshed through the water. Holding on for dear life to her seat cushion otherwise known as a floatation device, she made her way out of the back of the plane.

The water was ice cold. She gasped as she was merged neck deep in the water. People littered the ocean surrounding the broken wreckage of the plane.

Passengers continued spilling out of the back of the plane. Swimming to the left of the plane she waited for Brody to join her. She was starting to get worried about him when she saw him but he wasn't alone.

Spotting her he swam towards her. He had a little girl with him. "Here," he pushed the little girl towards her, "Her dad is stuck in his seat. I'm going back inside. I'll be right back."

As he was swimming back to the plane it exploded. Shrapnel and debris flew through the air. "Hold your breath," she told the little girl. She sucked in her breath and dove underwater taking the little girl with her.

When her lungs were close to exploding she resurfaced. A wave hit her in the face she was sputtering and still holding on to her cushion and the girl. The plane was on fire and sinking fast, well what was left of the plane.

A large chunk of the plane was floating near them. Swimming towards the make shift raft she pulled the little girl with her. Other people had the same idea and were swimming towards it as well. An older gentleman had made it on top to it first. He reached his hand down to help pull the little girl up. Then he helped her up as others crawled on as well.

She searched the ocean looking for Brody. She scanned the horizon and the faces in the ocean. The rain was coming down hard and she did not see him. About eight people fit on the piece of the airplane. Several other people were hanging on to the sides. A smaller piece of wreckage nearby had three people on it another one had five people. Most were still floating in the ocean holding onto their floatation devices.

Turning to the little girl she said, “My name is Kara. What’s your name?”

“Daphne.” She managed to get out her teeth chattering and her hair was matted down to her scalp.

She tucked Daphne’s hair behind her ears, “Listen honey-Daphne I need you to be a good girl and stay here.” The man that had pulled them up was sitting close to them. She addressed him directly.

“My friend is still out there. I need to try and find him. Will you watch her for me? Her name is Daphne.”

He held his hand out to her, “I’m George.”

Taking his hand she shook it, “I’m Kara. Thank you George.” He nodded his acknowledgement.

She jumped back in the water and swam in the general direction of where she last saw Brody. It took her a long time and her arms were aching, her body cold. She found him with another man. Brody was unconscious and the man had his arm tucked up and under his arms as he held on to the cushion with his other hand.

She swam toward them, "Hi, this is my friend, Brody. I'm Kara. I have a piece of airplane we are sitting on if you want to come with me."

The dark skinned man nodded his head. They worked together to swim back to the make shift raft. George and another man helped pull the still unconscious Brody up out of the water and the other man that had saved his life. They pulled her up next.

Susan a nurse about fifty years old came over to assess the damage done to Brody. She also learned the name of the man that had saved Brody was Neil.

They were in the water for several hours shivering and scared. Brody had finally regained consciousness. She was cradling a now sleeping little girl. Poor thing was exhausted and had cried herself to sleep. She wished she could do the same but stayed strong for little girl with dark hair and big brown eyes.

The equivalent of the coast guard showed up and rescued all the survivors. They were given warm blankets to wrap up in. She found someone in charge, "My husband and" she pointed to Brody, "his wife are still out there. The back of the planed broke off and they would have been that way." She pointed in the general direction.

"I'm sorry ma'am but we came from that way and we didn't see anything. No signs of wreckage. Sorry." Brody had to drag her away from the man.

When they showed up in port they were bussed to a local hotel. They were told they could shower and were given clean, warm clothes. They were then told to meet downstairs in the conference room to record who had survived.

Brody and Kara kept Daphne with them. She knew she should have felt better being showered and warm but she just felt numb. They all walked downstairs together and were told to stand in line to record their information.

As they were standing in line they heard a large booming voice. "Daphne!" All three of them turned around. Daphne who had been holding Kara's hand let go and started running. She tried to catch her but Brody put his hand on her arm stopping her.

Daphne sprinted through the crowd that was making way for the little girl. A large gentleman knelt down on one knee scooping her up and twirling her around. Her joyous laughter brought a smile to people's faces followed by spontaneous clapping.

When Daphne's Dad put her down she tugged him towards Kara and Brody. "Come on Daddy, you have to meet these people. They saved me."

Brody put his hand out to meet the man but instead the man scooped both of them up into a giant bear hug.

"I can never repay you for saving my baby girl. Anything you ever need you just let me know. I mean that."

"Not necessary, we have kids and we would like to think anyone would do the same."

"You folks are real fine upstanding citizens. You ever change your mind you just call me." He pulled out his wallet and opened it to find a soggy business card. Paul Connors was his name.

"My name is Brody and this is Kara."

He shook both their hands his other hand desperately clinging to Daphne who was practically wrapped around his leg, "That's just wonderful. How long have you two been married?"

Kara looked away tears stinging her eyes. "I do apologize." Paul said immediately realizing he had erred in his questioning although he didn't know how.

"I don't think-" Brody's voice broke off. "I mean, our spouses were in the back of the plane."

Realization crept slowly over Paul's face. Crest fallen and with tears in his eyes he offered his sincere condolences.

George and Susan who were nearby also heard the exchange. Susan pulled Kara into her embrace and Kara took the comfort as she began sobbing. Brody rubbed her back as George did the same for him.

"We had no idea." He explained.

"How could you know?" Brody asked him even though he didn't expect a response.

"Come on," George started pulling them to some upholstered chairs and sofas set in a circle around a coffee table.

"But we are supposed to fill out our information." Kara a rule follower tried to explain as her hand gestured to the table. Susan was guiding her where George was leading them.

"They will be here all night. Please sit. If they need our information that badly they can come to us."

The entire group including Paul and Daphne joined them on the chairs. Neil joined the group minutes later when he had spotted them. Susan got him up to speed. Daphne's Dad was alive. Brody and Kara's spouses were dead.

He sat down heavy in one of the chairs, "Oh man that sucks."

They sat for hours talking and crying. George was right a couple of people with clipboards did come over and take down all their information. They saw the sun come up through the windows.

Susan suggested they should all get some sleep. "They said they were going to get us out on flights to go home later today. They also said we should call our families. They left calling cards in our rooms."

Brody and Kara looked up at each other. Their families. If they had heard the news they had to be devastated and they also had to inform them that only one parent from each family was coming home. They said their good-byes and went back to the room.

"You first," Brody told Kara.

She picked up the phone and used the calling card. She called the phone number that had been the same number for forty years. Her Dad John Sr. picked up the phone.

"Hello?" it sounded abrupt and anxious.

"Dad." She cried so happy to hear a familiar voice.

"Kara?! Judy! Kara's alive! She's fine. Oh thank god. We were so worried. Is everyone else okay?"

There was a long pause as she tried to keep her tears silent, but they were choking her throat, causing a burning sensation.

"Honey, what's wrong? Tell me." She could hear mom questioning him. She could almost picture her tugging his arm, and him waving her off.

"I think Bennett is dead, Dad." She said the sentence in a rush fearing she wouldn't be able to get it all out. Brody was sitting next to her on the bed rubbing her back for support.

She heard him swear under his breath then, "Honey, I'm so sorry."

"Harper too." She was crying in earnest now. Sobbing.

"What? What about Brody?"

"He's here with me."

"Holy-"

"Dad, what am I going to do? What am I going to tell the boys?"

"We will figure that out together. We won't tell them anything now. We will sit them down together and we will be here for you. You just get home safe."

"Okay. Tell Mom I said hi. I love you guys. I have to go Brody needs to call his family."

"Okay, baby girl. We love you."

John hung up the phone his eyes full of tears. He raked an unsteady hand through his thinning hair. "John, you tell me right now." Judy demanded.

"It's not good. Let's go sit."

"I don't want to sit. Tell me."

"Bennett and Harper didn't make it."

Her hand flew to her mouth and she collapsed to the ground. "Oh my god. That's awful" She wailed.

John's own legs were giving way so he sat down next to her on the kitchen floor. He pulled her into his arms and they cried together. They were so thankful that Kara was alive but Bennett and Harper had both been surrogate children of theirs. They had taken each of them into their homes and treated them like their own kids.

It was a huge loss. It was crushing and devastating and he couldn't imagine how Kara was dealing with the death of her spouse and best friend.

Meanwhile Brody made a phone call to his parents and broke the same news to them. After hanging up with them he asked. "Who should call Harper's parents, you or me?" He pinched the bridge of his nose.

She wiped her eyes. "I can do it if you want."

"Please, I just don't think I can tell Frank and Rachel their only daughter isn't coming home."

She held her hand out and he handed her the phone. She dialed the home phone number of her best friend's house that was next door to hers. Her parents were staying at their house while they watched the grandkids.

The phone was picked up on the first ring. "Hello?" again an anxious voice came across the phone. It was Rachel.

"Hi, Mrs. Stewart."

"Kara? Oh thank god." She could hear the relief and the false hope. She was nervous about crushing that feeling, "Is everyone okay?"

"I don't think so-" she started.

"What do you mean you don't think so? Is Harper hurt? Brody?"

"Brody is fine."

"Kara," her voice was firm. "Tell me what happened."

Tears gathered again, "I'm so sorry to tell you this, but I don't think Harper made it."

"What do you mean you don't think?"

"Well when the plane crashed the back of the plane severed off from the rest of the plane. Harper and Bennett were both in the back of the plane. We haven't seen them since. The Coast Guard said they haven't found them and it doesn't look good. I'm so sorry."

Half way through her explanation Rachel started sobbing but she kept talking. Frank ended up picking up the phone, "Kara?"

"Yes, Mr. Stewart. I'm really sorry but Harper and Bennett didn't make it. Brody is fine. We are going to be taking a plane home in a few hours. Please don't tell the kids anything. We will break the news to them when we get home."

"Kara, I'm real sorry to hear about Bennett."

"Thank you. I'm really sorry about Harper. I loved her like a sister and I'm not sure how I'm going to get through this."

Frank choked up, "We love you Kara and we will help you and Brody anyway we can. Just come home."

"We will, give my condolences to Mrs. Stewart."

"I will. Good bye."

She hung up the phone and looked over to Brody who had stopped pacing and collapsed in a chair. He was sobbing. She went to him. Standing in front of him she put her hands on his shoulders. He hugged her to him and they tried to comfort each other.

They didn't end up sleeping. After answering a knock on the door they were informed that their flight would be leaving shortly.

Chapter Twenty

At the airport they were met by Judy, John and Rachel. Frank had stayed home with all the kids. Hugs and tears where abundant. The ride home was sober and quiet. Kara sat in the back holding the hands of her parents and Brody rode up front with Rachel.

They pulled into Brody's driveway where everyone was gathered. The kids all ran out to greet them. Giving hugs and kisses Lucas asked Kara, "Where's Dad?"

"Let's go inside." She suggested. She could tell the other kids were now looking around.

"Where's Mommy?" Paige demanded.

Panic started to rise in the front yard. All the adults ushered the kids inside. They settled in the living room. Kara's boys sat together looking worried. Rachel sat down and pulled Paige on her lap. Frank and John sat with Colton and Chloe in between them.

Kara and Brody sat on the sofa facing their family. On the airplane ride home they had discussed who was going to talk and how they would handle questions. They were as prepared as they could possibly be but they were not ready for it.

They had both felt that Brody could keep himself contained emotionally.

Brody took the lead, "We were in a plane crash on the way home. That's why we are late. That's also why you didn't go to school today. The plane broke when it crashed in the middle of the ocean. Your mom," he looked to his kids, "and your dad," he turned to Lucas and Griffin, "were in the back of the plane. They-" his voice broke.

"Mom," Lucas asked.

"Dad's not coming home." Kara said softly.

Chloe chimed in, "Where's Mom? She has to be coming home. Dad," she had tears in her voice, "Mom's okay right?"

Brody was shaking his head. "I'm sorry guys, but they were never found. They sent a rescue team out looking for them but the back of the plane was never found and neither were they. They are not coming home."

Chloe jumped up, “I don’t believe you!” she yelled at them.

“Honey,” Rachel tried to console her granddaughter but it was too late she was already turning and running out of the room.

Colton was crying and his Grandpa Frank pulled him onto his lap. Paige wasn’t quite sure what to do. Rachel took her upstairs to her room. Brody went after his daughter.

Kara went to her sons. Lucas and Griffin stood up and wrapped their arms around her. Griffin was crying and Lucas was trying really hard not to. Judy and John stood up and joined the group hug.

They decided to go home, saying goodbye to Frank. They sat around the table for a long time talking about what this means and how everyone was feeling.

There was a knock on the door. It wasn’t a light inquiring knock, it was loud and demanding. “I’ll get it,” John offered getting up from the table to answer the door. Judy had gotten up to make coffee.

Loud voices started coming from the front of the house. Getting up she told the boys to stay put. Kara walked to the front door. Hank was standing there looking wild.

“I saw the news. Where’s my son?” he demanded.

Her heart quickened. She hadn't thought to call him. Bennett had not spoken to his dad in years. He didn't allow him around his kids. She had only met him a couple of times.

"Hank, come in. We were just making some coffee."

He looked at her and she could see the pain in his eyes. "I'm really sorry Hank but Bennett didn't make it." She went to him. Her dad stood guard next to her.

"NO!" he shouted. "No!" he backed away from her.

She reached for him, "Please Hank, come inside and sit with us."

He pinched the bridge of his nose. She put her hand on his back and gently led him into the kitchen. Her dad, John, closed the front door.

If her mom was surprised she didn't show it she just poured him a cup setting cream and sugar out on the table. Her boys eyed the near stranger at their kitchen table.

Hank took the coffee and drank it black. Kara added cream and sugar to hers taking a seat next to Hank. Her dad sat on the other side of him. Her mom took a stool at the kitchen breakfast nook.

"What happened?" Hank wanted to know.

Kara began explaining it again.

Over at Brody's house he was dealing with his own drama. Chloe had locked herself into her bedroom and it took a half hour of coaxing to convince her to let him in. When he finally got into her bedroom she was inconsolably crying on her bed.

When he finally got her to talk he hated what she had to say and he wasn't sure how to answer her. "Dad, Mom is never going to see me get married!" She wailed. "I won't have a grandmother for my kids. Who is going to help me pick out a prom dress? What if I have questions about sex? Who am I going to ask, you? I don't think so!"

They had a long conversation, "Listen, if you don't feel comfortable talking to me you have two grandmas whom I'm sure would love to take you shopping or talk to you about girl stuff. I'm sure Kara wouldn't mind either.

This is uncharted territory we are going through, but we will get through it. It won't be easy but we will make it through."

"I miss her." Chloe confessed.

"Of course you do. I miss her too."

They hugged. "I need to go check on your brother and sister. Are you going to be okay for now?"

She nodded, "Thanks Dad. I love you."

"I love you too honey."

He walked by Paige's room it looked like Rachel had things under control there. He found Frank and Colton in the backyard they were in the tree house. Frank came down and Brody went up. Frank patted him on the shoulder as he walked by.

Brody crawled up the ladder that he had nailed to the tree years before. Colton was in the corner of the tree house with his knees up to his chin and his arms wrapped around them. When he saw his dad he scrambled towards him.

Brody wrapped him up in his arms holding him tightly. "I'm sad, Dad."

"I know Bud, me too."

He just held him for a really long time. The sun started to set. He talked him into coming inside.

Frank had called for some pizza to be delivered. They sat down as a family to eat. Most of them just picked at the food on their plates.

That night Brody had tucked each one of the kids into bed and was in his room pulling all the pillows off the bed when there was a knock on the door.

"Come in," he called. The door opened and all three of his children were standing there.

Paige had her baby doll tucked in the crook of her arm. "Can we sleep in here," she asked.

He looked at his big empty king sized bed then at the kids with their sad eyes. "Yes." He told them. Instantly he saw relief in their eyes and all three of them jumped into bed and settled under the blankets.

He crawled in next to them reaching his arm over all of them they snuggled closer.

Kara had put her two boys to bed. When she went downstairs she found Hank and her dad talking in the living room. Her mom was in the kitchen cleaning up. Her mom gave her a sad look and held her arms out to her.

She ran to her crushing her mom to her. Together they rocked back and forth. "Oh, Mom, what am I going to do?"

"You are going to do the best you can." She told her. "We will be here every step of the way."

"Me too."

The women turned to see John and Hank standing in the doorway. Hank was the one that spoke.

"Listen, Hank I really appreciate it but-"

He cut her off, "I'm quitting drinking, cold turkey, tonight. Kara, I swear to you. My family needs me. I was not there for my son and I can never take that back but I'll be damned if I am going to let another chance slip by me. Please give me that chance."

She looked at her dad who was resting his hand on Hank's shoulder while her Mom was rubbing her back comfortingly.

"Please don't let me down. I can't take any more heartbreak."

"You won't regret it." He seemed relieved. "Can I stay here tonight? Please?"

"Sure, Hank. Is the couch alright? I'll get you a pillow and some blankets."

"Thank you Kara."

She left to retrieve the items. After she had him settled she said good night to her parents and headed for her own bed.

She walked into her room and closed the door behind her. Her room was just as she had left it. The bed was made and the room was empty. She was not used to not having Bennett around. He was a larger than life personality and it was lonely.

She stripped out of her clothes, that weren't hers, that had been given to her by the airline. Walking over to her dresser she put on her pajamas. Crawling into bed on her side she laid there. Pulling his pillow towards her she could still smell his cologne on the pillow.

Hot wet tears streamed down her face as she held on to the pillow pretending it was him, knowing it wasn't. It took her a long time to fall asleep and when she did it was restless and fitful at best.

Chapter Twenty-One

The next day they were bombarded with funeral plans. Kara and Brody planned together while the grandparents took care of the kids. They decided against a wake because there was no body and they didn't think they could put themselves through that.

They met with their priest after the funeral home. They needed to pick out cemetery plots. They got out of the car. The priest showed them some plots by the road.

"No," Kara said "this is all wrong."

"Okay," Father Donavan looked down at the cemetery map. "We can go over here." He led them to the right side of the cemetery.

"No." Kara said. "It needs to be special, secluded and pretty."

He looked at the map again, “I don’t have four plots together, but…” he trailed off.

“Can we see it?”

“Sure.” They meandered through the headstones to the back of the cemetery. There was a stone wall along the back edge of the cemetery. When she turned around she could see the whole cemetery from here. She could see glimpses of the lake from here through the trees.

“This is perfect. What’s wrong with it?” she asked Father Donavan.

“Well the couple divorced and sold back their plot. There are only two of them here. So one of you could pick this plot and the other one can be buried here or you could bury Bennett and Harper here but you couldn’t be buried with them.”

She looked to Brody who had been awfully quiet this time. “What do you think?”

“It’s a really nice spot. I don’t want to think about us not being with them. Is there any way we could be buried on top of them and share the plot?”

“Oh, that’s a good idea.” Kara whipped around to Father Donavan.

He hesitated. “It’s highly unlikely but I could ask for you.”

"Good. Then it's settled." And she walked away leaving the two men to follow in her wake.

Brody's family had flown in from Ohio. They were staying at a nearby hotel. The media had picked up on their story and continued to hound them for an interview. Both of them declined. The people they had met on the plane had done interviews telling the world what little of the story they knew.

Reconsidering their decision not to hold a wake she scanned the crowd of hundreds of people crowding the church. Not all of them followed them to the cemetery for the burial but at least a hundred people did. It was sad and tears flowed down her face constantly behind the dark shades she chose to wear. Her boys stood solemnly on either side of her.

Afterwards they went back to their houses where both were open for company and food was piled high in both places. People talked and remembered the dead. After hours of small chit chat and endless condolences people left except Hank and her parents.

They took care of putting the kids to bed. She sat down in the kitchen her shoes thrown off and her feet resting on one of the chairs. She was still in her black dress she had worn to the funeral. She was uncomfortable in her clothes and her feet ached. She wished this nightmare would end. She rubbed her temples with her hands.

The phone rang. Absentmindedly she answered a tired, "Hello?"

"Mrs. Treadwell?" a voice asked.

"Yes?"

"This is Sampson Clarke, I've been appointed by the airlines to settle with the victims of Flight 924."

She looked at the clock on the wall it was eight past nine. "Are you kidding me?" she asked incredulous.

"No ma'am. We are authorized to give each passenger five thousand dollars."

"What?!" her brain was having a hard time comprehending what was going on.

"I apologize, you and Mr. Treadwell will both get five thousand dollars so that is a total of ten thousand dollars. Now I just need to verify your address so I can mail this out to you immediately."

"I can do math Mr. Clarke," her voice was cold, "but what I fail to comprehend is your inadequacies. I just buried my husband today-actually," she talked over him as he tried to interject, "an empty coffin because he was never recovered from the crash your company is responsible for. You can shove your ten thousand dollars where the sun don't shine and I will be having my lawyers contact you in the morning at a reasonable hour." And with that she hung up the phone on the sputtering, apologetic, Sampson Clarke.

She whipped the phone across the room and it shattered against the wall. She turned around in time to see her Mom, Dad and Hank standing there watching her. “I’m sorry.” She apologized.

“You have nothing to apologize for.” Her Dad told her.

“This sucks,” she told them as she threw herself into the chair she had vacated. They all nodded their agreement.

Each of them took a seat surrounding her and talked well into the night. She was not looking forward to going up to an empty bed again tonight.

The next morning she called the law firm she worked for and was given the name of the best lawyer to handle the suit she would be bringing against the airlines. She gave them the name of George, Susan, Neil, Daphne and her Dad to be contacted.

She also informed work that she would be coming back to work the following Monday. They protested and suggested she take another week but she told them it was best if she and her family got back into the swing of things. Kara couldn’t stare at the walls in her house anymore.

She made arrangements with her parents and Hank to pick up the kids after school and watch them until she got home at night which sometimes was pretty late. Returning to work was awkward but she kept her head down and powered through with her cases putting all her time and energy into the career she had tried so hard to build.

Brody offered to buy her out of Bennett's half of the company. She accepted his more than fair valuation of their company. Life moved on slowly at first then picked up the pace, and things were off and running.

Chapter Twenty-Two

Brody didn't have help like Kara did. After about a week of Frank and Rachel helping out they needed to get back to their life in Connecticut. They had offered to move here to help him out but he didn't think that was fair to ask. His parents went home the day after the funeral.

He contacted a live in Nanny Service to see if he could get someone to help him out with the house and the kids.

They sent a German woman by the name of Gretchen. She was near sixty and tough. Strict rules and not at all what the kids needed at a time when they were missing a mother figure. He called and requested someone different. They sent him three different people all of them not acceptable.

Rebecca Buchanan was their last hope. Her dad had walked out on her and her mom when she was little. It had always been the two of them. Her mom worked two jobs and she started working as soon as she was able. Rebecca worked non-stop to put herself through college.

She had light brown hair and blue eyes. She was a pretty girl the guys would check out but she didn't have time for them. When she graduated she was approached by The Agency. She was pleasantly surprised with how well nannies did for themselves.

When Brody opened the door and saw her standing on his front door in leggings and boots with a white button up shirt and a hint of cleavage he said. "I'm sorry this isn't going to work." Brody tried to close the door on her.

She looked dumbfounded. "Excuse me?" she asked her boot wedging itself in the door frame before fully closing on her face.

He opened the door slightly as to answer her and not slam her foot in the door. "The position has been filled." He told her.

"No it hasn't. They just sent me. I don't understand."

"That's because you're twelve," he muttered under his breath but she heard him.

"Listen," she said as she picked up her suitcases and barged in the front door. "I may look young," she pushed past him and into the kitchen, "but I am more than capable of taking care of your children."

Paige walked by her and she acknowledged her, "Hi, Sweetheart."

"Hi." Paige's face lit up with the new arrival.

She addressed Brody again setting her bags down. "I have a degree in Child Psychology and I'm working on my Masters. This is my job and I do it well." Colton was running by throwing a football up in the air which she caught with one hand. Handing it back to him she told him he could do that outside.

Without questioning this stranger he did. Looking back at Brody who had his hip propped up against the center island was watching this all in amazement she concluded. "The least you can do is give me a chance."

He looked at her for a long while debating. "Let me show you your room." He finally said. He couldn't tell but he thought he saw her shoulders relax just a little. He waved her off of her bags and picked them up.

"This way," he told her as he walked to the French doors leading out to the patio.

"Daddy, can I show her, her room?" Paige asked excitedly.

"Sure, honey."

Paige took Rebecca's hand and led her to the door. They walked outside and to the pool house on the right side of the pool. Inside was a cute living room fully furnished with a couch and two chairs. A small round glass table was behind the couch and behind that was a kitchen.

Paige pulled her to the room to the right of the living room. It was a pretty little bedroom with a queen sized bed with a sage green comforter and silver accents on the walls and around the room. There was a dresser with a mirror and two end stands with matching lamps. To the right was a walk in closet and to the left was a bathroom.

"This is very pretty." She told Paige, "Did you pick it out?" she asked.

"No my Mommy did, but she's dead."

"Paige!" Brody shouted dropping the luggage.

Rebecca and Paige both startled at the outburst.

"It's okay." Rebecca soothed Paige when she could tell she was about to cry.

"Paige go in the house," Brody commanded.

Paige ran. Then addressing Rebecca, "I am home tonight for dinner so you have tonight off to settle in. Tomorrow I need you to come in at 6:30 get the kids up and ready for school. Make their lunches or arrange for them to buy lunch. I have a petty cash box set up for that. Make sure their school work is packed and drive them to school at 7:20.

At home I need the house kept up, laundry, dishes etcetera. The kids need to be picked up after school at 3:20. There is a schedule inside to let you know who has what for after school sports or activities. You are responsible for getting dinner on the table."

He waited. "Okay." She said and with that he turned around and left. When she heard the front door close she let out a long pent up breath, "Wow!"

Rebecca called her mom, "This guy is not nice." She told her. "I think he is a workaholic though so hopefully I don't have to see him that much. I feel bad for the kid, their mom died."

Her mom made a sad noise on the other end. "It can be tough loosing someone. You know that Rebecca." She did know that. Even though her dad hadn't past away he might as well have.

"I know. But he is such an ass! Did I tell you he tried to fire me at his front door?"

"Yes."

"And did I tell you what I said to him to have me stay."

"Yes." Her mom told her but not that it mattered she went into the whole story again. After getting off the phone with her mom she unpacked and went into the kitchen which was fully stocked. "Wow. Well at least my little sanctuary is nice." She said aloud to herself.

She made herself a sandwich and sat down to watch a little T.V. before setting her alarm and taking a shower. She crawled into the super soft bed and fell asleep. The alarm woke her up on time the next morning. She got up straightened her hair, applied make up and got dressed in a pair of jeans, a pair of converse sneakers and dark pink top.

She walked into the kitchen at 6:29. Brody was waiting for her. He was dressed sharply in a navy blue suit, light blue button up shirt and a red tie. He looked at his expensive watch on his wrist and nodded his head.

"I'm off to work. I left you my contact information here. This is the address to the schools." He pointed to a paper on the kitchen island next to a key. "This is your house key. If you need anything don't hesitate to call me. The kids are up the stairs, the first three bedrooms. The one down on the end is mine, it is off limits."

"Aye, aye Captain." And she gave him a salute realizing too late he was not in the mood. She turned and went into the kitchen to find what she would need for the day.

"I will be home at six," he told her then left through the door she assumed went to the garage. A minute later she heard the garage door open and close. She ran upstairs and went into the bedrooms to wake the kids.

Groggily they got out of bed and headed for the bathroom or the closet to get dressed. She helped Paige get dressed for the day. "Do you think you can help me with lunches?" she asked Paige.

She nodded her head. They headed downstairs together. Paige put her hand in Rebecca's. Down in the kitchen she found Chloe and Colton sitting at the island eating pop tarts. She introduced herself to the kids. They barely paid her any attention. She had heard they had, had a parade of nannies before her so they were probably trying not to get attached.

The backpacks were set out on the kitchen island. She took out their lunch boxes and set them up on the counter. Opening the fridge she searched for what they had. Paige helped her find the bread to make sandwiches.

The morning went pretty smoothly. When she returned home she gave herself a tour. Off the entrance of the house to the left was a home office. She just peeked inside not wanting to invade his privacy. To the right was a large sitting room. Straight ahead was the kitchen eat-in area and family room. Behind the kitchen was a formal dining room. Off the hallway to the left was a three car garage and a large laundry room and bathroom.

Upstairs was a large game room for the kids and four bedrooms. She made the kids beds and picked up their dirty laundry. She started a load of laundry then dusted. Switching over the laundry she went through the kitchen and made a list of groceries she would pick up.

She vacuumed then folded laundry and put it away. She looked up grocery stores online and ran the errand. When she got back she put the groceries away. She made a salad put it in the fridge. She marinated a pork tenderloin with a teriyaki glaze. She peeled and diced potatoes and put them in a pan of water on the stove.

She swept the downstairs hardwoods then went to get the kids. She had taken a photo of the kid's schedule so she had it with her on her phone. She found Colton's soccer bag in the front closet and brought it with her grabbing a bottle of water to put inside.

She picked the kids up. Colton put on his gear in the backseat and she dropped him off at practice. She dropped Chloe off at music then sat and waited for Paige to finish gymnastics.

Picking them all back up she headed home an hour and a half later. When they got home she turned the oven on and started cooking the potatoes. Rebecca emptied out all the backpacks and set them up at the kitchen island to do their homework.

Paige had a color by numbers page and Colton and Chloe both had math and English homework. She helped them with questions they had along the way. She made them their lunches for the next day and put them in the fridge.

The kids were just finishing up with their homework when Brody got home. The kids lit up when they saw their dad. Calling out to him they all jumped up and bombarded him at the door. He scooped them up and for the first time she witnessed his face soften.

"Dinner's ready," she called as she set the table. The kids started running for the table, "Go wash your hands," she called. They immediately changed course and ran to the bathroom down the hall. He looked at her trying not to be impressed.

"Dinner smells good." It was compliment and she beamed at him and he practically frowned at her. Rebecca tried not to let that dampen her mood.

"What can I get you to drink?"

"A beer would be great."

She went to the fridge and pulled one out. She found a tall pilsner glass and poured it in for him. She set out four glasses and filled them with cold milk.

"Bring your milk to the table, please." She held them out for the kids as they came out of the bathroom.

They all sat down to eat. She helped serve the kids. She sat next to Paige. Chloe and Colton sat across from them. Brody sat at the head of the table. The kids kept up endless chatter about school and sports. After dinner she cleared the table and sent the kids up to take showers and get into their pajamas.

She started a load of dishes then went upstairs to see how the kids were doing. Colton was already showered and was in his pajamas. She found Chloe in her room, "Can I help you brush your hair," Rebecca asked from the door.

"Sure," she held out the brush to her. She walked into the room and sat down on the edge of the bed. She brushed out her wet locks. "I can blow dry your hair for you. It will help keep it nice for tomorrow."

"Okay." She jumped up and headed for the bathroom. Paige was splashing in the tub. She blew dry Chole's hair then told her she could go have dessert downstairs. Pulling Paige out of the tub she toweled her dry and blew dry her hair too then helped her into her pjs.

When she went downstairs she found Brody had retired to his office. The kids had turned on the Disney channel and were settled down in front of the TV. "Do you guys want popcorn?" she asked.

"Yes!" they all shouted.

Rebecca looked in the pantry and pulled out a bag of popcorn and put it in the microwave. Putting it in a big bowl she settled down with the kids. When the show finished she sent them upstairs to brush their teeth.

They went upstairs and she put the popcorn bowl in the sink. When they came downstairs to kiss their dad goodnight she inspected their teeth to make sure they did a good job. Rebecca escorted them back upstairs and tucked them in.

Once they were all settled for the night she knocked on Brody's office door. "Come in," he called. She opened the door to find him on his phone in front of his computer.

"I'm just going to go," she whispered.

"Just a minute," he said into the phone and put it up against his chest.

"Kids are in bed. I will see you in the morning," she reported.

"Okay, no problems today?"

"No everything went fine." Except your attitude she didn't mention.

"Good night," he said before he was back on the phone.

She closed the door behind her. She walked to her little home out back. She threw herself down on the couch exhausted. She watched a little TV before taking a shower and crawling into bed.

Chapter Twenty-Three

In the office Brody hung up the phone and tossed it on the top of his desk. It landed with a thud. His head rolled back against the leather chair. Tears stung his eyes and he pinched the bridge of his nose. How was this his life now? His wife was gone. God he just couldn't believe it. Now a stranger, a beautiful stranger was tucking his kids into bed. He was frustrated beyond belief.

His phone vibrated on his desk. Picking it up he noticed the time, it was after ten. He had a text from Kara, "You awake?"

Quickly he replied, "Yup. You ok?"

"Not really."

"Come over."

"I'm at the back door."

He jumped up from his desk and hustled to the back of the house. She was standing there in her pjs and holding two beers. He unlocked the door Rebecca had locked and let her in.

"Hey, come in." She did and offered him one of the beers. He took it and held his hand out to the couch. She walked past him and flopped down on the couch. He sat down in the chair next to her. He set his beer on the coffee table took hers from her and opened it then handed it back. He then picked up his beer and opened it taking a deep swig. Then he sat back in his chair and waited.

Kara tucked her feet up under herself and took a drink staring off into space. "The court settled today."

He sat forward, "Really? Was it not good?"

"7.9 million."

"Ok so split between how many families?"

"No 7.9 million for each family that lost someone. 1.3 million dollars went to each family that survived."

"Holy shit. That's crazy money."

"They also graciously threw in free flights for life."

"Who the fuck wants that? I don't ever want to get on a plane again that's for sure."

"I know." She took a swig of her beer. "I think the worse part for me is realizing Bennett isn't coming back."

His lips tightened into a thin line. He reached over and squeezed her hand and she squeezed back. He had bowed out of the court proceedings. He had given her power of attorney to accept whatever deal she felt fair. He couldn't deal listening and recounting the day he lost Harper.

It had been eight months since the plane crash. She looked at her hand that still held the ring Bennett had picked out for her it was a princess cut with round diamonds on the band. "I don't know when I'm supposed to take this off."

He lifted his own hand with his platinum ring still intact, "I don't know. I haven't even thought of it."

"I feel like life is just moving on without them and I'm not sure what to do."

"I know. I miss her every day and I miss hanging out with Bennett. I miss us as couples."

She nodded her head in agreement, "How's the new nanny?" she asked conversationally, changing the subject.

He snorted.

"That good, huh?" she asked.

He sighed, "No. She fine."

"Then what's the problem?"

"She's not Harper."

"Honey, no one is ever going to be Harper. If she's good take the help to try and relax a little. Are you going to send the kids to private school now?"

"No. Even if I wanted to I wouldn't want to change their lives around at all. I'll keep them with their friends."

They talked about what they were going to do with the money. He offered to invest for her and come up with a plan. She told him whatever he thought was fine with her, just send over the paperwork to her office and she would take a look.

The family fell into a routine with Rebecca in the house. Everyone adjusted well except Brody. He tried to keep his distance from her. The kids loved her and she did amazing with them and the house.

The summer was tough for Brody. He saw Rebecca more than once in a bikini. One night she came and knocked on his office door. "Come in," he called.

She peeked her head in. "Can I talk to you?" she asked. She seemed a little nervous. He sat up straight in his chair. Was she going to quit? He really hoped not.

"Sure, have a seat." He gestured to the chairs across from his desk.

She came in and closed the door. She sat down with her hands wiping sweat off the palms of her hands on her shorts. "I'm not really sure how or if I should tell you."

If she should tell him? What's that supposed to mean?

"I had to deal with something with Chloe today."

"Okay." He said slowly still not sure where this was going. He sat forward folding his hands.

"She reached a milestone in her life today. She wasn't sure what was happening to her. So I did have a talk with her and took her to the store to get her some supplies."

Dawning registered on his face and it drained all of the blood from his face causing him to go ghostly white. He rubbed his hands over his face. He didn't know if Chloe was ready for this but he most assuredly was not ready for this.

"I hope I didn't over step. I didn't really think you wanted to have that conversation with her."

"God no." he confirmed. "Thank you for dealing with that. Is she okay?"

“She was really freaked out at first but we talked it out and I did give her some Midol for cramps.”

“Thank you.” He told her sincerely grateful she had dealt with it and it hadn’t happened on his watch.

Chapter Twenty-Four

Christmas Eve Rebecca exchanged gifts with the kids. They gave her homemade presents they had made at school. "I love them!" she exclaimed. "Thank you so much." She kissed and hugged them all. Rebecca read them 'Twas Night before Christmas' and tucked them in.

"Good night," she called to Brody who was sitting in front of the fireplace. She tried sneaking out the back door.

He stood up, "Hold on," he walked over to the tree and picked up one of the presents. "I got you something."

She stopped short at the door. "The bonus check you gave me was more than adequate."

He held out a small box wrapped neatly in sparkly paper and a red bow. "The kids helped me pick it out."

Unwrapping the present she found a Pandora Charm bracelet. It had a piano charm from Chloe, a soccer ball charm from Colton and ballet slippers from Paige. "It's beautiful." She looked up at him. He looked sheepish. "Thank you." She told him.

"You're welcome."

"I have something for you!" she exclaimed. "It's in my apartment." He followed her out to her place. She had put up a mini Christmas tree in the living room. She had presents prettily arranged under the tree.

She handed him a present wrapped in blue and white snowflakes with a silver ribbon tied on top. He opened it up not really knowing what to expect. What would she get him he wondered?

"I wasn't sure what to get you." She prefixed.

Inside was a long black box with his name engraved on top. Pulling the top off top lid he found was a shiny silver bullet with his name engraved on it. It was a bottle opener. One night they had been watching Shark Tank with the kids and they had seen this. He thought it was cool and had said so. He was surprised she remembered.

"Thanks." He smiled at her.

She smiled back, "You're welcome. Do you like it?"

He picked it up and turned it around in his hand. "I do. It looks really nice. It's awesome."

"Good," she seemed really happy, "I'm glad you like it."

"Are you leaving tonight?" he asked her.

"Yes. I'm already packed." He noticed the bag by the door.

"Can I help you with your bags?"

"Sure! I just have to pack up the presents." She walked to the kitchen and grabbed her keys off the hook on the wall. "Thanks." She handed him the keys.

He took the keys and the bags and walked them out to her car. She quickly loaded the presents into plastic bags and had them by the door when he returned. She picked up her purse and one of the bags. He picked up the other and she shut off the light and they walked out together to her car.

They loaded her things inside and she shut the passenger door.

"Well, I will let you go. Drive safe. We will see you when you get back." He turned to leave but stopped. "Merry Christmas." He told her.

"Merry Christmas," she said and leaned in for a hug. It was a warm embrace and it lasted longer than either one expected. She smelled like apples and cinnamon.

He pulled away from the hug, "Drive safe." He told her again as he walked away.

"Thank you," she called out. She looked down at her new bracelet she still had in her hand. She absolutely loved it.

"Um…" she held out her hand stopping him. He stopped and turned around. "Can you help me put this on?"

He walked back slowly taking it from her. She held her wrist out to him. His fingers grazed the inside of her wrist as he clasped the bracelet. His hands fell away from her. She turned it around and admired how it sparkled in the twinkling Christmas lights on the house.

She looked up at him smiling, "Thanks again for the bracelet, I love it."

"I'm glad."

There was an awkward silence then she was her chipper self again, "I guess I will see you in a week."

"Sounds good." He stepped back as she got in the car. He watched her pull out of the driveway and waved when she got to the end and he was happy when she waved back.

Frank and Rachel arrived Christmas morning to see Brody and the kids. Rebecca had prepped their whole Christmas dinner and left a note telling him when to put the turkey in and how long to cook it. She had done the same with everything else in the fridge.

"Wow, this is great," Rachel said when she got there and read the list. "What's she like?" Rachel wondered. She hadn't yet met her because they only came up on weekends and she went home to her Mom's house.

"She's really nice Grandma." Chloe came up behind them.

"She is really smart too." Colton chimed in. "She helps me with my math homework."

"Rebecca is funny," Paige chimed in.

She looked at Brody who shrugged his shoulders.

"And very pretty." Paige continued.

"How old is she?" Rachel asked.

"I don't know." Brody said as opened the oven and basted turkey.

"Hmmm…wild guess. 30s, 40s 50s?"

"Twenties," he said into the oven.

"Really," Frank asked.

Brody closed the oven door, he felt like he was being interrogated. "She is a college graduate."

"What was her major?"

"Child psychology."

"Why is she a nanny then and not practicing?"

"I don't know. She said something about getting her Master's. Frank would you like a drink?" he opened the fridge.

"That would be great. Rachel, leave the poor man alone." He told her when he saw she was clearly not done with her questioning, "The kids are doing great. The house looks great. Obviously we will be eating on time because of this girl. What's her name?"

"Rebecca." They all said in unison. Brody used the bottle opener Rebecca had given him the night before to open Frank's beer.

Frank smiled, and then changed the subject much to Brody's relief. They had a great meal and he set his in-laws up in the bonus room upstairs where the pull out couch was, because they had refused to take his room.

During the week he found himself looking out the French doors expecting Rebecca to come waltzing in. When she came back he tried not to be excited but he was.

It was late Sunday night, the kids were in bed and he was up watching T.V. The light in the guest house came on. He sat upright his heart started thudding wildly in his chest. He put the bottle of beer down on the coffee table because suddenly his palms were sweaty.

He rubbed them on his pant legs. Should he go over and welcome her back? Would she come over and say hi? He wasn't sure what to do about these feelings he had for this woman. She was much younger than him about ten years younger.

Rebecca was beautiful inside and out. She loved his kids and they loved her. She had unknowingly filled a void in their home. He still loved Harper more than anything and missed her every day but she wasn't here and he had felt like he was drowning.

Since Rebecca had come into their lives he slowly felt like he was treading water and was now on solid ground. As much as he thought about her he realized that she was technically his employee.

If anything happened with them and then it didn't work out where did it leave his kids? Again without a mother figure. He sat there so long contemplating that the light went off next door and he was left with feelings he couldn't describe.

Maybe he should starting dating? He could meet someone that wouldn't be a complication. Someone that didn't work for him and someone that was his own age and if something happened it wouldn't ruin his whole world.

Chapter Twenty-Five

Over the next several days he started to broach the subject of the possibility of starting to date. One night at dinner with all the kids and Rebecca at the table he went for it. "What do you kids think if Daddy went out on a date?"

Silence except the clank of a fork hitting the plate all eyes were on him.

"With who?" Chloe asked.

"I don't have anyone in mind," he told her, "I wanted to make sure you guys were okay with it if and when I decided to ask someone out."

His son Colton just shrugged his shoulders.

"I think you should date Rebecca." Paige piped up.

They all looked at Rebecca. Whose mouth was gapping open but she quickly recovered. "Your daddy and I can't date." She told the children calmly.

His heart sank. He almost wished she would look at him and say "Why not?"

"How come?" Chloe and Paige asked at the same time. All eyes were now on her.

"Well," she explained patiently to the group, "I work for you dad and it's against the rules for us to date."

"It is?" Paige seemed sad by this revelation and if he was correct, his other kids looked just as dejected by this announcement as he felt. Were they all routing for him and Rebecca?

"Well only if she is as nice as Rebecca." Paige said.

"Deal." Brody raised his glass to the table, "Only someone as nice as Rebecca." He looked at her and he saw something in her eyes he couldn't quite place. Maybe it was wishful thinking on his part.

After dinner he put the kids to bed and came back down to find her doing dishes. "Let me help you."

"You don't have to do that," she told him. Even though he came around to the other side of her and started washing the silverware as she loaded the plates.

He reached around her once he had a handful scrubbed and dropped them into the plastic bins to hold them.

"What was with the kids tonight?" she wondered. "Did they say anything to you when you tucked them into bed?"

"About what?" he fringed ignorance.

"About me and you? Crazy huh?"

He circled around her again dropping more silverware into the dishwasher. She added the last bowl into the dishwasher, added the detergent, and then started it. He dried his hands and leaned against the kitchen island facing her.

She dried her hands and turned around to look at Brody leaning up against the kitchen sink. He had not answered her question and she was starting to get nervous about why. He noticed she was still wearing the bracelet he had given her for Christmas and his chest swelled. "Do you think so?" he asked.

"What?" she was confused. Did she think what?

"Do you think it's a crazy thought? Me and you?"

She didn't know what to say. "It's definitely not a good idea."

"Okay, I'll give you that, not a good idea, but other than that…" he trailed off.

Oh God. She looked at him, really looked at him not as her boss or as the kid's dad but as a man. He was attractive she would give him that. He was clean cut and dressed nicely and she had noticed he smelled really good too. That and he had softened up considerably since she had arrived.

He was going to kiss her. She could feel it. She could see it in his eyes. They were only three feet away from each other. She could stop it she knew. Just walk away she told herself, but she was curious. What would it be like to kiss him? Maybe it would be nothing. They would get it out of the way and both of them would realize that it wasn't something they wanted and-

Brody was across the distance in one long step. His hands gripped the countertops on either side of her. Ducking his head he captured her lips. His body pressed hers into the cabinets. When she didn't reject him he scooped her up into his arms.

This was not a nothing kiss. Her hands wound around his neck and pressed herself to him. It was intoxicating. Her tongue slipped into his warm inviting mouth and he groaned into her.

"Daddy?" they heard Paige's voice at the same time. They jumped apart. She was standing next to the refrigerator rubbing her eyes. Her cute little feet were bare and she was wearing pink and green frog pajamas. "I need a drink."

Rebecca quickly turned around and opened the cupboard pulling out a plastic cup. Brody went to scoop his youngest daughter up in his arms. "What are you doing up Sweetie Pie?"

"What were you doing kissing Rebecca?"

"I think you are dreaming." He told her. Rebecca handed Paige the cup of water. She took a sip and looked from her dad to Rebecca. He carried her back to bed and got her settled in. He hurried back downstairs to find it empty.

After a moment's consideration he strode out the back door and pounded on her door. She opened it immediately. She grabbed him by the front of his shirt and pulled him towards her. Their lips met once again.

He kicked the door shut behind him. They stumbled back onto the couch together. Their breathing became heavy as they kissed and caressed each other. She was half lying on top of him. She wanted him. She had a deep aching need for him. Damn the consequences too. She wasn't thinking of them just him in this moment.

One of his hands was in her hair his other roamed down her back and across her ass. Something he had been fantasizing about since this summer when he saw her in a bikini. She started unbuttoning his shirt and pulling it out of his pants. She managed to take it off and admired his upper chest with dark springy curls covering a sculpted body. She had noticed how many days of the week he went to the gym and it paid off.

He sat up, she was straddling him when he lifted her shirt up over her head. His eyes were heavy with lust as he saw her perky breasts in a lime green bra with a little bow nestled between her cleavage. That's where his lips went and she cradled her arms around him pulling him closer. His fingers made quick work of releasing her breasts from the confines of her bra.

Gliding the straps over her shoulders he removed her bra and dropped it to the floor. Reality was much better than his fantasies had been. Her hands gripped his hair and pulled his head back until he was looking into her eyes.

His hands cupped her breasts and she gasped at the feeling. She dipped her head down and captured his mouth. He stood carrying her to the bedroom. Setting her down on the edge of the bed he stood in front of her. She reached out and unbuckled his pants pulling them down.

He stepped out of the rest of his clothes and she was pulling her pants down and tossing them on the floor next to his clothes. Joining her in bed they kissed again rolling around tangled together. Quickly he was inside her. She gasped out and thrust her hips to meet his. The sensation was so strong and it had been so long for him that their passionate lovemaking was over soon.

Collapsing and rolling off of her they were both breathing heavily. They lay on their backs looking up at the ceiling. “Well that went from 0-60 in no time at all.”

“I’m sorry,” he apologized, “It’s been a long time and-”

She burst out laughing, “No silly,” she rolled onto her side putting a hand on his chest as his arm went around her back. “I’m talking about the, “I think I should start dating” conversation an hour ago to now. That was fast work.”

He sat up his knees raised he put his elbows on his knees with his arms out straight. “I didn’t plan this.”

She sat up next to him. “I know that, but this seriously complicates things.”

“I know. I’m sorry.”

“We will figure it out.” She reassured him her hand on his back. “We are both adults. We shouldn’t tell the kids anything yet. We need to figure out if this is anything we need to concern them with.”

“I agree. I don’t want them to get their hopes up.”

He rolled out of bed and started putting his clothes on. “Where are you going?” she asked.

“I need to get inside in case any of the kids wake up.”

She pulled her sheet up over her chest feeling a little dejected. Of course he needed to go. “Oh, right.”

Brody leaned over and kissed her then he was gone out her front door. She threw herself back down in her bed. What did she just do?! Holy shit! Rebecca covered her face with her hands and groaned.

The next morning when she went next door he was waiting for her. “Hey-” she started but was immediately cut off by Chloe at the top of the staircase.

“Rebecca! I need your help this morning.”

She looked at Brody and he shrugged. “You’re up early.” She told her.

“I am running for class president today and I have to give a speech. Can you help me curl my hair? Please? Oh, and I need help picking out an outfit.”

“Sure.” She walked past Brody.

“I’ll see you ladies tonight.” He told them and gave Chloe a kiss goodbye and wished her luck with the speech she had been rehearsing the past week.

Rebecca arranged Chloe’s beautiful hair in fat ringlets and using a butterfly clip she put half of it up and left the rest cascading down her back. Together they picked out grey leggings and a long teal sweater and black boots. Chloe had started to develop over the summer so Rebecca had taken her out buy some bras.

She ran next door and let her borrow one of her long silver necklaces.

"Really?" she was excited.

"Absolutely. This is a special day for you. I think this will bring you good luck."

"Thanks Rebecca!" She threw her arms around her and she patted her on the back.

"You're welcome. Knock them dead kiddo." And she lightly rapped her knuckles across her chin.

After school Chloe made the announcement that she had indeed become class president. "Congratulations!" Rebecca exclaimed.

"Yeah!!!" Paige clapped her hands for her big sister.

"Nice work," Colton gave his sister props.

Rebecca texted Brody at work to give him the good news.

He responded immediately. "Great! Tell her I said Congratulations. I will take everyone out to dinner tonight. Don't bother cooking anything."

Rebecca relayed the information to the kids which they were extremely excited about putting in their recommendations of where they thought they should go. Rebecca texted Brody back to let him know the kids were excited about his plan.

That night after dinner and after she had tucked the kids into bed she came downstairs. She found Brody sitting on the couch. "Goodnight," she called trying to make an easy escape.

"Rebecca," he called. She stopped. This wasn't going to be so easy. She turned towards him. "Would you like to watch T.V. with me?"

She looked at him. He was serious. She walked slowly back past the kitchen table to the couch. She glanced up at the T.V. some cop drama was playing. "Sure." She plopped herself down on the overstuffed chair next to the couch.

"Um, I was kind of hoping you could sit over here on the couch." She looked over at him. He was sitting in the middle of the couch so no matter which end she picked he would be close.

"Okay," she said slowly. She stood up, walked the two steps towards the couch, and sat down. Pretending to watch T.V. she had a heightened awareness of him by her side. Brody turned towards her his leg bent at the knee his shin was close to touching her thigh. His arm rested on the couch behind her head. Turning to face him she wondered what he had to say.

"I'm sorry about last night. About everything, I did not handle it well."

"No you didn't," she told him.

"I know," he picked up her hand and looked into her eyes. "Please forgive me. I don't want to screw this up and I want to do this right. Spend time with me. Go on a date with me. I'll have Chloe watch the kids, she is getting old enough. If not we can ask Lucas to come over to help watch the kids. What do you think?"

She took a minute to respond. "Wow, you've thought a lot about this."

"Yes I have, but if you think this is a mistake," he trailed off searching her eyes.

Her heart was beating wildly in her chest. She had thought about him all night and day. Rebecca had fantasied about how he had caressed her, kissed her, licked her, how he had moved inside her. Brody was holding her hand now and it felt, right.

Leaning towards him he met her half way their lips caressed. She pulled away she didn't want to get sucked in like last night. "We shouldn't kiss in the house." She told him nodding towards the stairs where the kids could come down at any moment.

"Do you think holding hands on the couch is safe?" he asked.

"I think we can manage that."

They sat on the couch holding hands talking about themselves. She asked about Harper and he told her. He asked about her family and she told him about her Dad leaving and her mom. They shared stories of their childhood. They talked about the kids. It was two in the morning when they realized what time it was.

"Can I walk you home?"

She smiled, "Sure."

They stood up still holding hands while he walked her across the patio to her door. At the door she turned towards him. "I had fun tonight." She told him.

He leaned closer. "Me too."

Her hand reached around his neck and drew him closer. He pulled her into his arms and they kissed both wanting more but trying to stick to their promise of taking it slow. He pulled away from her first. "Can I take you out tomorrow?"

"Yes." She said breathlessly and he kissed her again. She moaned and it was almost his unraveling, instantly hard. Her hand ran down his chest then gently pushed him back.

"Goodnight," she whispered.

"Goodnight," his voice was raspy. Reluctantly he pulled away from her. "Sweet dreams," he told her.

"You too." Then she disappeared inside.

Chapter Twenty-Six

The next morning she practically skipped into the kitchen. He was there waiting for her as always clean cut dressed in a navy tailored suit and vest and a grey striped tie. "Good morning," he said with a grin.

She replied in kind, "Good morning Mr. Quinn."

"Would you mind walking me to the door?" he asked her.

"Sure," she responded curious as to where this was going. He picked his briefcase off the counter and walked in front of her to the front door. When he reached the front door he pulled her into his office. Shutting the door behind him he had her up against the built in book case and he was kissing her.

She kissed him back her hands running from his sides up under his coat and up his back her breasts pressing against his chest. His hand slipped down to cup her backside. She gasped breaking the kiss but he continued the assault on her neck. One of her hands came up to rub his head her hands gliding through his hair.

"I thought about you all night," he whispered.

"Me too," she confessed.

"I can't wait for tonight." He told her, "I don't think I'm going to get any work done today."

She giggled. She loved the idea that she was a distraction for him like he was for her. He kissed her again then he was opening the door and putting on his coat. "If I don't leave now I never will." He told her.

"Go," she told him knowing he was right. "I'm looking forward to this evening."

"Oh," he said as he had his hand on the door. "I'm going to text Chloe after school and tell her I have a meeting tonight and I already asked you to work late tonight but you have to leave a little early tonight because you have to go to…" he trailed off wondering if she could come up with a good excuse.

"I have a college reunion coming up soon. I could say I'm going to that?"

"Perfect. I'll text you the address of the restaurant. Say seven?"

“Okay, see you then.”

Chloe was excited to be able to be in charge of her siblings for a few hours and didn’t even question their made up story. Chloe actually helped her pick out her outfit. A red dress with a handkerchief multilayer skirt with a halter top with a rhinestone nestled in between her breasts. She put on a cream color pea coat over her outfit. She chose black strappy high heels which made her calves look phenomenal and made her three inches taller.

She took her time curling her hair and spraying it into place. She applied her make up carefully adding lip gloss that made her lips appear kissable. “You look beautiful.” Chloe told her. She was sitting on her bed watching her get ready.

“Thank you, Sweetie.” She kissed her, then said good bye to the others and glowed at their compliments as well.

“Have fun!” they told her.

“I will,” she promised.

Brody met her as planned outside with a kiss. They walked quickly out of the cold and into the restaurant. She removed her coat and handed it to him. He was staring and it made her beam with delight.

“You look absolutely beautiful,” he told her.

“Why thank you.”

They sat and enjoyed their meals. They were escorted in front of a fireplace which gave off a romantic glow. Afterwards neither was ready to end the night. "Do you want to go for a ride?" he asked her.

"Sure."

He had the valet bring his car around. Inside it was cold and they cranked the heat and he turned her seat warmer on. He drove out of town and up to a parking spot for hikers. The dirt parking lot was hidden off the main road and was empty. The moon was out shining bright into their car.

He parked the car and shut off the headlights but left the car running. He played with the radio stations until she told him she loved a song. He used the buttons to pull his seat away from the steering wheel giving him some room to stretch out.

He was looking at her in her seat wanting desperately to touch her. So he told her so. "I want to touch you." He breathed.

She sat back in the seat. "You do?" she played coy. "Where?"

"I want to run my hand from your knee up your thigh under your skirt."

Her breath hitched in her throat as she imaged what he said. "Then what?"

"I would play with you my finger slipping inside you."

"Ah, yes" she breathed her hands clutching the door handle and the console as if she could already feel him doing it.

"Then I would slip your breast out over your dress so I could see them in the moon light and I would use my finger and thumb to roll your nipples getting them sensitive so that when I suck on them you will cry out in pleasure."

She un-buckled her seatbelt and crawled over the console to straddle him. "That was hot." She told him. His hands slid up under her dress on her outer thighs.

"You think so?" he asked.

"Mmm, hmm." She leaned forward her hands on his face and kissed him her tongue rubbing against his. His hand ran further up the inside of her thigh and discovered she wasn't wearing any panties. She was smooth and wet for him.

His finger rubbed against her and she rocked her body back and forth against him gasping as he kept hitting the right spot. Her hands went down to his pants and rubbed finding him hard and ready for her under the confines of his clothes. She nimbly unbuckled his belt and unzipped his pants. Her hand slipped under his underwear and grasped him firmly.

His free hand cupped her behind her neck and pulled her in for a kiss. Her breast tightened as the sensation overcame her. She was whimpering into his mouth. His hand slid down her bare shoulder and scooped out one breast then the other. He did exactly what he said he would with his fingers rolling her nipples taunt.

She made quick work of unbuttoning his shirt. Her hands explored his chest, liking the feeling of his strength under her hands. He took one of her nipples into his mouth and suckled. Rebecca jumped and her head hit the roof of the car.

"Ouch." He stopped instantly. She leaned back and bumped the steering wheel causing the horn to honk.

She jump again, "Oops."

"Are you okay?" he was concerned, it was sweet. She cupped his jaw and started laughing. He chuckled. "I feel like we are in high school." She sat down on his lap and ran her hands through his hair.

"Did you do this often in high school?" she asked not in jealousy but out of curiosity.

He laughed. "No. I was kind of a nerd in high school. Glasses and braces did not make for a desirable date."

"I find that hard to believe." She kissed his neck and his hands wandered down over her backside. She sucked on his earlobe, "I would have dated you in high school." She told him.

He groaned as she used her teeth on him. She helped him pull his pants and underwear down to his ankles. She guided him into her. She rolled her hips and he met her thrusts. They found a rhythm their cries of pleasure filled the car. Steam fogged up the windows.

His arms wrapped around her back and his fingers gripped her shoulders the feeling getting more intense. With one hand gripping the headrest behind him and her other hand on the roof of the car she manipulated her body on his. She reached her orgasm first her body convulsing around him. He joined her seconds later.

They wrapped each other up in their arms as their breathing returned to normal. He tucked her hair behind her ears and told her, "I never thought this was possible."

"What?" she asked.

"You and me."

"When did you first think about it?" she asked.

He grinned. "You don't want to know."

"Well now I really want to know." She said as her hand trailed down his chest towards his belly.

Reaching up his finger caressed her face. "The day I saw you at my front door."

"Is that why you tried to get rid of me?"

"Yes. I wasn't ready to think of anyone else and there you were looking beautiful. I tried to shut you out and I was mostly successful until I saw you in a bikini."

She giggled, "I did that on purpose."

"Really?"

"Yes. I wanted to see if I could soften you up."

He laughed long and loud. It made her smile.

"What?" she wanted to know what had made him laugh so much.

"You made me harder."

She gasped at his meaning, shocked at his words yet felt a little triumphant. She playfully slapped him on the shoulder.

Chapter Twenty-Seven

The next morning it was the same as the morning before. She walked him to the door and he pulled her inside his office for a good bye kiss. Around lunch she had headphones on and was dancing around the kitchen wiping down the cabinets when Brody walked in.

He stood for a minute watching her. She was wearing grey yoga pants and an oversized black Boston Bruins tee shirt. She was so at home in his house it sent a feeling over him he couldn't explain. She was spinning in circles with her hands up in the air when she noticed him.

Gasping she jumped and ripped her headphones out of her ears. "Oh my God, Brody, you scared the crap out of me."

"I'm sorry."

"What are you doing here? Are the kids okay?"

He held his hands up, "Kids are fine."

Her hand clutched her chest, "Oh good."

"I couldn't stop thinking about you." He told her as he started stalking her. "This is where we had our first kiss. If we weren't interrupted that night who knows what else would have happened in this kitchen."

They made love on the kitchen island. Then next day when he surprised her at home they made love on the couch in the living room. The next day he found her in lingerie sitting on his desk in his office.

"Damn you're sexy," he said at the door as he stripped out of his clothes to meet her open arms.

Then it was the weekend and she wasn't working and it was him and the kids. On Monday it had clearly become a hide-and-seek game for them. He found her in the laundry room dressed in a hot pink nighty with white thigh high stockings held on by a garter belt.

The next day she was in the dining room wearing a purple lace ensemble. "How many of these do you have?" he asked.

"I had none a week ago. I have to keep going back to the shop to pick up more."

"Which shop? I'll open an account for you."

"Seriously? Am I a kept woman?"

“If you would like to be.” His hand trailed down her bare arm. “I’d like to take care of you. I have a better idea for today.” He took her hand and led her up the stairs.

“Where are we going?” Rebecca asked but she knew. Brody was taking her to his bedroom. It was his off limits bedroom. It was where he had spent so many happy years with his wife.

She stopped him at the door. “Brody, are you sure?”

He turned to her. “I’m positive.” He took her into his arms and kissed her. They stumbled into the bedroom. They fell onto the bed together. He propped her up on the pillows then slid down in between her legs.

Her legs bent at the knees. He caressed her inner thigh with his tongue. Her hands reached up to grasp the headboard. His warm tongue touched the center of her causing her hips to rise. He took his time coaxing her into submission giving herself over to him. She withered under him moaning.

“Brody!” she called out his name. Continuing to love her she cried out her pleasure. When she climaxed he stood and stripped out of his clothes joining her naked on the bed. He was fully aroused listening to her enjoying herself. Listening to her enjoy him, what he was doing to her body.

They kissed wrapped in each other's arm she rolled on top of him. Straddling him she looked down at him. Her look was seductive her hair falling down over her shoulders her hands on his chest. She took him deep inside her, "Ah!" she exclaimed.

"Mmm..." he reached up to touch her, his hands skimmed down to her hips. She moved on top of him his hands reached around her holding her bare backside. The strain of the reach flexed the muscles in his arms and chest turning her on.

She slid down his chest lying on top of him. She was looking at his lips she sucked in her lower lip wanting to kiss him. He reached up and pulled her to him. His kiss was sweet and gentle and she melted into him.

Afterwards they lay sated in their embrace. He was playing with her hair and she was rubbing circles around his nipple. "I love you." He confessed.

"Ah, crap!" She sat up straight in bed, "You can't tell me that!"

He sat up next to her, "What? Why? You don't want me to love you?"

She looked into his eyes, she knew he loved her she could sense it. She touched his jaw bone and he kissed the palm of her hand. "Of course I do, but what am I going to tell people when they ask about the first time you said, I love you?"

"People ask that?" he wondered.

"Women do." She told him.

"Well, you can tell them about the time when I first knew I loved you."

"When was that?" she was curious.

"When I had you bent over my desk." He said with a wicked grin.

She gasped and punched him in the arm. He tackled her and held her hands above her head. "It was a few months ago. You were at the kitchen island you were helping Colton with his reading homework and Paige brought you a brush and you managed to brush her hair and still help Colton with his homework. Meanwhile, Chloe was trying to cook herself an egg and you walked her through it. You looked so beautiful and composed. I knew then."

"Do you want to know when I knew?"

"Knew what?" he asked.

"When I knew I loved you." She told him. Bending over, his lips, brushed hers she lifted her chin wanting more but he pulled away.

"Tell me."

"Do you remember when we all went to the Patriots game at Gillette Stadium?" When he nodded she continued, "We had a really good day with the kids, they were all getting along. We were losing and Colton got upset. You sat with him while everyone was standing up yelling. I don't know what you said but he listened to you and when we got the winning touchdown and everyone was high fiving each other. You looked at me your eyes were lit up and I just got this feeling that came over me. That's when I knew."

"What am I going to tell my friends?"

"I'm sure you'll think of something."

"Guys don't talk about the specifics."

"That's a shame, we have really juicy specifics."

"I want to keep them all to myself."

Chapter Twenty-Eight

Brody had to go back to work and when he was there he started thinking more about Rebecca and their conversation. He picked up his phone and made a call.

Kara picked the phone, “Hey Brody, how’s it going?”

“Do you have time for a coffee?”

He could almost picture her looking around her desk at her pile of work. He heard her shuffle some paperwork, “I do.” She told him even though he knew she didn’t.

“I’ll meet you in the lobby in about twenty minutes?”

“Deal.” They hung up and Brody grabbed his coat again.

Twenty minutes later Kara and Brody had taken a seat in a booth near the window at the small café on the bottom floor of her law firm. They both sipped their coffees for a minute before Kara put hers down, "Okay Brody spit it out."

"I've fallen in love."

If she would have had coffee in her mouth she would have spit it out. "With who?" she was shocked. "I didn't know you were dating anyone."

"Rebecca."

"The nanny?"

"Yes, but she's more than that."

"Obviously."

"Kara," he warned.

She looked at him, "You're happy." It was almost an accusation.

"I am. Is that wrong? How long should I grieve? How long should my kids grieve?"

"No," she said slowly, "It's not wrong. What is she like?" she asked.

"She's amazing, great with the kids, she has it all together. She is a great cook. She is well organized. She smart and funny and she makes me happy."

Kara reached over and squeezed his hand, "I'm happy for you. If you were looking for my blessing you have it. Do the kids know?" at his head shake she continued, "I think the boys and I should come over for dinner and I can get to know her."

He let out a pent up breath, "Thanks Kara."

"Have you told her you love her?" she wondered.

He laughed, "Rebecca told me you girls liked to talk about this stuff."

"She sounds like a smart girl."

"How are you doing?" he asked.

"I'm good."

"Is there anyone?"

She laughed. "I am a workaholic my job is my someone. I don't have time for anyone anyways. I'm not really sure I want anyone. I'm content. The boys and I are doing fine. My parents are a huge help and Hank has really turned his life around. I'm just sad that Bennett wasn't around to see it.

"They should all come. I think I'll even invite Harper's parents. What do you think?"

Kara raised an eyebrow at that. "Well, they are still the kid's grandparents and they have no other children so I think it is nice of you to keep them in the loop. How are they are going to take it?" she shrugged,

"I'm not sure. I guess we'll have to find out. Listen, thanks for the coffee, but I have to go." She eased out of the booth and leaned down and kissed him on the cheek. "I'm glad you called."

Months later Kara was in her office when her secretary told her that her next client was there. "Send Mr. Wentworth in please." She smoothed down her skirt and walked around the desk to greet him.

She had looked him up when she had learned that her firm was going to be taking him on as a client. He had been in Forbes magazine when they had done an expose on him two months before. He was the CEO of Wentworth Enterprises. He was about forty years old with dark hair with a little salt and pepper at the temples that made him look distinguished.

Mr. Wentworth strode into the room like he owned the place. He exuded confidence and it was extremely attractive and slightly intimidating. He was dressed nicely in a sharp five thousand dollar suit tailored to fit his slender athletic physic. He looked even better in person than the magazine.

"Mr. Wentworth it's nice to meet you," she held out her hand for him to shake.

"David, please." He told her in a British accent. His warm dark brown eyes met hers.

"David. Please call me Kara."

“A beautiful name for a beautiful woman.” He told her.

“Flattery will get you everywhere.” She told him.

“Good to know.” He informed her.

“Please sit,” she gestured to the chairs in front of her. He unbuttoned his suit coat so he could sit comfortably. She walked back around to the other side of her desk and had a seat.

“So, David, what can I help you with?”

“I am in need of a lawyer in Boston. I acquire and merge with other companies and I need someone to handle the paperwork and vet the companies for me.”

“Very well.” She opened his file with his contact information. “I see here you are looking into Vespa Tech and Bio Corp. I can look into these for you and let you know what I think.”

“What do you know about them now?” he asked.

He was testing her she knew. She had already looked into these companies. “Well Bio Corp is a solid buy. They turn a good profit. Vespa Tech on the other hand is a sleeper company. I think with the right management they could do really well for themselves.”

“You’ve done your homework.” He seemed impressed. “I can do five million for Vespa and up to twenty million for Bio Corp.”

"I will draw up the paper work and get a proposal together. I can schedule a meeting for early next week with the owners if you like."

He stood and re-buttoned his suit coat. "I think that works nicely. I will see you next week."

She walked him to the door. "Good-bye, David. It was nice to meet you."

"The pleasure was all mine," He took her hand and kissed it, then sauntered away.

"Oh, my," came from her left. Her secretary was practically swooning at her desk.

She was leaning against the door jam for support but quickly pushed herself off it, "Nothing to see here." And she walked back into her office and shut the door. With a huge sigh her back went against the closed door.

Her heart was beating wildly and her palms were sweaty. It had been years since she had lost Bennett. She hadn't so much as looked at another man. She had buried herself in her work and family.

She set up the meeting for the following week and made sure her homework was done. She picked her outfit carefully this morning changing several times before deciding on black high heels a black pant suit with a raspberry blouse. Normally she wore her blonde hair up at the office for ease but she spent extra time this morning in the mirror curling her long locks.

She applied her makeup and stood back to assess herself in the mirror. Wow, she hadn't seen this version of herself in a long time. She started to hope it wasn't too much that people would take notice and mention it to her.

Before she could change her mind she left the house and drove to work. She anxiously waited for the eleven o'clock hour when David Wentworth showed up at her door. Marcy her assistant hovered by the door.

Rather than stay in her office where she was feeling flustered she walked him down to the conference room. They were the first to arrive. They took their seats in comfy chairs with their backs to the floor to ceiling windows so they would be able to see through the glass doors when the others arrived.

The lawyer for Vespa and owner of the company showed up. They were able to easily settle and come to an arrangement. Bio Corp. arrived shortly afterwards and it was a hard fought battle on her part. He sat back and watched her work. She tuned him out completely and got her client the best possible deal without batting an eyelash.

After they left he invited her to lunch. "I really can't," she told him. "I have a lot on my plate right now."

"What's the harm? You need to eat. You can charge it to my account. I would like to talk to you about another deal I'm interested in."

"If you insist," she agreed. The law firm was over the moon interested in Mr. Wentworth's connections and money. They would not be happy if she turned down his offer of a business lunch. "Let me go get my coat." He followed her back to her office.

They had both switched into professional mode. There had been no flirting. She was beginning to think she had imagined the feelings of last week. He was looking at photos she had displayed on her bookcase along the wall.

He saw two handsome teenage boys. They sported longer blonde hair with shaggy curls around their ears, and Kara's emerald green eyes. They were smiling with their arms around each other. "Nice looking boys." He commented.

Kara was behind her desk putting her coat on. "Thanks."

"What are their names?"

"Lucas and Griffin."

"It suits them." He put the photo back down.

Throwing her purse strap over her shoulder she hurried towards the door. She knew what question followed. It didn't come. The question she feared, where is their father?

He followed her out to the hallway and they took the elevator down thirty-two floors. His cell phone rang.

David checked it then excused himself, “I need to take this. I do apologize. Hello?” he said into the phone.

She checked her own phone trying to give him privacy while she replied to an email. When they arrived in the lobby he had hung up and escorted her past security and past the glass doors.

“I have a driver at my disposal while I’m in town. Thank you Conrad.” He said to the well-dressed gentleman holding open the car door for them. He stepped aside and allowed her to enter. She got in and the door closed behind her. The men walked around to the other side of the car and David joined her in the car.

“Where would you like to go?” he asked her.

“Oh,” she hadn’t thought about it, “Where ever you want.”

“Where would you recommend? I live in London most of the year and part of the year in New York. I just bought a place here while I’m in town for business.”

“Well what are you in the mood for? Would you prefer Italian, Sushi, hibachi, pub style, fine dining, or Steak house?”

“I do enjoy a good steak.”

Kara gave an address to Conrad and he pulled away from the curb.

"So you just bought a place here?" she asked trying to make small talk and she wanted to get a glimpse into his life.

"On Beacon Hill, it's a small townhouse. It beats staying at a hotel all the time."

"That must be hard. Does your family travel with you?" she asked.

"No, no. I'm not married no children."

She wanted to ask more but refrained. Instead she asked about his business. "I graduated from Oxford and went into business with my Dad and older brothers. When my Dad passed away he left me the business to me. My brothers were not happy."

"What happened?"

"They took me to court, but they had no case. They both resigned and went into business for themselves." Before she asked he added. "They are doing well for themselves but they don't speak to me. I'm lucky my Mum still does."

"I'm sorry to hear that." She didn't add that sounded like a lonely existence. She wondered why he had chosen to reveal such intimate details of his life. Was it as simple as that she had asked?

They arrived at their destination and Conrad had pulled the town car over. He opened her door and she crawled out with the help of his hand. David scooted out behind her. They walked in and were seated at a nice table with white linen tablecloths. The restaurant was slowly filling up with patrons.

They ordered the same thing, bacon wrapped filet mignon with twice baked potatoes and broccoli. She ordered sweet tea and he got a diet coke. When the waiter left he sat back resting his elbows on the arms of the chair and folded his hands.

"Well Kara, I have to say I am impressed with you. I like the way you handled yourself today. You got me the best deal possible and you did your homework."

"Thank you." She was pleased with his praise.

"I have another deal I would like you to work with me on."

"Okay."

"It's in New York."

"Don't you have a lawyer in New York?"

"I do, but I haven't been happy with them lately."

"Why not find another lawyer that's actually in New York?"

"I would prefer to work with you."

"I'm not sure my firm would be okay with me jet setting to New York."

"They are. I've already cleared it with them. They are eager for our relationship to move forward.

"Excuse me? Our relationship?" she did not like how this was feeling. Kara felt like she was being manipulated by this man, David Wentworth whom she had just met a week ago. The fact that her firm was just offering her up to him made her skin crawl. Eager? They were probably ecstatic. This was probably her chance to make partner and she was sure if she had a conversation with them that's exactly where they would lead the discussion.

He could see her hesitancy and rushed to assure her. "Our professional relationship, Kara, I promise you that's all."

Well that was the other problem she thought she wasn't sure she just wanted a professional relationship with him. That was crazy talk though she was a widow with two kids at home to think about. The deals she would make with him would more than cover college for her kids.

Although, the settlements with the airline and Bennett's life insurance had assured her of her kids safety already. Time spent away from her family was also a concern.

"I can have you home every night." He promised her.

That also meant getting on a plane, which she hadn't done in two years of being home after the crash. It wasn't a conscious decision she had made but it also made her a little fearful at the same time.

"Can I think about it?" she asked.

"Of course, take your time." He steered the conversation in another direction.

Chapter Twenty-Nine

Months later after considering his offer seriously and with the partners at work pushing her towards it she gave in. One night David and Kara were racing to the airport in downtown New York City traffic. They had lost track of time trying to close a deal. "I'm going to miss my flight." She said for the ninth time.

"I really do apologize," he kept telling her.

His driver George, in New York pulled up to the curb and they both jumped out. Running inside they searched the monitors to find her flight and gate number but it was too late the flight had just left.

Kara let out a frustrated sigh, "What am I going to do now."

"Listen I know this probably isn't the best scenario but you could stay with me tonight and I could have you on the next flight out of here in the morning."

She gave him a skeptical look.

"I have a spare bedroom." He said as if that would help the situation. It did not.

She pulled out her phone and called her mom. She worked it out with her that she would spend the night with the boys and get them to school the next day.

He picked up her bag and they headed back to the car. George was standing outside. He went over to open the door for them. They drove to his apartment. She had been there once before but had never made it out of the two story living room. She could see the state of the art kitchen from there though. He walked her down the hallway and led her into a nice bedroom with floor to ceiling glass windows like the rest of the apartment.

The room looked like it came out of a magazine. There was a king sized bed with a fluffy white down comforter black hardwood floors and mirrored end stands, adorned with silver lamps and abstract art on the wall over the bed.

"The bathroom is right across the hallway. And if you need me I'm the next room over."

"Okay, thank you."

"Would you like a drink or anything?" he asked.

"No thank you it's late, I just want to go to bed."

He laughed, "No, no you misunderstand. Do you want a bottle of water in here for you for the night? I like one in my room, would you like one?"

She gave a nervous laugh, "Oh, sure, that would be great. Thank you." She added as he went back down the hallway to grab her one from his fridge.

When he returned he wished her good night and retired to his bedroom. She closed the door. She didn't like the windows where everyone could see in if your light was on. She looked for blinds and found a switch on the wall that controlled them.

Once she slipped out of her clothes leaving on her panties and camisole she crawled in under the covers and almost melted. No hotel, hell not even her own bed at home felt this good. She shut off the side lamp and snuggled down and reached for the blind switch putting them back up. Sitting in bed in the dark she could see all the twinkling lights of the city and buildings around them. It was beautiful.

Sighing she laid down and promptly fell asleep. She woke up early the next morning. She opened the hallway door and listened. The apartment was quiet. Running quickly across the hallway she dashed into the bathroom.

When she was washing her hands she wished she would have brought her stuff in with her so she could have taken a shower and got back into her clothes. She opened the door and ran back across the hallway. She collided into a warm brick wall.

David had been walking down the hall when Kara had flown out of the bathroom. He caught her in his arms as she ran into him. She was scantatedly clad in red panties and a lace camisole.

He had gotten up, he thought early enough, to go start some coffee before taking his shower. He had not slept a wink tossing and turning thinking about Kara lying in bed down the hallway from him. He was only wearing a pair of grey athletic pants which luckily he had the foresight to put those on because he usually slept in the nude.

Kara thought she was going to die. Her hands were resting on his naked forearms. His naked toned forearms. She tried not to look but she would never have guessed he had such a great physique under all those suits. Looking down so as to not to look directly at him she saw his naked feet. She hadn't ever pictured what those would have looked like either under his shiny shoes. Seeing his feet seemed even more intimate to her.

Looking up at him he seemed unconcerned about the fact they were standing in each other's arms half naked in his house. "I'm so sorry," she apologized.

"Quite alright," he assured her. "Did you sleep well?"

"So good," she assured him. "Your bed is very comfortable. Oh, God" Realizing what she said she quickly added, "I meant your guest bedroom." She corrected.

"Good, you were my first guest."

She wanted to ask him more about that but she really needed to get dressed. Her hands came off of him and he instantly let go of her.

"I'm going to go start some coffee." He told her.

"Good idea." She disappeared into her room. She made the bed then took a shower. Grabbing her bag she walked down the hall and into the kitchen. He wasn't out there yet. The coffee smelled delicious she looked through the cupboards and found a plain white coffee mug.

She poured herself a cup and found cream and sugar. David came into the kitchen looking the way she was used to him looking professional and dressed.

"I've called George he should be here shortly to pick us up. You have a ticket waiting for you at the airport."

"You're not coming?" she asked realizing too late she should not have asked.

"I would but I realized I have an early meeting this morning. He is going to drop me off at the office then bring you to the airport. I hope that is okay. Again

I do apologize for the inconvenience it won't happen again."

"Stop apologizing I know it wasn't intentional." He looked down into his coffee mug.

"Right?" she was beginning to wonder if this whole thing might have been a set up. Not that he would have known she would have run half naked into his arms this morning.

He looked up, "Quite right."

She eyed him for a minute and decided to let it go.

It was weeks later after they had seen each other during their little sleep over. Kara was working at her desk when her assistant, Marcy knocked on the door.

"Come in," she said absentmindedly.

The door opened, "I'm sorry to bother you," she started.

Kara looked up. "What is it?"

She seemed concerned, "Mr. Wentworth is here to see you. He doesn't have an appointment."

"That's alright. Tell him to come in." She signed one more paper and he was through the door. Her assistant closed the door behind them.

"I do apologize for arriving unannounced."

She stood straightening her skirt as she walked around the desk, "David," she held out her hand, "is everything okay?"

Ignoring her outstretched hand he strode purposely towards her and took her into his arms. "I can't stop thinking about you." He told her. He looked down at her his hand caressed her face.

"Oh," was all she managed. She was feeling breathless her chest heaving. Her throat felt dry. His mouth captured hers. She wanted this. She wanted more and for a second she gave into the kiss. Unfortunately her mind wouldn't stop to enjoy this moment.

A moment she had thought of and dreamed of since she was half naked in his arms. She also thought of Bennett and the fact that she had only ever dated one boy and had married that boy. Now he was gone and she hadn't kissed anyone else since.

She shoved him away from her. "David, I'm sorry, I can't." her hand covered her mouth.

"Kara, I apologize," he reached out for her and she took another step back. His hand dropped to his side. "I thought you felt the same way." His hand raked through his hair. "I'm sorry, I shouldn't have come." He turned to leave.

"David wait," he stopped and turned around. "You took me by surprise. I don't know if I'm ready for any of this. Also I'm your lawyer. I can't ethically be involved with a client."

He seemed relieved, "I understand. We can take it slow. Can I take you out to dinner tonight?"

"Sure, we can talk then."

"Very well, I will pick you up downstairs in the lobby at seven?"

"I will be there."

He left the room and the air still felt thick. She collapsed into her chair. Picking up the phone she called her mom.

"Hello?" the all too familiar, comforting voice came across the phone.

"Mom."

"What's wrong?"

"Umm… you know that client of mine that has me going to New York for him all the time?"

"Yeah…" she said hesitantly.

"Well, he just kissed me."

"What?!" she said it so loudly she had to pull the phone away from her ear for a second, "That's sexual harassment! Are you going to sue him? Divorce him as a client? Did you hit him? Were you arrested? Do I need to bail you out of jail?"

"Whoa, whoa, whoa! Slow down, Mom. It wasn't like that. I think I kind of wanted him to kiss me and I sort of kissed him back. I don't know what to do." She put her head in her hand.

"How old is this man?" her mom asked.

"About forty. Never been married, except to his work."

"Is he gay?"

'"Mom! No, he just kissed me, but thanks for that."

"I don't know dear. It's been a while since your mom was in the game. Do you want to see him? Is that legal?"

"Not really. I would have to drop him as a client."

"Well he does make you work all sorts of hours. Would that be the worst thing? It's not like you have no money."

"I know. I'm just not sure I can move on from Bennett."

"Nonsense, listen, I know you loved Bennett. We all did. But honey he isn't here anymore and if you have a chance to be happy you should take it."

Tears stung her eyes as she thought of her past and her potential future. "He wants to take me out to dinner tonight."

"Go!" her mom urged her. "I'll watch the boys for you. Have a good time."

"Thanks, Mom. I mean it, you have done a lot to help me and the boys. I love you."

"I love you too, honey. I would do anything for you, you know that right? You are never too old to spoil you know?"

"I'll see you tonight."

"Hopefully late, wink, wink."

"Mom!" she sounded outraged but she was grinning. She hung up and had a hard time concentrating on work the rest of the day.

At seven she walked into the lobby and found David waiting for her. He looked so handsome. "How was your day?" he asked her.

"Productive," she lied.

"Good to hear. Are you ready? Kids are taken care of?"

"Yes, my mom is going to be watching them."

"I would like to meet your Mum one day." He told her.

"You would?" she asked.

"Of course, she must be a lovely woman to have raised such a wonderful daughter."

She smiled up at him. "Thank you, that is nice of you to say."

"I only speak the truth."

She honestly hoped so. She had some questions for him and wanted the truth.

He led her out of the lobby. "Hello, Conrad." She greeted his driver with a smile.

"Good evening Ms. Treadwell." He responded as he opened the car door for her.

Once they were sitting inside he reached for her hand. "I'm nervous," she told him.

"It's okay to be nervous." He told her his voice soothing.

After several lunches and dinners together he knew what her favorite restaurant was and that's where they went. She felt awkward her palms were sweaty and she felt like her chest was constricting. By the time they got to dessert she had begun to relax a little bit.

He was smiling at her from across the table.

Her laugh was apprehensive. "What?" she asked.

David took a sip of his wine. "I find you are radiant."

"Wow." She took her own sip of wine. She also thought that the two glasses she had of wine was also helping ease her distress.

"Are you concerned about firing me as a client?"

"Yes," she told him honestly.

"What if we took that out of the equation?"

She sat back in her chair. "I think that even with that out of the equation…" she trailed off.

He waited.

"My husband-Bennett, he was the only. My only love and to move on from that is hard to contemplate."

"I understand. Do you think maybe you would consider trying?" He reached across the table and caressed her hand.

She smiled, "I can."

"That's all I ask."

He insisted on driving her home even though her car was at the office. He held her hand in the backseat his thumb massaging her knuckles. He walked her to her front porch. "You have a lovely home," he commented.

"Thank you," she murmured.

At the door he pulled her close and she let him. She looked for anything to say, "Thank you for dinner." Was that the best she could up with?

His head bent towards hers and she raised her eyes to him. His lips grazed hers and she lifted up on her toes pressing them more firmly together. His kiss was nice and it stirred some feelings in her she had thought had shriveled up and died with Bennett. She tried to push him out of her mind and give into this kiss.

For a blissful minute she did. She lost herself and it was magical.

Chapter Thirty

One weekend Rebecca went to her Mom's house for a visit. Brody sat the kids down in the living room. "I want to talk to you guys about Rebecca."

"Okay," Chloe said a little apprehensively.

He sat down facing the three of them on the couch with his hands folded. "I don't want her to be your nanny anymore." He told them.

"What?!" Colton seemed outraged.

"Dad!" Paige whined.

"How come?" Chloe demanded.

"Well I'm thinking I would like her to be your stepmom instead."

They all sat forward. The girls squealed in delight and Colton grinned.

"That's awesome!"

"Woo Hoo!"

"Are you serious?" this from Chloe.

"Yes." He answered her seriously. Paige was already wrapped around his neck. "Are you okay with that?"

"It's cool with me Dad." Colton responded but Brody was still watching Chloe. This didn't work unless everyone was on board and he really prayed they were on board.

Slowly a smile crept over her face, "How are you going to propose?" she asked. "Unless you already have?"

"No." he reassured her. "I have not asked her yet. I wanted to check with you guys first. I was hoping you could help me think of how to propose."

Paige squealed in his ear.

"Did you get the ring yet?" Chloe asked.

Brody pulled out his phone. "I haven't bought it yet but this is what I was thinking." Paige ripped the phone out of his hand to look at the picture on his phone.

"It's beautiful, Daddy."

Chloe pulled it away from her sister to take a look. The ring was stunning. It was a princess cut diamond with smaller princess cut sapphires on either side. The band itself was an antique style with tiny diamonds encrusted in it. She handed the phone to Colton who glanced at it not nearly as long as his sisters.

"Her favorite color is blue, so I thought…" Brody tried explaining.

"It's perfect Dad." Chloe assured him.

They all sat back down to discuss how the proposal was going to happen. They all had different ideas on what would work and what would be the biggest surprise for her. After a lot of discussion and excitement they came up with a great plan.

The kids all wanted to go with him when he picked up the ring. They did it before Rebecca came home. They even picked out the exact diamond that was going in the ring. The lady behind the counter was friendly and happy to see the kid's excitement.

A week later, Rebecca walked into the kitchen, "Hello?" she called out. She picked up Colton's sweatshirt off the back of the stool and walked it to the front closet. No one responded to her. "Hello?" she called out again. She ran up the stairs and found the house empty.

When she came down stairs she noticed a note on the kitchen island. Picking it up she read, "Rebecca, You are standing in the spot where we shared our first kiss. I would like to take you on a walk through our courtship. Your first destination is where we had our first date. Have fun, see you soon. Love, Brody."

She grinned at the note. This was unexpected. She wondered if this was a birthday surprise. He had been hinting around for the past couple of weeks. He was so sweet.

She ran out the back door and grabbed her purse. Hopping in her car she drove to Salvatore's Restaurant and she wondered if they were even open at this hour.

Inside she was greeted by the same hostess they had that night. "Ms. Buchanan?"

She was taken aback a little, "Yes?"

"Right this way." She walked her through the empty restaurant to the same table her and Brody had shared in front of the fireplace. Sitting at the table unexpectedly was her Mom.

A smile lit up her face, "Hey, Mom! What are you doing here?"

Her mom stood up and hugged her daughter, "Sit down and have a coffee with me." She gestured to the vacant seat that already had a steaming coffee ready for her.

She gladly joined her. When the hostess left her mom leaned forward to tell her, "I like Brody."

"You met him?" she asked surprised.

Her mom laughed, "He called me."

"How did he get your number?"

"I'm not really sure, but he said he thought we should meet and I completely agreed with him. How come you haven't introduced us?"

"I don't know. His kids don't even know we are involved. I guess I didn't want to rock the boat."

"Well I think the boat is getting plenty rocked and it's a good thing." She sat back in her chair assessing her daughter. "You seem really happy."

Rebecca was taking a sip of her coffee after adding cream and sugar to it. Grinning she set the cup back down on the table. "I am Mom. He is great, definitely not the same guy I first met. He is kind and considerate he is great with his kids. And Mom his kids are amazing. I love each one of them too. Colton is so quiet but has such a great sense of humor. Paige is adorable such a love bug. Chloe is growing into such a nice young lady."

"You helped raise those kids." Her mom pointed out.

"They were already great kids. I would like to think that I help keep them on the right track."

Her mom sipped her coffee, “I’m supposed to give you the next clue.” She rifled through her purse and pulled out an envelope and handed it across the table to her daughter.

Rebecca ripped it open and read the next clue, “Rebecca, my Love. My family is extremely important to me as I know yours is to you. You are important to me. Your next destination is waiting. Love, Brody.” Enclosed was a ticket to the Aquarium.

She looked up at her, “Are you coming with me?”

She shook her head, “No, dear, but I will see you later.”

“Okay.” She leaned over and gave her a hug and a kiss, “I love you.”

“I love you too honey. I’m really happy for you.”

She smiled, “Thanks, Mom.”

At the Aquarium she met with Brody’s parents. She had met them a couple of times before. Brody’s mom hugged her followed by his dad. “Hi guys!” she said, “This is a surprise! I didn’t know you guys were going to be in town.”

They gave her another envelope. Inside it read, “Rebecca, You’re getting closer. Are you having fun? I hope so. Next go to the place where you knew you loved me. See you soon. Love, Brody.”

She drove to Gillette Stadium. A man met her at the door and escorted her through the gate. The place was deserted but he walked her to the seats they had that day for the game. She found Harper's parents waiting for her.

Frank and Rachel stood up to hug her. "Hi Honey." Rachel called her. She was happy that she had come around to like her. They didn't seem so sure about her when they first met her but they had come around.

"Are you having fun, dear?" Frank asked.

"Yes thank you," she told him as they all sat down.

"So do you have any guesses as to what's happening?" Rachel asked her.

"I'm thinking a birthday surprise."

Frank and Rachel looked at each other and smiled. She had guessed correctly. Rachel dug through her purse and produced an envelope. Inside was not another letter from Brody but instead was three pieces of paper.

The top one was a drawing from Paige. It was a picture of her family and she was included in the picture. They were standing outside of their house and the sun was shining and blue birds were in the air. In the corner was a picture of a brown dog with an arrow pointing to it saying, "Maybe." She laughed.

Flipping the page was a letter from Colton. It was a short and sweet letter thanking her for all she had done for him and his family. His letter made her laugh.

Chloe's letter was much longer, "Dear Rebecca, We as a family have experienced a great deal in our short lives. We have had great loss. You have come into our lives and brightened our world. You have done more than you know for this family and we couldn't be happier.

I think you are fun to hang out with. You have helped me with some pretty big moments in my life, you know what they are."

Tears were blurring her vision as she finished reading the rest of the letter. Wiping her tears she laughed looking up at her audience. She said loudly, "Okay! What's next?"

Frank handed her another envelope. Inside was another letter. "Rebecca, I hope you see that everyone that's important to me loves you like I do. I have one more surprise for you. Come to the last place our family shared a meal outside of the house. I love you more than words can say, Brody."

"Well I guess I know where I'm headed to next. Will I see you guys later?"

They nodded. She hugged them good bye.

The last clue led her to the park where she and Brody had taken the kids recently. They had a picnic down by the lake. That's where she found him. He had a large blanket set out on the grass and a large picnic basket.

Brody was standing there waiting for her. He was so handsome. He was dressed in relax fit jeans and a blue sweater with a white plaid collared shirt underneath. His hands were casually looped in his pockets. When he saw her his face lit up.

Rebecca ran to him. He scooped her up into his arms. She laughed, "What is all this?" she asked. She was holding all the clues in her hands.

He turned serious and her heart started thudding in her chest. "I think it's time I fired you."

It was so unexpected she sputtered, "What?!"

He got down on one knee and pulled out a black ring box from his pocket. "It's because I have fallen madly in love with you. Will you marry me and help me raise our kids together not as their nanny but as my wife."

She started crying, her knees felt weak and she wasn't sure she was going to be able to stay standing. He had put on such an elaborate ploy to get her here. It was his way of telling her the kids knew and that his parents, her mom and even his dead wife's parents were now on board with their relationship.

He misunderstood her reaction and stood up. "Rebecca are you okay?"

She nodded then managed to get out, "Yes!" He was holding her elbows trying to look into her eyes.

"This wasn't quite the reaction I was looking for." He told her.

She started laughing through the tears, "You are the sweetest man I've ever known. You did all this showing me how much I mean to you getting everyone involved. I thought this was a birthday surprise, not a proposal."

"Are you disappointed? Is it too soon? Are you saying no?" he asked in a rush.

She kissed him hard and passionately then pulled back, "No, no, no. I'm saying yes! Of course I'll marry you. I love you so much!"

He crushed her to him and kissed her back just as hard, just as passionately. Pulling away he said, "Oh wait, you haven't even seen the ring." He opened the box for her inspection. She gasped when she saw the diamond and sapphire engagement ring.

"Brody it's beautiful, I love it!" He took it out of the box and slipped it on her shaky left hand. She held her hand out at arm's length to inspect it. It sparkled in the sunlight.

"Here, why don't we sit? I made us a picnic. Well the moms did." He confessed. They sat down on the blanket and they pulled out the food. He popped the cork on a champagne bottle and produced two flutes. She held the glasses while he poured.

"To a life time of happiness together." He raised his glass and they clinked them together in a toast then drank the bubbly liquid.

They sat and talked about wedding plans and her moving into the house, no more sneaking around. She told him about Paige's drawing and the possibility of a dog. They laughed together and kissed at every opportunity.

When they were done eating he told her that when she was ready the kids were anxiously waiting for them at home. When they arrived home they were greeted by the whole family including the kids.

Chapter Thirty-One

Kara was in the kitchen cooking dinner when the phone rang. Stirring the caramelizing onions she picked up the phone and tucked it in between her ear and shoulder, "Hello?"

"Is this the Treadwell residence?"

"Who's asking?"

"I'm sorry this is Bob Charter from Tidal Wave Industries and I don't know how to put this."

"Is everything okay?"

"Do you know a Bennett Treadwell?"

Her heart skipped a beat then sank. A tear sprung to her eye. "He is deceased, he was my husband."

"No ma'am, we have reason to believe he is alive."

The phone clattered to the ground. The wooden spoon stopped stirring the onions. She dropped to her knees and scooped up the phone. "Hello? Hello?"

"Yes Mrs. Treadwell I'm still here. We have cargo ship that rescued him from an island. They are going to be docking in Florida tomorrow morning."

She was laughing and crying. Tears streaming at free random down her face but she was overjoyed. Her husband was coming home to her.

"We have a ticket ready for you at the airport so you can meet him in Florida. He is currently on a boat and you should arrive roughly at the same time."

"I will be right there. Thank you so much." The smell of burning onions did not stop her from running out of the house and nearly collided into Brody.

"Harper's alive!"

"Bennett's alive!"

They spit it out at the same time. "Wait what?" Brody was grasping onto her upper forearms to steady her.

"Bennett's alive! Wait, Harper is too?!"

"YES!"

"Oh my God, this is unbelievable."

They hugged each other then she jumped up and down clapping her hands. The fire alarm started beeping.

Brody pushed past her and removed the pan from the stove then opened the window behind the sink.

"We need to go the airport right now. I'll call my mom. Do you want ride to the airport together?"

"Yes. I'm going to pack a couple of things and make sure the kids are all set. I will meet you out front." He shouted the last sentence because she had already ran up the stairs with the phone to her ear.

Book Three

Chapter Thirty-Two

Present Day

Kara and Brody stood shell shocked as they came face to face with Bennett and Harper and what they assumed was their baby on her hip. They could tell it was them but their appearance had changed quite a bit. They were golden brown from the sun and they had obviously lost weight.

Kara's eyes started filling with tears. She was faced with this beautiful miracle of having her husband come home to her. But he wasn't coming home to her he was bringing home two people, her once best friend and what she assumed was their daughter.

Harper stood rooted in place. She couldn't believe her eyes. They had seen an explosion! No one had come for them. "We thought you were dead," she said quietly.

“We thought the same thing,” Brody told her. Kara confirmed with a head nod.

“We buried you.” Kara told them.

“We made you a memorial site on the island,” she told them. Bennett nodded in confirmation.

Ellie cooed and waved her hands up and down, drawing everyone’s attention towards her. The elephant in the room had demanded their attention.

Kara took some tentative steps towards them. “What’s her name?” she asked.

“Ellie,” Bennett told her.

She looked at him her eyes sad, “After your mom?” She held her hand out to Ellie who waved her hands excitedly at this stranger. Kara looked at Harper.

“May I?” she asked.

“Of course,” she handed her daughter off to Kara. Ellie had only ever been in either hers or Bennett’s arms in her short life.

When she handed over her daughter she walked slowly towards Brody who had started walking towards her. He opened his arms to her and she walked into his embrace like the last three years had never happened.

She started crying in his arms and he held her. Brody looked over her head and saw how uncomfortable Bennett was in this situation. He didn’t like it either.

Kara was cooing with Ellie she was trying to pretend none of this was happening. She looked over Bennett's daughter's head at him he was not looking at her but staring at Harper who was in Brody's arms. She had a deep pain in her chest.

At that moment he looked at her and he could see the hurt in her eyes, the betrayal. "I'm sorry," he told her.

A tear slipped down her face as she bounced Ellie up and down. "I know." She told him.

He walked to her. She shifted Ellie on her hip and held her arm out to him. He hugged her.

Harper pulled away from Brody. "How are the kids? Is everyone okay? Tell me everything." She demanded. Brody chuckled.

"The kids are all great. Everyone is healthy and doing well. Chloe is a full-fledged teenager into music and boys, giving me grey hair," he pointed to three grey hairs at his temple and she laughed. "Colton is on a premier soccer team his voice is starting to change. Paige is a social butterfly and doing really well in school, actually all the kids are. They all made honor roll."

"That's great!"

"What about the boys?" Bennett asked.

"Lucas is going to Notre Dame in the fall on a football scholarship. Griffin is going to be driving soon.

He just got his learner's permit so we have been practicing."

Bennett grinned ear to ear. "You did great with them. I'm so happy they had you guys. The whole time on the island we figured they would be orphans and we weren't sure which relatives they would have ended up with or if they would have to move out of our house away from their friends."

"I brought a picture," Kara told them. She handed Ellie to Bennett and put her purse down on the table in the room as she rummaged through it. Finding the photo she pulled it out and held it for him.

He took it and stared, "My boys have become men," he said.

Harper turned to Brody, "Did you bring a picture?" she asked.

He seemed hesitant, "I didn't think to bring one…" he trailed off because he had one. The look in her eyes had him reaching for his wallet; she wasn't going to like it.

He produced a photograph to her. She ripped it from him and studied the photo. It was a picture of a happy family, all smiles. Paige was grinning ear to ear missing a front tooth. She had gotten so big and her curly red hair had started to soften into waves and her hair was more of a deeper richer auburn red. Chloe was beautiful and looked like a mini Harper tall and thin. She was wearing the latest fashion trend and her hair, nails and make up was all done to perfection. Colton who had always been cute was now a handsome teenager with a mouth full of braces.

Brody was behind the kids with a smile on his face and his arms wrapped around a beautiful young woman whose hand was on Colton's shoulder.

"Who's this," she asked. She knew she had no right to be jealous, she had been with Bennett and Brody had been left to raise their three kids by himself. He had every right to move on but it hurt.

"That's Rebecca, she's my wife." She looked up at him the pretty woman had a name, Rebecca. She had been replaced.

"You're remarried?" she knew that was a dumb question he had just told her he was.

"I thought you were dead," his eyes were just as sad as hers.

Harper turned around to look at Kara who looked about as devastated as any of them. Bennett was looking to her asking with his eyes the same question Brody had just answered.

Harper voiced it, "What about you Kara? Did you? Move on?" The answer to this question was important. She dreaded the answer. If Kara had moved on too then it wouldn't be so bad that her and Bennett had moved on as well but if she hadn't moved on where did that leave her?

Bennett could easily choose to go back to his legal wife and not stay with his island wife and daughter. Her husband was already remarried. She wasn't sure how she felt about all of this or how Bennett would feel.

"No," it was a simple answer but one that held a lot of weight. They all stood there staring at her not really knowing what to do.

"I'm sorry," Kara took her purse and left the room. Harper looked at Bennett they exchanged a glance. He handed Ellie to Harper and walked out of the room after Kara.

Harper sighed, "Let's sit," she suggested to Brody. They pulled out chairs from the table and sat down, Ellie on her knee. She bounced her up and down.

"Well this is complicated," she stated the obvious. He reached out and squeezed her hand on the table.

"I still love you," she told him a tear slipping down her cheek.

"I never stopped loving you," he told her.

A sob slipped out of her. Ellie started fussing.

He leaned forward like he was going to kiss her. "I love Bennett too." She told him. His head dropped and he nodded.

"I know." He said quietly. "I'm in love with Rebecca."

"What does your wife think about me being alive?"

"I haven't told anyone yet. We thought it was best not to get anyone's hopes up in case it was a false report of some kind."

She nodded trying to absorb the information.

"How do you think she is going to take it? What about the kids? I've been gone so long."

"I think everyone will be ecstatic. Your parents are going to be thrilled. They have been so great and supportive. I can't wait until they see you."

Her face lit up when she thought of Frank and Rachel. "I've missed everyone so much."

"So what happened to you guys? They never found the back of the plane."

"We managed to get the raft out of the door panel of plane. We saw the explosion." She explained but then continued, "We were out to sea for three days before landing on Survivor Island."

"Survivor Island?" Brody asked.

She smiled, "Yeah, Bennett came up with the name. We found fresh water, shelter, and food. We kept a log," she told him, "we wrote down each day. We saw a plane once! We built a raft, Bennett tried going out by himself. He got attacked by a shark and caught in a storm that got him back to the island."

"Wait," Brody interrupted her, "Bennett left you on the island by yourself?" he seemed outraged.

"We had a really big fight about it," she continued.

Bennett found Kara down the hall she had found a couch near a window. She had her knees drawn up to her chest her arms wrapped around them. She was crying and it tore at him. He sat down next to her his arms pulled her to him.

"Kara, you have no idea how sorry I am. If I would have known there is no way I would have started anything with Harper. In my defense we thought you guys were dead and we were on that island for three years. Who knows how long we could have been there? We didn't know if that was it for us or not."

She looked up at him face was tear stained. Tentatively her hand came up to cup his jaw that was overgrown with a beard. "You look so different, but the same. Is it really you?" she asked.

His hand covered hers, "It's really me." His hand kissed her palm. She pressed her lips to his and for a second he allowed it but quickly pulled away.

"Kara," he said.

She cried out, “I’m losing you all over again.”

“I’m not going anywhere. I plan on being around a long time. We will figure this all out. I promise. I want to be a part of the boy’s life.”

“Just the boys?” she set back away from him hurt.

“Kara, I don’t have all the answers but I want to be in your life too.”

She stood up and wiped her tears. “We need to get going. There is a car waiting for us out front. Our flight home leaves shortly. I’ll meet you out front.” With that she turned and walked away.

Bennett stood there for a moment as he let her go. He was devastated and happy at the same time. Kara had survived along with Brody he would have given anything for that to be the case. Now he was in love with his wife’s best friend and his best friend’s wife. What a mess.

He walked back to the room he had left Harper in. Opening the door he found Harper and Brody seated closely together talking like old times. Why hadn’t his and Kara’s exchange gone like that?

“We need to go.” He told them.

He walked past them and pick up their only possession, Daphne’s suitcase.

They all walked out and found Kara in the driver's seat of their rental car. Brody and Bennett stood outside of the car all of them trying to decide where they should be sitting. Harper made the decision for them and hopped in front with Kara.

Kara turned to Harper. "I'm sorry we didn't have a car seat for you. We had no idea."

"I know," she told her.

Bennett opened the door, "Can you pop the trunk please?"

Kara did so without commenting.

"Thank you," he told her.

He put Daphne's suitcase in the trunk then climbed into the backseat next to Brody. Harper handed Ellie back to him. "Can you buckle her in back there please?" she asked him.

"Yes. Come here baby girl." He talked to Ellie who was taking her first ever car ride.

The ride to the airport was filled with tension. The radio played music they had never heard before. Harper turned around and smiled at Bennett, "You don't have to listen to me sing anymore."

"Thank God," he joked, and they laughed. It did not help break the tension only making it worse that they were sharing an inside joke.

She looked at Brody, “You don’t have any of my clothes anymore do you?”

He was just now noticing they were wearing the same clothes he had last seen them in. They had been in the same clothes for the past three years. They had become thread bare in some spots, stained in other areas.

“I’m sorry,” he told her, “I donated all of them except Chloe kept your Boston College sweatshirt.”

Memories came flooding back to her, “Ah, I loved that sweat shirt.”

“I remember,” there was a twinkle in his eye as he looked at her. She noticed Bennett was glaring at him. She turned back around to face the front of the car.

“Do we have time to stop for clothes?” she asked Kara.

Kara turned to look at her. “I wasn’t even thinking that you would be in the same clothes.”

“It’s alright, just happy that a change of clothes is an option.”

“Was it horrible?” she asked sincerely.

“Parts of it were. It’s a long time to be on an island with nothing and no one. We had no one to talk to except each other-oh and you guys!”

“What?” Kara and Brody asked at the same time.

"I told you we had a memorial site for you guys on the island. We would sometimes sit and talk to your crosses. It made me feel better but you annoyingly enough never responded."

Brody laughed at her joke Kara did not.

"I miss food, meat. Can we have steak for dinner tonight?"

"That would be amazing." Bennett chimed in, "With mashed potatoes!"

"All we have eaten for the past three years is fish, which you all know how much I hate fish. We also had almonds, mango, pineapple, and bananas. Lots and lots of bananas."

"Sure thing," Brody told them. He got on his phone and started texting.

"What happened with our business," Bennett asked.

"It's doing well. I bought your share out. If you want to buy back in you can."

"Good to know," Bennett said.

Kara informed them that they weren't going to have time to stop for clothes but they could pick some up at the airport.

"How are they going to let us on a plane?" Bennett wondered, "We don't have any IDs."

"Yeah we are legally dead right?" Harper asked, "And we obviously don't have a birth certificate for Ellie."

"We have people." Kara told them.

"You have people? What are you talking about?"

"Well we sued the airlines and won. They know who we are and we have free flights anywhere. They are aware you are coming and have guaranteed no issues getting you home."

"Wow, still a kick ass lawyer I see." Harper told her.

She got the faintest of smiles out of Kara, "I made partner." She told them.

"Congratulations, Kara that's great, you deserve it." Bennett congratulated her.

"Thanks," she murmured.

"That's awesome Kara. I knew you could do it." Harper praised her.

She nodded more tears blurring her vision.

Chapter Thirty-Three

They made it to the airport and returned the rental. They made it through security with an escort and boarded the plane. When they sat down Kara noticed their luggage.

"Where did you get that?" she wondered pointing to the polka dotted suitcase.

"This old thing?" he told her, "We found it when we crashed. It was actually quite the lifesaver. It was a little girl's named-"

"Daphne." Both Brody and Kara said at the same time.

Harper stared at them, "How did you know?"

"We saved her life after the crash. She is a great little girl. Her and her dad live in-"

"Texas!" Harper chimed in, "Yeah we know it says on her id tag."

"How was it a life saver?" Brody wanted to know.

"Well Harper made a blanket out of Daphne's clothes. There were things we could use like flip flops for Harper and hair brush. And for a long time we had shampoo and conditioner but even using it sparingly we ran out of that. Oh and the best part was the coloring book."

"The coloring book?" Kara asked.

"Yes," Harper was excited about showing them the book. She took it out of the bag and handed it to Kara. She flipped through it.

Her heart sank as she looked at over one thousand tick marks in all different colors over the pages. Her hand circled the day that had the raft launch written on it. "You tried leaving the island?" she asked.

He sat down next to her, "Yes I told Harper that I couldn't die without trying."

"You tried coming home?" he had already answered the question but she wanted to hear it again.

"Yes."

"What happened?"

"I was attacked by two sharks then was knocked unconscious during a storm. I was out to sea for five days, I'm not even sure how my boat made it back to the island."

"Oh my God you could have died!"

"But I didn't."

The stewardess came by and asked them to take their seats. Brody put their luggage in the over-head bin and took a seat next to Harper. She was in the center isle and Bennett was in the center isle on the other side of her and Kara on the other side of him.

Harper held Ellie on her lap as the plane started to take off. Harper reached for Bennett and he was right there for her as they held hands in the isle. Once they gained altitude they released their hands that were being watched like a hawk by Kara and Brody.

Harper talked to Brody about the kids not able to get enough details about them. "So…" she broached the subject slowly, "how did you meet Rebecca?"

He told her how he had needed help around the house and what a disaster the first few nannies had been. He tried to gently ease her into his new love story trying to spare her all the details.

"What's Ellie's middle name?" Kara wanted to know.

"Kara," he said softly looking down at her to see her reaction.

She looked up at him wide eyed then looked to Harper for conformation. "Really?"

Harper nodded, "Yes, we both love you very much and wanted to keep the memory of you alive."

"I missed you guys so much," she said.

"Ah, sweetie," Harper said as she quickly unbuckled her seat belt and stood up with Ellie in her arms. Bennett already knowing where this was going stood and took his daughter from her. Harper threw herself in Kara's arms, "I missed you too," she told her as they rocked back and forth.

Bennett stood smiling bouncing his daughter up and down in his arms. He went to walk to the back of the plane and all three of them shouted at the same time, "No!"

He stopped and turned around, "You sit down right now, Bennett Paul Treadwell." The old Kara came bubbling to the surface. They all smiled and he was happy to sit down.

They landed and made their way to Kara's new car. "This is nice," Bennett told her.

"Thanks, I got it with the promotion."

"That's great," Harper told her.

They drove to Brody's house. "I need to go in first," Brody told them, "Just wait here for a minute. They all agreed and watched him run into the house. Harper and Bennett were in the backseat with Ellie.

Brody ran into the house, "Rebecca!" he shouted.

"Hi Daddy!" Paige skipped past him.

"Hi Sweetheart, can you go find your brother and sister for me please? We are having a family meeting."

She groaned but wandered off to find them.

"Hey, Honey," a familiar voice came from the kitchen.

He walked into the kitchen to find Rebecca unloading the dishwasher. "How was your meeting?" she asked. At first he was taken aback. What meeting? Then he remembered that's what he had told her he was going to do.

He walked to her and kissed her soundly. She smiled up at him, "Well welcome back. Maybe you should have more meetings." She told him as her hand ran down his backside and gave it a tap.

He grabbed her wrist, "I need to talk to you." He pulled her up the stairs to their bedroom and shut the door.

"Brody," she giggled, "what has gotten into you?"

"Listen," he told her seriously. She sobered up quickly sensing his urgency.

"What's wrong?"

"I have some good news and some bad news."

"I don't like bad news." She told him.

"I know. First I want you to know how much I love you," when she started to respond he forged ahead, "I want to apologize to you. I lied to you about where I've been." She backed away from him. "I didn't have a meeting. I was told something that I didn't want to tell you until I confirmed it." He stopped and took a steading breath.

"Brody, you're scaring me." She told him.

"They found Harper and Bennett alive. They have been surviving on an island for the past three years."

"Oh my God, are you serious?" That's crazy!"

The weight of what he was telling her hit him. "I know."

"What does this mean for us?" she asked worry in her voice.

"One, she was declared dead so our marriage is legitimate. Second she has been sleeping with Bennett this whole time! They have a daughter for Christ sake."

Her brain was reeling with all this information, "Oh, poor Kara. How is she taking this? Does she know?"

"Yes, I don't think she is doing too well with the situation. They are outside."

"What?! Well go get them! Harper must be dying to see the kids."

"I know I just needed to prepare you first."

She leaned over and kissed him, "Thank you, now go!"

Brody ran outside and gave the thumbs up sign to the car. Kara turned around, "I'm going to grab the boys I will bring them in the back door." She tossed them her phone, "I will text you when we are ready."

She ran next door and into the house. Rounding up the boys and her parents she ushered them out the back door and into the Quinn's backdoor. She asked Brody to text her phone that she was ready.

"What's going on?" Lucas asked.

"I thought this was a family meeting?" Chloe said.

"It is. This affects all of us." Brody told them.

They all turned when they heard the front door open all eyes fixed on the opening in the kitchen. In walked Harper and Bennett who was carrying Ellie.

"Mom?!" Colton jumped to his feet. He leaped right over the back of the couch and ran into her open arms. She was knocked back a bit; he had grown as tall as her.

"Dad!" Griffin ran to Bennett, Lucas right behind him. The girls followed suit of the boys. Paige and Chloe were squealing and jumping up and down with excitement.

Once everyone had hugged and cried and squealed with excitement and Brody had introduced them to Rebecca, which was awkward. The questions came. Who was the baby?

"This is your sister, Ellie." Harper told them.

"Whose sister? Our sister?" Chloe asked, "Or their sister?" She pointed with her thumb the boys.

"Both." She could see the confusion on their faces. The older kids got it.

"Are you serious?" Lucas asked, "Mom has been at home pining over you and you were off-" He stopped himself short of what he was about to say and ended with, "making babies?"

"Lucas," Bennett's tone warned. The two men had a stare down and Lucas caved first.

"She's so adorable." Paige was holding Ellie's chubby fingers.

"Is dinner ready?" Brody asked.

"Almost," Rebecca was thankful to do something. She had received Brody's text with the request hours ago for a steak dinner. Now she knew why.

Rachel and Frank had gotten an invite from Brody for dinner and thought it a little strange in the middle of the week but because it was such an odd request they thought they should honor it. Maybe someone had some exciting news to share. They hopped in the car and made the two and a half hour ride to see their grandkids.

When they pulled in the driveway they also took notice that Kara's car was in the drive which was funny because she lived just next door. "I wonder if Kara is staying for dinner tonight."

Frank just shrugged his shoulders. They walked to the door and after knocking the door flew open. It was Paige. She was bouncing up and down unable to contain her excitement.

"Grandma, Grandpa, come see! You are never going to believe this!" she squealed as she took both grandparents arms and dragged them through the front door and towards the kitchen, "I have the biggest surprise you will never guess what it is!"

Rachel was laughing at her precocious granddaughter and Frank had a big smile on his face. As they rounded the corner they stopped abruptly frozen in place by what they saw. Paige was jumping up and down clapping her hands as she looked from her Mom to her grandparents.

"Isn't this exciting?" she asked.

Rachel fainted and Frank was quick thinking enough to catch her. Everyone gasped as they rushed to her side. Rebecca ran to the kitchen to get a cold compress.

"Mom?" Harper's voice showed concern.

"Harper." Frank's voice was rough with emotion. She looked up and touched her hand to his face that had grown a beard. It looked good on him. Rachel began to come around underneath them and they pulled back a bit.

"Harper, is that really you? Tell me I'm not dreaming."

"You're not dreaming, Mom. I'm home."

She cried out and the two women wrapped each other up in an unbreakable hug. It had been too long and a lot of grief over the course of three years. It was a lot to take in within the span of a few seconds. The tears flowed easily and Frank joined in the hug wrapping both women up in his grizzly bear hug. Neither woman minded.

He kept saying over and over again as he rocked them back and forth, "My two girls." It was sweet and touching and everyone watching had some emotion that tugged on their heart strings.

When they finally separated still all sitting on the floor Harper told her mom, "I need to introduce you to someone." She told them.

They looked up not knowing what to expect. An eight month baby was not what they were expecting. "This is Ellie." Looking to her for clarification she confirmed what they were thinking, "Your granddaughter, Ellie."

They looked from Harper, to Ellie and Bennett who was holding her. The shock was apparent but they quickly recovered. "Frank, help me up." Rachel commanded.

Both Frank and Harper helped her up. She walked over to her new granddaughter. "Hi, pretty girl," she cooed. Ellie waved her hands up and down excitedly and bounced in her Daddy's arms.

"May I?" she asked.

Bennett handed off his daughter to her grandmother. Rachel pulled her close and swung her gently back and forth. She inhaled deeply the scent of baby and sunshine.

"I'll go up to the attic and see if I can find a high chair." Brody offered.

"It's in the back to the left." Harper told him automatically before stopping herself, "Well last time I checked. Oh, and if you find a pack and play can you bring that too?"

He nodded.

"I'll help you," Bennett told him.

They went up the attic together. When they were alone Bennett asked him, "Are you okay?"

Brody who was pushing and pulling boxes aside to get to the baby stuff in the back corner, right where Harper said it was turned to face him. He punched him right in the jaw. Bennett was half expecting it and took it on the chin.

"What the hell, Bennett? My wife?"

Bennett rubbed his jaw and worked it back.

"I'm sorry, man."

He sighed deeply. "I know." He told him.

"Friends?" Bennett asked.

They shook hands, enough said. Done.

The two men carried down the items that had been requested. When they got back downstairs they had another family member waiting for them. It was Hank, Bennett's dad.

"What the hell are you doing here?" Bennett's voice was cold.

Hank looked crest fallen. Kara came quickly to his defense. "Bennett," she warned, "Hank has been with us since the beginning. He has turned his life around. He has stopped drinking, he goes to meetings. He has been helping me out, helping the kids out."

"Great time to start showing up." He said to his dad replying to Kara's praise of him.

Hank flinched at the harsh true words he spoke. "I'm sorry I wasn't there for you Bennett. When I thought I had lost you I was bound and determined not to let it happen again with your boys. If I could take your whole childhood back I would."

Everyone stood back and assessed father and son gauging their reactions.

"Dinner is ready," Rebecca called out.

People jumped into action, bringing the food to the table. People walked around them like they didn't exist.

Bennett didn't know how he was supposed to respond. He had spent most of his life hating the fact his dad hadn't been there for him. He resented that he had to be the adult in the relationship with him. He had taken care of his dad and when he was old enough he had moved out and never looked back.

Hank's heart was breaking in half knowing his son didn't want to trust that he had changed. That he hadn't changed for him, but only when he thought it was too late. Hank spoke first, "If you need time to think it over, I understand. It's a lot to spring on someone."

Bennett nodded. "You have a new granddaughter." He told him.

Hank's eyes widen in surprise as he looked to Kara for conformation. She didn't look at him. He looked to Harper who was holding a beautiful baby. "Her name is Ellie." He told him.

Hank looked back to Bennett, "After your mom?" he already knew the answer. "Can I hold her?" Harper looked to Bennett and he gave a curt nod. She smiled at Hank and walked towards him to place Ellie in his arms.

He bounced his only granddaughter up and down and cooed at her. He looked over her head towards his son.

"Come on you two, come make yourself a plate and sit down." Rachel called. The two men broke eye contact and Bennett made sure he sat as far away as possible. The conversation at the table was lively as everyone tripped over each other trying to catch up on the past events of three years.

Chapter Thirty-Four

Bennett and Harper said good night to everyone and retreated to the guest house in the back yard. They set up Ellie's crib and put an already sleeping baby to bed.

They closed the bedroom door and went to sit out in the living room. He flopped down on the couch and she sat down next to him his arm going around her. Her head rested on his chest with a deep sigh. "What a mess."

"I agree." He said solemnly.

"Do you want to be with Kara?" she asked dreading the answer, dreading even more if he lied about it.

"What?" he tipped her chin up to look at him, "I made you a promise."

"You made one to Kara long before me." She pointed out.

She could see the turmoil inside him, "Will you think about it for me please? I want to make sure this is what you want."

"But-" he tried to interrupt and she shushed him putting her finger to his lips.

"What about you? Is this what you want?"

She kissed him and he kissed her back but they were both aware that she hadn't answered the question. They went to bed and slept cuddled in each other's arms.

Meanwhile Kara tossed and turned in her bed. She was beyond sad she was devastated. This was just as bad if not worse than the day she had lost Bennett and Harper. She punched her pillow and stuffed her head into it.

When that didn't work she flopped onto her back her fists clenched and stared at the ceiling. Her phone that was charging next to her bed dinged. It was a work email by the sound of it. She grabbed it thankful for anything to take her mind off her dilemma and responded to the email.

When she was done she started scrolling through her phone contacts. Who should she call? Brody? No, he had Rebecca to talk to. Maybe she should have moved on. Maybe she wouldn't have felt so miserable now.

David. The name and feelings come rushing back to her. Her heart rate actually quickened. She went to messages and sent him a quick text.

"Hey." And waited. She looked at the clock. Shit it was after ten.

Her phone dinged and she quickly checked it. It was a response from David. She opened it and read, "Hey, yourself."

She grinned and texted, "What are you wearing?" Then quickly deleted that. Think Kara, "What are you doing?"

"I'm in bed. You?"

"Same. Which bed?" she wanted to know if he was local or in London or New York.

He texted, "Which bed would you like me to be in?"

Oh God! She groaned. He was flirting with her and she liked it. She was thinking about what a good response would be when he sent his next text.

"I'm in town."

Her palms started getting sweaty.

"Can I come over?" Send. She threw the phone away from her. She couldn't believe she had just invited herself over. What was she thinking?

Ding. She dove across the bed for the phone. "I can send Conrad to pick you up."

"No! Don't you dare." She sent it quickly knowing he had probably already called the poor man to wake him up. "I'll be over soon." She jumped out of bed. She needed to get dressed. What do you wear to go over to a man's house at ten thirty at night?

Ding. "Hurry." His text read.

She felt faint. She put on a cute blue halter top dress that was knee high and put on the wedge sandals she was wearing earlier. She looked in the mirror. She quickly brushed her hair and applied light make up.

Sneaking out of her room she could hear the boys in their rooms both still watching T.V. She closed her door she didn't think they would even notice her gone. She grabbed her purse and ran next door where her car was still parked and drove to David's townhouse.

Kara tried not to think about what she was doing. She drove, parked and got out. She walked purposely to the front door and knocked. The door swung wide and her heart skipped a beat as she was confronted by a face she hadn't seen in too long.

David looked amazing. He was wearing a t-shirt and shorts. She had never seen him in casual wear. Except the one time in New York where he was half naked. He had a day's growth of beard she had never seen him look so good. "Can I come in?" she asked.

He stood back and let her come in. He closed the door behind her. "It's great to see you, love. What do I owe the pleasure of your company?" His British accent made her heart do summer salts. She dropped her bag and threw her arms around his neck.

"I've missed you." She told him and she pulled his lips to hers. She was greedy and she took what she wanted from him. He did not disappoint and he returned her kiss. It was even better than she remembered. His arms slipped easily around her waist and pulled her close.

Kara opened her mouth up to him. He took full advantage and swirled his tongue around hers. David was the one to pull away first. He looked down at her cupping her face with his hands. "Hey, Sweetness." His voice vibrated through her body.

She grinned up at him, "You're not dating anyone?" she wanted to make sure she hadn't missed her chance.

"Not at the moment." He grinned back at her.

"Good." Her lips sought him out again and instantly they were kissing. Her hands slid under his soft t-shirt and found his warm hard muscles. She tugged his shirt up over his head. She admired his chiseled chest, gliding her hand up and over his pecks.

His lips descended on her bare shoulder, his right hand caressed her slowly down her arm resting at her elbow. His left hand curled at the crevice of her slender neck and shoulder opposite of the one he was peppering with light kisses. His lips made it over to her neck and he enjoyed listening to her exaggerated sighs and deep moans.

David's fingers played with the ribbon at the nape of her dress holding her breast up. Slowly he tugged on the piece of fabric and she didn't stop him, letting the upper half of her dress peel off of her.

He stepped back to admire her breast clad in a pale yellow lace bra, her nipples straining against the fabric demanding to be touched. His lips crushed hers, she staggered back a step and his came with her his strong hand supporting her lower back.

He picked her up and threw her over his shoulder. She screeched out loud laughing as he carried her up his grand staircase. His hands were taking liberties under her skirt with her bare thighs. He was almost to the top when he stopped suddenly. She thought for a second that she had gotten too heavy for him and figured she was right when he set her down in front of him.

She was standing two stairs above him and was eye level with him. He looked serious and her good mood quickly vanished. "What's wrong?" she asked. Her hand caressed his face.

He kissed the palm of her hand then held it in his. "I was going to ask you the same thing. Why are you here? Don't get me wrong, love, I'm thrilled, but what has changed for you since we last spoke? Is there something else going on?"

Tears welled up in her eyes. He was so damn perceptive. "My husband is alive."

The look on his face was priceless, "Wow, not what I was expecting. How is that possible? I know we never discussed how he died, but I had assumed it was cancer or an automobile accident?"

She swiped at the tears on her face. "No we were in a plane crash and his body was never recovered along with my best friend. Everyone thought they were dead. They were just found living on an island together for the past three years and they came home with a baby!"

She sat down on the stairs and he sat down next to her. "I'm sorry." She told him. "I'm a little overwhelmed and…" she trailed off.

"Are you trying to get back at him with me?"

She turned her head towards him, “I’m not sure.” She answered him honestly as she tied her dress back up behind her neck.

“As much as I would love to have passionate revenge sex with you, I do have to decline. That’s not to say that I will never make beautiful sweet love to you, but you need to first figure out where your head is at.”

She nodded, “I know.”

“Would you care to have a drink and talk it over?”

She smiled, “I would love one.” He stood and held his hand out to her which she took and he helped her stand. They walked downstairs and he picked up his t-shirt off the floor and put it back on. They walked through the living room and into the kitchen.

There was an alcove with a round glass topped table centered under a pendant light. She took a seat at the table and he got out two glasses. “I have scotch.” He told her.

“Perfect.” She replied.

He poured two fingers worth and brought it to the table where he joined her. She took a sip and instantly started sputtering and coughing. He slapped her back with one hand and took the drink from her with his other hand.

“Oh my God, that’s strong.”

"Are you okay?" he asked.

She coughed and choked some more holding up her hand. "Would you like some water?" he asked. She nodded her head. He jumped up and went to the refrigerator where he filled a glass with ice and water.

David sat back down as she drank the water. "I thought I could look cool throwing back all the Scotch in one swig. I didn't get even one sip down."

He laughed. "Don't worry about it, Love. I think you're cool."

She smiled at him. "Thanks."

"Feeling better?" he asked. When she nodded he said, "Okay, why don't you talk me through this. Start from the beginning."

She did. She told him everything and he sat back and listened. Afterwards he walked her to the door. He didn't tell her to call him but he did wish her luck. She thanked him for listening and understanding. When she left he sighed his hands on the door and placed his forehead there as well.

He prayed she would be happy.

Chapter Thirty-Five

Early the next morning Harper eased out of bed and quickly got dressed in yesterday's clothes which were still better than the three year old clothes she had worn each day before that. She and Bennett had happily disposed of them at the airport yesterday.

She had fed Ellie about an hour ago so she knew she would sleep for a couple of more hours. Tip toeing out of the guest house she saw a light on in the kitchen. She tapped on the window and Rebecca unlocked the dead bolt letting her in.

"Couldn't sleep?" Harper asked her.

She gave a slight smile, "Not so much. Um, Brody's not awake yet."

"Good," Harper told her, "I wanted to talk to you."

Rebecca seemed a little taken aback but quickly recovered. "Would you like some coffee or tea?"

"Coffee would be amazing. Thank you."

"Sure thing," she went through the kitchen and poured her a cup, "Cream? Sugar?"

"Yes please." Rebecca added it and handed her the cup then took her own.

Harper sat down at the kitchen island and Rebecca joined her.

"The house looks great," Harper told her

Rebecca looked around, "I haven't really changed anything." She told her.

Harper laughed "I noticed but I never kept it this clean." She took a sip of the coffee, "Oh my God this is amazing. I missed coffee so much."

"I'll bet. I couldn't imagine life without coffee."

Rebecca put down her coffee mug "Do you want Brody back?" She was clear and to the point and tried hard not to sound like a bitch.

Harper put her coffee mug down, "No." she could see the instant relief in her, her shoulders relaxed. She put her hand on her arm and squeezed, "I'm happy he met you," she told her. Rebecca's lips pursed together in a sad smile in response.

"I offered Bennett an out last night."

"What?" Rebecca seemed surprised, "What did he say?"

"I told him to think it over."

"Are you worried?" she asked.

Harper nodded. It was Rebecca's turn to squeeze her hand.

"I wouldn't worry about it. I saw the way he looked at you all night. I just feel bad for Kara. I don't think she ever got over losing Bennett and I think it's painful to see him alive and not with her."

"I know. I feel terrible. Do you think she will ever forgive me?"

"It might take her some time."

"I want to talk to you about something else."

"Shoot." Rebecca took another sip of the coffee.

"I don't want to use a lawyer because I'm hoping we can come up with an arrangement with the kids. I've missed them so much and I need to see them and have them in my life."

"Of course," Rebecca assured her, "You have every right as their mother-"

"I don't want to take anything away from you and Brody. You guys have done an amazing job keeping the family together and I don't know how to repay you for that."

"We will work something out that works for all of us."

"Good morning ladies," Brody announced from the stairs. They both jumped as he came down and helped himself to a cup of coffee.

"What did I miss?"

Harper jumped up from the kitchen island, "Rebecca can fill you in. Thank you for the coffee it was delicious." Rebecca stood as well and she hugged her. "Bye Brody."

"Bye Harper."

Harper left the kitchen and instead of heading back to the guest house she went next door to Kara's back door. The light was on like she knew it would be. Kara opened the door and held it wide. "Come on in. I've been expecting you."

"How did you sleep?"

"Not good."

"Me either."

"Would you like some coffee?"

"No thank you. Do you have the stuff to make chocolate milk? Would you mind making me one of your famous omelets?" Kara had made the best omelets in college she would use whatever they had left over and put it in eggs and it was always delicious.

Kara smiled at the memory and went to the fridge. She pulled the milk and fixings for an omelet out of the fridge and opened the cupboard to get the powder to make chocolate milk. Harper went to the cupboard she knew Kara kept her cups and poured herself a glass. "Do you want me to make you one?" Harper asked her as she mixed the drink.

"No thanks, I have a coffee."

Harper put the milk away and sat down at the counter and watched her whip up an omelet. "Soooo…." Harper tried to start up a conversation with her longtime best friend.

Kara smiled, "Soooo…." She threw back at her.

"What have you been up to?"

"I told you guys yesterday that I made partner."

"Yeah, yeah, I know that but I want to know the stuff you didn't say."

Kara gave her a suspicion look, "What do you mean?"

Harper gasped and pointed, “I knew it! There is something you haven’t said. What is it? I’m not leaving until you tell me what it is.” She gasped again, “You have met a guy!” she pointed accusatory at her.

Kara looked at her wide eyed. She started to sputter, “Not really.”

“Yes, really. Details.”

“Honest to God it’s like you never left.” They smiled at each other. “Nothing happened.”

“What’s his name? How did you meet him?”

“His name is David. He was one of my clients.”

“Was? What happened?”

“I met him about a year ago. He brought a lot of business to the company and he is how I made partner. He doesn’t live here full time but in London and New York. He would fly me out to New York for business. He wanted more but I wasn’t ready to move on. I fired him as a client because I couldn’t be around him anymore.”

“So you don’t see him anymore?”

“No.” she embellished the truth.

“Do you miss him?”

She hesitated then responded honestly. “Sometimes, but I’m so busy I don’t have time to miss anyone.”

"You need to not be so busy. What does he look like?"

The look on Kara's face was priceless, "He's tall and thin. He has salt and pepper hair, clean shaven, nice looking with an English accent."

"Wait. He has an accent?"

Kara giggled, actually giggled. She folded over the egg to melt the cheese.

"Now we are getting somewhere. What exactly happened?"

"We kissed and-"

"Was it good?"

Kara sighed as she thought back to the kiss they had shared just last night. It was heavenly. She was actually sad she didn't have Harper to call and talk to about all these things that had happened. She missed her friend. She missed this interaction. She eased the omelet out of the pan and onto a plate handing it over to Harper.

She dug into her breakfast and groaned. "Oh my God this is so good. I missed this so much." She reached her hand across to her and squeezed her hand. "I missed you."

Kara came around the island with her arms open "I missed you too." They hugged not wanting to let go.

When Kara pulled away Harper told her, "You've avoided my question. Was David a good kisser?"

Kara pulled up a stool next her. "Very good."

Harper took another bite. "Okay, very good. Then you fired him?"

"I was nervous. I've only ever been with Bennett. I thought I could live my life as the lonely widow." At Harper's sad eyes she responded, "What? I was more than ready to be the independent widow. I was okay with it. I was here for my boys. I was capable of putting them though college. I had it all planned out. I would cry myself to sleep only once in a while."

"Oh, Kara. I'm so sorry with how this all turned out. Really I am. I didn't want any of this to happen. We should have never crashed. I should still be with Brody and you with Bennett, but that is not the life we were dealt."

Kara wiped fresh tears away from her cheeks. "I know. This really sucks. I should hate you, you know?"

Harper nodded solemnly, "I do know. Don't you?"

She shook her head, "How could you not fall in love with Bennett, he is a great guy."

"The best," Harper agreed.

"Let's go shopping," Kara suggested.

“Okay! I have to bring Ellie and tell Bennett.” She ran back to the guest house and told Bennett her plans.

“Have fun,” he told her.

“I will.” She called out. She stopped over at her old house and collected her other kids as well. After talking to Brody and Rebecca she asked the kids if they wanted to go shopping with her. She thought for sure the girls would want to go but was surprised when even Colton agreed to go along. She missed them all so much she was ecstatic to be home and to be around them.

Kara wasn’t at all surprised when her friend showed up at her back door with all the kids. They spent the day shopping and Kara took her to a spa where she got a haircut, pedicure and manicure. She let Chloe and Paige get pampered by a make-over too and gave Colton money to go play at the arcade while they were inside. Then they all had lunch together.

Kara pulled in her driveway and sat in the car for a while thinking long after Harper and the kids went in through Brody’s house. When that didn’t help she went inside. She found Bennett hanging out with the boys. They were playing video games in the living room. “Hi guys.” She tried to sound chipper and even to her own ears she sounded false.

Bennett got up and followed her to the kitchen. “Did you girls have fun?” he asked.

She looked up and realized he too had gone shopping. He was wearing new clothes she was pretty sure their boys had picked out for him. Stylish jeans and a graphic t-shirt and in his new physique made him look ten years younger. His beard was gone and he had his long locks styled to a more manageable length. She noticed how he had kept his hair in a longer style and not the short hair he used to have. She wondered if Harper had liked the longer locks, but didn't comment on it.

When she didn't respond he asked, "How do I look?"

He looked freaking fantastic but she told him, "Fine."

"Can we talk?" he wondered.

"Fine let's talk."

"Not here. Let's go somewhere." She gave a dramatic sigh and he knew he had won.

They drove up to a deserted area up on a hill. Getting out they went up to the hood of the car and sat down on the hood like they used to in high school.

"You look really pretty, Kara."

She looked down at her Bermuda shorts and pink blouse. "Thanks." She murmured.

"I missed you." He told her.

She looked at him. What was he getting at she wondered. Yesterday he wanted nothing to do with her, he was all about Harper. "Cut the crap Bennett. You forget I know you too well."

He took her hand, "I did miss you. Moving on from the memory of you was the hardest thing I ever had to do. I did not do it lightly and I still kept a piece of my heart for you. I want to be here for the boys" he lifted her chin, "and for you."

He leaned down and kissed her. Her arms went up around his neck and she kissed him back. She had missed him so much, this is all she ever wanted. The kiss was comfortable, familiar. It didn't have the same spark they had once shared for so many years. It would be easy to fall back into step with Bennett. They had a past and the boys would be happy.

She pulled away from the kiss and looked at him. "I think it is really honorable of you to "do the right thing" she used air quotes, but let's face it. That kiss was not your best material."

"Hey!" he fringed being hurt.

She smiled. "You've moved on and without realizing it I have moved on too. This would be wrong for us to try and pick up where we left off. I didn't think I was, but I'm happy for you and Harper. Bitch, stole my husband, but she is still my best friend."

He chuckled. He felt so relieved she felt the same way. He still loved Kara and always planned on loving her, but he wasn't in love with her like before. He had fallen in love with Harper and she was his future now.

"What do you mean you've moved on?" he asked.

"I mean I had accepted the fact that you were never coming back. I'm glad you are back I really am but-things are different. You have Harper and a beautiful baby girl. I feel like I can now finally move on without guilt."

"I really hope that you do Kara."

"What happens now?" she asked.

"When we were on the island I proposed to Harper."

"You did?"

"Yes, before Ellie was born. I want to see if she will still have me. We have your blessing?"

"Yes." She told him.

"We will need to find a house to live in. We can't stay in the guest house."

"I'm sure you can while you guys look for somewhere to live."

"I want to make sure we are close to everyone. I want the boys to be able to come over whenever they want. I've missed so much. I'm sure Harper won't want to be too far away from her kids either."

"I'm sure. We also need to talk about the money. I've spent some paying off the mortgage and making accounts for the boy's college and a retirement account. We received quite a settlement. I can write up some paperwork for you to sign giving over a portion to you."

"You write it up. I'll sign it." He told her.

"Deal. Are we good?" she asked.

"I think we are more than good."

She nodded in agreement. "Are you ready to go home?"

"Yes." He said. They climbed off the hood of the car and drove home.

"Will you stay with the boys tonight? I have something I need to do."

He gave her a sideways glance. "I'd love to."

"Great, thanks." She leaned over and kissed his cheek.

Harper, who was inside waiting inside for them saw the exchange in the car.

No! Her heart tightened up squeezing inside her chest. Backing away from the window she walked through what used to be her home.

"Are you okay?" Rebecca asked. She was bouncing Ellie up and down on her knee.

"I'm fine. Do you mind watching her for a minute? I need to go do something."

"Sure. Take your time."

Chapter Thirty-Six

Kara ran inside and up to her bedroom. She needed to change. She found a pink and white floral dress that had a wrap-around belt of material that gathered at her hip. There was a sharp V-neck on the dress showing off cleavage. She took her hair out of her ponytail and shook it out.

Going downstairs she kissed the boy good-bye. "Dad is going to stay here with you tonight." She told them.

"Where are you going?" Griffin asked her.

"Your Mom has some business to do. We will be fine." Bennett told the boys. "Have fun." He told her.

She hugged him. When she pulled back she saw Harper standing in the doorway between the living room and kitchen. The look on her face said it all. She thought she had lost Bennett.

"Honey, no." she walked quickly to her. She gave her a hug and whispered in her ear. "I'm going to see David."

She pulled back to look at her. She was looking at Bennett hurt still on her face but late registration of what she was saying started to sink in. She looked down at her then back at Bennett.

"Really?" she let out a long breath. She scooped Kara up into her arms. "Go get him, tiger." She told her.

Kara laughed. She left the house feeling light and airy and free and most importantly guilt free. She thought of texting or calling David first but though better of it. What if he wasn't home? She would wait for him she decided. She wanted it to be a surprise.

He was. Opening the door he saw a vision on his doorstep. "You're back." He stated the obvious.

She stepped over the threshold. He shut the door behind her. He was back to the way she was used to seeing him. He was in black slacks and a crisp white shirt with a cobalt blue tie. She took his tie in her hand and slowly wound it in her fist bringing him closer to her. When he was a breath away she whispered to him looking deep into his eyes. "I'm ready."

He captured her mouth crushing her to him. She welcomed him. He picked her up her legs winding around his waist. He pressed her back up against his front door. She gasped at the contact.

He pulled away slightly. She looked at him and ran a hand through his hair. He had shaved today. "You're home early." She observed.

"I worked from home today."

"Why?" she wanted to know.

"Because I hoped you would be back."

Pulling him back to her she kissed him again. His hands were up under her skirt and it wasn't long before he realized she wasn't wearing any panties. He grew hard instantly. He wanted to bring her up to his bedroom. She started kissing his neck.

"I want to bring you upstairs," his voice was rough.

"No." she told him.

He was crest fallen. She suckled on his ear. "I want you right here." Her tongue flicked against his earlobe. She barely had it out of her mouth and he was unbuckling his pants then he was inside her.

She gasped. It felt incredible. He pumped inside of her. Kissing her neck he listened to her words of encouragement. His hands were cupping her bottom.

Her hands clawed at his back. He kissed her and played with her tongue causing the tip to tingle.

He nibbled on her lower lip. Her nipples tightened and her head leaned back against the door. She held him tightly to her as she reached her climax. Her body clenched around him causing him to join her orgasm. He pressed her up against the door his head on her shoulder.

He kissed her gently one more time then slipped out of her and gently set her down. “I want to spend the rest of day in bed with you.” He told her.

“Okay.” She agreed breathlessly.

He pulled his pants back up and fastened the button. He picked her up and carried her upstairs. At the top of the stairs he turned left and walked down the hall. At the end of the hall was his room.

It was sleek and modern. The bed had a high tufted fabric headboard up against the left wall across from it were large white built ins with a large flat screen TV. Gleaming hardwood floors held a tan fluffy throw rug at the base of the bed. Two white fabric chairs sat on the fuzzy carpet at the end of the bed facing the TV. Along the back wall were large floor to ceiling windows with French doors leading out to a balcony. Sheer window treatments offered privacy.

He set her down on the floor. “I would like to see you naked.” He told her.

"I would like to see you naked." She threw back at him.

He lifted an eyebrow, it was adorable. "Same time?" he suggested.

"Sure."

He kicked out of his shoes and removed his socks. She stepped out of her shoes as well. Stepping forward she started removing his tie. He let her knowing she would feel more comfortable taking control of the situation. She tugged it out of his shirt then began unbuttoning his shirt. She made sure she undid the cuffs too before slipping it off his shoulders.

She undid his pants and let them fall to the floor. She appreciated he was allowing her to go at her own pace. He stepped out of his pants standing still in his plaid boxers. She stepped back to admire him. Reaching up she untied her dress and let it fall to the floor. She was in a hot pink bra and nothing else.

"Bloody hell, woman." He ground out.

She laughed, "What?"

"You're stunning."

She looked at his chiseled body and waved her hand up and down, "You're one to talk. I can't look at you with out wanting to jump into bed with you."

It was his turn to laugh, "Nothing wrong with that, Sweetheart." He walked slowly towards her. He kissed her buttering her up as she stripped naked. She removed his underwear and when their bodies came together, skin touching skin it was electric.

He backed her up to his bed that was neatly made and fell onto it together. This time they made love, slowly and passionately they explored each other's bodies. Afterwards they lay sated in each other's arms under the covers. Kara lay in his arms. He played with her hair and ran his hand down her arm resting it on her petite hand.

He kissed the top of her head. He couldn't believe she was here. He was shocked enough when he got her text yesterday and even more when she showed up. Sending her away was the hardest thing he had ever done. When she had called things off months ago he had been devastated.

He kept his promise to her and they hung out in bed all day. They cuddled, talked, laughed, kissed and made love. At dinner time he called for food to be delivered. After dinner they took a bath together.

"Can you spend the night?" he asked her.

"Do you want me to?" she asked.

"You can stay as long as you like."

Bennett and Harper had a great evening with his boys. They played card games and ordered Chinese take-out. They had brought over the pack and play and put it in Kara's home office. They put Ellie to sleep and sat around the kitchen table talking.

Harper could tell that Lucas didn't like the fact that she was with his dad and not his mom, but he was doing a good job of pretending. Griffin had always liked her and he might have been hurt that his parents were no longer together but was happy his dad was alive.

At about eleven o'clock the boys headed up to bed giving them both a hug and kiss goodnight. Harper and Bennett went outside to the back patio. Bennett threw himself down on the lounge chair and opened his arms up to her. She laid down next him and they stared up at the stars.

"I kissed Kara today," he confessed.

She sat up and looked down at him. "And what did that tell you?"

He tucked her hair behind her ear, "That what Kara and I had is gone and that I'm one hundred percent in love with you."

She leaned down and kissed him with all the pent up emotion she felt and he responded in kind. "I love you." She told him.

"I love you more."

Content she lay back in his arms and they watched the night's sky. A shooting star streaked across the sky.

"Will you marry me?" he asked.

"Only if you promise to love me forever."

"I promise."

Epilogue

Four Years Later

Lucas was graduating college. His little sister Ellie tugged on the wide sleeve of his graduation gown, "Lucas, pick me up." She demanded. Grinning he picked her up and settled her into his arms. She was getting big. She was all knees and elbows. She played with the tassel on his graduation hat.

Harper came over to relieve him, taking Ellie out of his arms. She gave him a big hug and kiss on the cheek, "I'm so proud of you, Lucas."

"Thanks, Harper." She was his step mom and had been since she and his dad had returned. They had a small ceremony with just the two families. It was nice. He had worried about his mom and how she was going to handle getting their dad back and losing him to another woman.

He did not need to worry about his mom. She had showed up at the wedding with a date. His name was David. He was a really nice guy who a year later became his step dad. They had debated where they were going to live but in the long run his mom won.

David had sold his company to his brothers in London along with the New York branch. He had kept the Boston branch separate and still ran a multimillion dollar company.

David's mom had come over from London and was living in his old townhouse. She was a sweet little old lady with an adorable accent. She made scones and tea every day and if the boys were around insisted that they have some. He liked her lemon curd the best.

Rebecca and Brody were doing great. Rebecca was pregnant again. They had a little boy named Mason and were expecting another boy in August. They had yet to decide on a name for him.

Brody had asked Bennett to come back to work with him but he had refused. Instead he had used some of the settlement money to start his own business. He was making his own furniture. He had learned so much on the island and with the modern tools he was able to purchase he was like a kid in a candy shop. Business was doing really well selling in Boston and New York and soon to be in L.A. He also did a lot of custom one of a kind pieces.

Harper and his dad bought a house in town, one of the old Victorian Mansions off the town square. It was huge and could sleep everyone at their house if they wanted to. They had said they didn't want to be isolated but in the heart of the town where there were people around. He couldn't blame them after being isolated for such a long period of time on the island.

Harper remodeled the entire house with her event planning business in mind. She hosts events all the time in the large mansion and gardens. They called it Jones' Jubilee.

Grandpa Hank and his dad had mended fences and he was glad to have both men in his life. He actually thought on occasion that Grandpa Hank and David's mom, Grandma Wentworth flirted a little. He tried not to think about old people's love life and pushed the image aside.

Following graduation he was on to law school, following in his mom's footsteps. His stepdad David had offered him a job as legal counsel for his business. Before starting law school he was planning on proposing to his longtime girlfriend, Arianna. He had already talked to her dad and had gotten his permission.

His little brother Griffin had graduated high school and was in college for graphic art design. He just started dating someone new but no one had met her yet.

He was living out in California and had flown in for his older brother's graduation.

Chloe was also in college as a business major in California and had flown home with Griffin for the summer for an internship in Boston. She was also being vague about who she was seeing. The entire family had it figured out but no one wanted to burst their bubble.

Colton graduated high school and had enlisted in the United States Air Force. He was going to basic training in San Antonio, Texas in two weeks. He wanted to be a fighter pilot and was going to be going to college and graduating as a ranking Officer.

Paige was twelve and going through some pre-teen drama that they were all dealing with. Rebecca thought she was having a hard time coping with not being the baby of the family anymore. Rebecca had finally gotten her Master's and had turned the guest house into her office where she saw clients.

He loved his big extended family. After so many years of loneliness he was happy to have so many great people and support in his life. Harper grabbed someone walking by and sweet talked them into taking a group photo of them. Everyone gathered around him for the photo. What was nice was it wasn't his family on one side and the Quinn family on the other side. They all mixed together.

Lucas picked up a running Ellie for the photo. His mom wrapped her arms around Rebecca and Harper.

Brody and his dad were next to each other. Brody was holding Mason and Bennett had his arm around Paige. Chloe and Griffin were standing close, Hank behind them with his hands on their shoulders. Frank and Rachel were standing next to David and Grandma Wentworth had her arm around Colton. His grandparents John and Judy stood on either side of him.

The woman taking the picture had to step back to get everyone in the photo. "Okay, say, Happy Graduation!"

In unison they are shouted happily, "Happy Graduation!"

Coming Soon

Amnesia at the Alter

Misty Jae Ogert

Chapter One

Beep…Beep…Beep…

What's that noise? she wondered.

Beep…Beep…Beep…

There it is again, she was slowly becoming aware of her surroundings. Her long eyelashes fluttered open and almond shaped emerald green eyes glanced around the room.

She was neatly tucked in a twin sized bed. No comforter just a crisp white sheet. One large window to her right revealed rain streaking down the pane.

What a miserable day, she thought.

Beep…Beep…Beep…

She turned her head to the left to locate the sound. The quick movement gave her a spitting headache. She noticed she was hooked up to some kind of machine which was the cause of the incessant beeping. When she put her hand to her head she found an IV in her arm. This can't be good, she thought.

When the pounding in her head began to ease she notice a man sprawled across a chair adjacent to the machine. He was handsome with jet black hair falling over his forehead. Except for the days growth of hair on his chiseled jaw he looked good. Then she noticed he was wearing a wrinkled tux, his tie hanging loosely around his neck.

The door opened and in walked an older man with salt and pepper hair. He was wearing a long white lab coat and carrying a clipboard. A big smile spread across his face when he saw her awake.

She weakly returned the smile.

"How are you doing this morning?" he asked. His voice seemed to fill the room. The booming sound made her wince.

"Fine," she managed to croak out. Her hand reached for her throat which felt like sand paper.

"Would you like some water?" he asked but he was already heading to a stand at the foot of her bed. He picked up a paper cup and a beige pitcher. She watched greedily, her thirst becoming more apparent as the water slipped out of one vessel and smoothly into the other.

She gladly accepted the water and drank all there was in the cup allowing the cool liquid to coat her throat. Sitting up now she set the cup on the bed side stand and folded her hands primly in her lap. Clearing her throat she asked, “Now this might sound like a dumb question, but who are you and where am I?”

The man gave a slight laugh before thrusting his hand out for her to shake, “I’m sorry. My name is Dr. Peter Chandler and you are at St. John’s Hospital. You were involved in a car accident yesterday morning.” He was watching her for some kind of reaction.

A frown marred her perfect heart shaped face.

“Car accident,” she whispered. “Okay, one more question?” She said this with one finger in the air.

“Of course,” Dr. Chandler assured her.

The finger she held in the air pointed to the man in the chair, “Who is he?”

The shock on Dr. Chandler’s face was unmistakable. Her mind started to scramble she was supposed to know.

“Charles Weber, your fiancé. Yesterday was to be your wedding day, but with the accident…,” his voice trailed off.

The man in question began to wake up as if he sensed he was the topic of conversation. When Charles saw her awake he rushed to her bedside and picked up her hand giving it a big kiss.

"Oh darling, I'm so glad you're awake I've been worried sick," Charles kept kissing her hand.

She looked up at Dr. Chandler and down at Charles and asked, "Are you sure?"

But she had seen the ring on her left ring finger so she knew the answer but why didn't she feel it. Shouldn't she know this gorgeous man was her fiancé?

"Sure about what?" Charles asked still kneeling by her side. He glanced from one to the other.

"Excuse me," Dr. Chandler all but shoved Charles away from the bed. He pulled a pen light from his pocket. "Follow this please." She did what she was asked with no problem except her head started to hurt again. "Can you tell me your name?" His voice had grown serious.

Her heart started to beat wildly in her chest, "Of course I can," she said confidently but her mind was a blank. She looked up at Charles but he was no help he looked as lost as she was beginning to feel. She looked up at the doctor. "I don't know." She said it in a whisper willing it not to be true.

Charles finally found some words and this time it was his turn to push the doctor aside. "Julie, darling, tell me you remember me." It wasn't a question.

"Julie? That's my name?" not ringing any bells she thought. "Julie what?" she asked.

"Julie Hart" Charles supplied her full name.

"What do you remember, Julie?" asked Dr. Chandler.

Remember? Julie thought. I can't even remember my name and he thinks I'm supposed to remember my life story?

"Nothing," Julie said sadly, "Not one simple thing."

"Doctor, how long is this going last?" Charles demanded.

"You can never tell with amnesia, it can be hours, days, months, even…years. In certain cases memories are never regained but that is worst case scenario."

Was he trying to be encouraging? Years! Never? Julie was getting frantic.

Dr. Chandler seeing this suggested Julie gets some sleep. Agreeing Dr. Chandler ushered Charles from the room who kept promising to come back soon.

Julie fell asleep with troubled thoughts.

****

Just outside of the room in hushed tones Dr. Chandler and Charles discussed Julie's amnesia.

"How can she regain her memory?" Charles asked his arms folded defensively across his chest.

"Sometimes people and places help. Getting her family and closest friends involved would be helpful." Dr. Chandler suggested.

"They are here now in the waiting room."

"I'll go talk to them. You go home get cleaned up and get some rest. You can come back tonight about six when visiting hours start. I'll tell her family the same."

"Okay I'll go," Charles shoulders slumped and he walked the opposite way of the doctor and waiting room towards the elevator.

Dr. Chandler walked into the lounge where seven worried people waited to hear some word about Julie. Mr. and Mrs. Hart stood when he entered and a young man stopped pacing.

"How's my baby?" Mrs. Hart asked anxiously. "Is she going to be alright?"

"Well she just woke up." Dr. Chandler explained.

There was a cry of relief from Mrs. Hart before she threw herself into Mr. Hart's arms.

The young man who was pacing moments before rushed forward. "Can we see her?" he asked.

"Not now she is resting. But there is more…"

"What?" asked one of Julie's sisters who was standing next to her parents.

"Well as a result of the car accident and some trauma she has suffered it has caused some complications. She has developed a case of amnesia." Dr. Chandler stated bluntly.

Mrs. Hart began to cry on her husband's shoulder while he patted her back. A dark haired young lady stood up next to the young man. Dr. Chandler assumed she was a friend because she did not possess the red hair of Julie and her sisters.

"She doesn't remember us?" she asked.

"She didn't even know Charles or her own name." Dr. Chandler tried to explain. He noticed the young man give a look to the dark haired friend and briefly wondered what that was about before continuing on, "As I told Charles people and places might help. She needs to rest right now, so why don't you all go home and get some rest and you can come back at six when visiting hours start."

They all agreed and Dr. Chandler watched them leave disheartened.

ABOUT THE AUTHOR

Misty Jae Ogert was born in Amarillo, Texas and currently lives in a small town in Massachusetts. This explains her love of both the Dallas Cowboys and the New England Patriots. Growing up she was a "Military Brat" traveling the globe living in Korea, Spain, Missouri, Illinois, New York and Texas three times. Her natural storytelling abilities helped procure friends wherever she went.

Misty is a Certified Dental Assistant by day, and a loving wife and mother, writing enthusiast, and horrendous housekeeper by night. She is addicted to TV dramas and Netflix. You can find her curled up with her two rescue dogs and a load full of laundry when she isn't losing the remote.

She dreams of one day owning a lake house where she can write and enjoy the view.

Made in the USA
Middletown, DE
22 July 2015